ONE WAY OUT...

The rebel leader's house had been gutted after the raid. Through a hole in the floor, Matt saw an aircar in the cellar. There was no way to get it out—it must have been stolen years ago and the house built over it. Useless—but . . .

He clambered down and inspected the vehicle. If he could figure out a way to use it, he might have a chance to save Polly and the others—but there was no hidden door, only the house and solid earth. How had the rebels hoped to fly it? Idly, he pressed the button marked *start*—and found out.

The house blew up around him.

Also by Larry Niven
Published by Ballantine Books:

ALL THE MYRIAD WAYS
CONVERGENT SERIES
THE FLIGHT OF THE HORSE
A HOLE IN SPACE
THE LONG *ARM* OF GIL HAMILTON
NEUTRON STAR
PROTECTOR
RINGWORLD
TALES OF KNOWN SPACE:
   The Universe of Larry Niven
WORLD OF PTAVVS
A WORLD OUT OF TIME
THE FLYING SORCERERS
   (with David Gerrold)

A GIFT FROM EARTH

Larry Niven

A Del Rey Book

BALLANTINE BOOKS • NEW YORK

A Del Rey Book
Published by Ballantine Books

ISBN 0-345-27548-9

Manufactured in the United States of America

First Ballantine Books Edition: September 1968
Eighth Printing: November 1978

Cover art by Rick Sternbach

TO HANK

A good critic, a good friend

CHAPTER I

THE RAMROBOT

A RAMROBOT had been the first to see Mount Lookitthat.

Ramrobots had been first visitors to all the settled worlds. The interstellar ramscoop robots, with an unrestricted fuel supply culled from interstellar hydrogen, could travel between stars at speeds approaching that of light. Long ago the UN had sent ramrobots to nearby stars to search out habitable planets.

It was a peculiarity of the first ramrobots that they were not choosy. The Procyon ramrobot, for instance, had landed on We Made It in spring. Had the landing occurred in summer or winter, when the planet's axis points through its sun, the ramrobot would have sensed the fifteen-hundred-mile-per-hour winds. The Sirius ramrobot had searched out the two narrow habitable bands on Jinx, but had not been programmed to report the planet's other peculiarities. And the Tau Ceti ramrobot, Interstellar Ramscoop Robot #4, had landed on Mount Lookitthat.

Only the Plateau on Mount Lookitthat was habitable. The rest of the planet was an eternal searing black calm, useless for any purpose. The Plateau was smaller than any region a colony project would settle by choice. But Interstellar Ramscoop Robot #4 had found an habitable point, and that was all it knew.

The colony slowboats, which followed the ramrobots, had not been built to make round trips. Their passengers had to stay, always. And so Mount Lookitthat was settled, more than three hundred years ago.

A flock of police cars fanned out behind the fleeing

man. He could hear them buzzing like summer bumble-bees. Now, too late, they were using all their power. In the air this pushed them to one hundred miles per hour: fast enough for transportation in as small a region as Mount Lookitthat, but, just this once, not fast enough to win a race. The running man was only yards from the edge.

Spurts of dust erupted ahead of the fugitive. At last the Implementation police had decided to risk damaging the body. The man hit the dust like a puppet thrown in anger, turned over hugging one knee. Then he was scrambling for the cliff's sharp edge on the other knee and two hands. He jerked once more, but kept moving. At the very edge he looked up to see a circling car coming right at him from the blue void beyond.

With the tip of his tongue held firmly between his teeth, Jesus Pietro Castro aimed his car at the enraged, ago-nized, bearded face. An inch too low and he'd hit the cliff; an inch too high and he'd miss the man, miss his chance to knock him back onto the Plateau. He pushed two fan throttles forward . . .

Too late. The man was gone.

Later, they stood at the edge and looked down.

Often Jesus Pietro had watched groups of children standing fearful and excited at the void edge, looking down toward the hidden roots of Mount Lookitthat, dar-ing each other to go closer—and closer. As a child he had done the same. The wonder of that view had never left him.

Forty miles below, beneath a swirling sea of white mist, was the true surface of Mount Lookitthat the planet. The great plateau on Mount Lookitthat the mountain had a surface less than half the size of California. All the rest of the world's surface was a black oven, hot enough to melt lead, at the bottom of an atmosphere sixty times as thick as Earth's.

Matthew Keller had committed, deliberately, one of the worst of possible crimes. He had crawled off the edge of the Plateau, taking with him his eyes, his liver and kidneys, his miles of blood tubing, and all twelve of his glands—taking everything that could have gone into the Hospital's organ banks to save the lives of those whose bodies were failing. Even his worth as fertilizer, not inconsiderable on a three-hundred-year-old colony world, was now nil. Only the water in him would someday return to the upper world to fall as rain on the lakes and rivers and as snow on the great northern glacier. Already, perhaps, he was dry and flaming in the awful heat forty miles below.

Or had he stopped falling, even yet?

Jesus Pietro, Head of Implementation, stepped back with an effort. The formless mist sometimes brought strange hallucinations and stranger thoughts—like that odd member of the Rorschach inkblot set, the one sheet of cardboard which is blank. Jesus Pietro had caught himself thinking that when his time came, if it ever came, this was the way he would like to go. And that was treason.

The major met his eye with a curious reluctance.

"Major," said Jesus Pietro, "why did that man escape you?"

The major spread his hands. "He lost himself in the trees for several minutes. When he broke for the edge, it took my men a few minutes to spot him."

"How did he reach the trees? No, don't tell me how he broke loose. Tell me why your cars didn't catch him before he reached the grove."

The major hesitated a split second too long. Jesus Pietro said, "You were playing with him. He couldn't reach his friends and he couldn't remain hidden anywhere, so you decided to have a little harmless fun."

The major dropped his eyes.

"You will take his place," said Jesus Pietro.

The playground was grass and trees, swings and teeter-totters, and a slow, skeletal merry-go-round. The school surrounded it on three sides, a one-story building of architectural coral, painted white. The fourth side, protected by a high fence of tame vine growing on wooden stakes, was the edge of Gamma Plateau, a steep cliff overlooking Lake Davidson on Delta Plateau.

Matthew Leigh Keller sat beneath a watershed tree and brooded. Other children played all around him, but they ignored Matt. So did two teachers on monitor duty. People usually ignored Matt when he wanted to be alone.

Uncle Matt was gone. Gone to a fate so horrible that the adults wouldn't even talk about it.

Implementation police had come to the house at sunset yesterday. They had left with Matt's big, comfortable uncle. Knowing that they were taking him to the Hospital, Matt had tried to stop those towering, uniformed men; but they'd been gentle and superior and firm, and an eight-year-old boy had not slowed them down at all. A honeybee buzzing around four tanks.

One day soon his uncle's trial and conviction would be announced on the colonist teedee programs, along with the charges and the record of his execution. But that didn't matter. That was just cleaning up. Uncle Matt would not be back.

A sting in his eyes warned Matt that he was going to cry.

Harold Lillard stopped his aimless running around when he realized that he was alone. He didn't like to be alone. Harold was ten, big for his age, and he needed others around him. Preferably smaller others, children who could be dominated. Looking rather helplessly around him, he spotted a small form under a tree near the playground's edge. Small enough. Far enough from the playground monitors.

He started over.

The boy under the tree looked up.

Harold lost interest. He wandered away with a vacant expression, moving more or less toward the teeter-totters.

Interstellar Ramscoop Robot #143 left Juno at the end of a linear accelerator. Coasting toward interstellar space, she looked like a huge metal insect, makeshift and hastily built. Yet, except for the contents of her cargo pod, she was identical to the last forty of her predecessors. Her nose was the ramscoop generator, a massive, heavily armored cylinder with a large orifice in the center. Along the sides were two big fusion motors, aimed ten degrees outward, mounted on oddly jointed metal structures like the folded legs of a praying mantis. The hull was small, containing only a computer and an insystem fuel tank.

Juno was invisible behind her when the fusion motors fired. Immediately the cable at her tail began to unroll. The cable was thirty miles long and was made of braided Sinclair molecule chain. Trailing at the end was a lead capsule as heavy as the ramrobot itself.

Identical cargo pods had been going to the stars for centuries. But this one was special.

Like Ramrobots #141 and #142, already moving toward Jinx and Wunderland—like Ramrobot #144, not yet built—Ramrobot #143 carried the seeds of revolution. That revolution was already in process on Earth. On Earth it was quiet, orderly. It would not be so on Mount Lookitthat.

The medical revolution that began with the beginning of the twentieth century had warped all human society for five hundred years. America had adjusted to Eli Whitney's cotton gin in less than half that time. As with the gin, the effects would never quite die out. But already society was swinging back to what had once been normal. Slowly; but there was motion. In Brazil a small but growing alliance agitated for the removal of the death penalty for habitual traffic offenders. They would be opposed, but they would win.

On twin spears of actinic light the ramrobot approached Pluto's orbit. Pluto and Neptune were both on the far side of the sun, and there were no ships nearby to be harmed by magnetic effects.

The ramscoop generator came on.

The conical field formed rather slowly, but when it had stopped oscillating, it was two hundred miles across. The ship began to drag a little, a very little, as the cone scooped up interstellar dust and hydrogen. She was still accelerating. Her insystem tank was idle now, and would be for the next twelve years. Her food would be the thin stuff she scooped out between the stars.

In nearby space the magnetic effects would have been deadly. Nothing with a notochord could live within three hundred miles of the storm of electromagnetic effects that was a working ramscoop generator. For hundreds of years men had been trying to build a magnetic shield efficient enough to let men ride the ramrobots. They said it couldn't be done, and they were right. A ramrobot could carry seeds and frozen fertile animal eggs, provided they were heavily shielded and were carried a good distance behind the ramscoop generator. Men must ride the slow-boats, carrying their own fuel, traveling at less than half the speed of light.

For Ramrobot #143, speed built up rapidly over the years. The sun became a bright star, then a dim orange spark. The drag on the ramscoop became a fearsome thing, but it was more than compensated for by the increase in hydrogen pouring into the fusion motor. The telescopes in Neptune's Trojan points occasionally picked up the ramrobot's steady fusion light: a tiny, fierce blue-white point against Tau Ceti's yellow.

The universe shifted and changed. Ahead and behind the ramrobot the stars crept together, until Sol and Tau Ceti were less than a light-year apart. Now Sol was dying-ember red, and Tau Ceti showed brilliant white. The pair of red dwarfs known as L726-8, almost in the ramrobot's path, had become warm yellow. And all the stars in all the heavens had a crushed look, as if somebody heavy had sat down on the universe.

Ramrobot #143 reached the halfway point, 5.95 light-years from Sol as measured relative to Sol, and kept going. Turnover was light-years off, since the ramscoop would slow the ship throughout the voyage.

But a relay clicked in the ramrobot's computer. It was message time. The ramscoop flickered out, and the light died in the motors as Ramrobot #143 poured all her stored power into a maser beam. For an hour the beam went out, straight ahead, reaching toward the system of Tau Ceti. Then the ramrobot was accelerating again, following close behind her own beam, but with the beam drawing steadily ahead.

A line of fifteen-year-old boys had formed at the door of the medcheck station, each holding a conical bottle filled with clear yellowish fluid. One by one they handed their specimen bottles to the hard-faced, masculine-looking nurse, then stepped aside to wait for new orders.

Matt Keller was third from the end. As the boy in front of him stepped aside, and as the nurse raised one hand without looking up from her typewriter, Matt examined his bottle critically. "Doesn't look so good," he said.

The nurse looked up in furious impatience. A colonist brat wasting *her* time!

"I better run it through again," Matt decided aloud. And he drank it.

"It was apple juice," he said later that night. "I almost got caught sneaking it into the medcheck station. But you really should have seen her face. She turned the damndest color."

"But why?" his father asked in honest bewilderment. "Why antagonize Miss Prynn? You *know* she's part crew. And these medical health records go straight to the Hospital!"

"*I* think it was funny," Jeanne announced. She was Matt's sister, a year younger than Matt, and she always sided with him.

Matt's grin seemed to slip from his face, leaving something dark, something older than his years. "One for Uncle Matt."

Mr. Keller glared at Jeanne, then at the boy. "You keep thinking like that, Matthew, and you'll end up in the Hospital, just like he did! Why can't you leave well enough alone?"

His father's evident concern penetrated Matt's mood. "Don't worry, Ghengis," he said easily. "Miss Prynn's probably forgotten all about it. I'm lucky that way."

"Nonsense. If she doesn't report you, it'll be through sheer kindness."

"Fat chance of that."

In a small recuperation room in the treatment section of the Hospital, Jesus Pietro Castro sat up for the first time in four days. His operation had been simple though major: he now had a new left lung. He had also received a peremptory order from Millard Parlette, who was pure crew. He was to give up smoking immediately.

He could feel the pull of internal surgical adhesive as he sat up to deal with four days of paperwork. The stack of forms his aide was setting on the bedside table looked disproportionately thick. He sighed, picked up a pen, and went to work.

Fifteen minutes later he wrinkled his nose at some petty complaint—a practical joke—and started to crumple the paper. He unfolded it and looked again. He asked, "Matthew Leigh Keller?"

"Convicted of treason," Major Jensen said instantly. "Six years ago. He escaped over the edge of Alpha Plateau, the void edge. The records say he went into the organ banks."

But he hadn't, Jesus Pietro remembered suddenly. Major Jansen's predecessor had gone instead. Yet Keller had died . . . "What's he doing playing practical jokes in a colonist medcheck station?"

After a moment of cogitation Major Jensen said, "He had a nephew."

"Be about fifteen now?"

"Perhaps. I'll check."

Keller's nephew, said Jesus Pietro to himself. *I could follow standard practice and send him a reprimand.*

No. Let him think he'd got away with it. Give him room to move around in, and one day he'd replace the body his uncle stole.

Jesus Pietro smiled. He started to chuckle, but pain stabbed him in the ribs and he had to desist.

The snout projecting from the ramscoop generator was no longer bright and shiny. Its surface was a montage of big and little pits, craterlets left by interstellar dust grains pushing their way through the ramscoop field. There was pitting everywhere, on the fusion motors, on the hull, even on the cargo pod thirty miles behind. The ship looked pebble-finished.

The damage was all superficial. More than a century had passed since the rugged ramscoop design had suffered its last major change.

Now, eight and a half years beyond Juno, the ramscoop field died for the second time. The fusion flames became two actinic blue candles generating a twentieth of a gee. Slowly the cargo spool rewound until the cargo pod was locked in its socket.

The machine seemed to hesitate . . . and then its two cylindrical motors rose from the hull on their praying-mantis legs. For seconds they remained at right angles to the hull. Then, slowly, the legs contracted. But now the motors pointed forward.

A U-shaped bar swung the cargo pod around until it also pointed forward. Slowly the spool unwound to its full length.

The ramscoop went on again. The motors roared their full strength, and now they fired their long streams of fusing hydrogen and fused helium through the ramscoop itself.

Eight point three light-years from Sol, almost directly between Sol and Tau Ceti, lie the twin red dwarf stars L726–8. Their main distinction is that they are the stars of

smallest mass known to man. Yet they are heavy enough
to have collected a faint envelope of gas. The ramrobot
braked heavily as her ramscoop plowed through the
fringes of that envelope.

She continued braking. The universe stretched out
again; the stars resumed their normal shapes and colors.
Eleven point nine light-years from Sol, one hundred million miles above the star Tau Ceti, the machine came to
an effective stop. Her ramscoop went permanently off. A
variety of senses began searching the sky. They stopped.
Locked.

Again she moved. She must reach her destination on
the remaining fuel in her insystem tank.

Tau Ceti is a G8 star, about four hundred degrees
cooler than Sol and only 45 percent as strong as its output
of light. The world of Mount Lookitthat orbits sixty-seven
million miles away, a moonless world in a nearly circular
path.

The ramrobot moved in on Mount Lookitthat the
world. She moved cautiously, for there were fail-safe fac-
tors in her computer program. Her senses probed.

Surface temperature: 600 degrees Fahrenheit, with little
variation. Atmosphere: opaque, dense, poisonous near the
surface. Diameter: 7650 miles.

Something came over the horizon. In visible light it
seemed an island in a sea of fog. A topography like a
flight of broad, very shallow steps, flat plateaus separated
by sheer cliffs. But Ramrobot #143 sensed more than
visible light. There was Earth-like temperature, breathable
air at an Earth-like pressure.

And there were two radio homing signals.

The signals settled it. Ramrobot #143 didn't even have
to decide which to answer, for they were coming from
only a quarter of a mile apart. They came, in fact, from
Mount Lookitthat's two slowboats, and the distance between them was bridged by the sprawling structure of the
Hospital, so that the spacecraft were no longer spacecraft

but odd-looking towers in a sort of bungalow-castle. But the ramrobot didn't know that and didn't need to.

There were signals. Ramrobot #143 started down.

The floor vibrated gently against the soles of his feet, and from all around came muted, steady thunder. Jesus Pietro Castro strode down the twisting, intermeshing, labyrinthine passages of the Hospital.

Though he was in a tearing hurry, it never occurred to him to run. He was not in the gymnasium, after all. Instead he moved like an elephant, which cannot run but can walk fast enough to trample a running man. His head was down; his stride was as long as his legs could reach. His eyes looked ominously out from under prominent brow ridges and bushy white eyebrows. His bandit's moustache and his full head of hair were also white and bushy, forming a startling contrast to his swarthy skin. Implementation police sprang to attention as he passed, snapping out of his way with the speed of pedestrians dodging a bus. Was it his rank they feared or his massive, unstoppable bulk? Perhaps even they didn't know.

At the great stone arch which was the main entrance to the Hospital, Jesus Pietro looked up to see a sparkling blue-white star overhead. Even as he found it, it winked out. Moments later the all-pervading thunder died away.

A jeep was waiting for him. If he'd had to call for one, someone would have been very sorry. He got in, and the Implementation chauffeur took off at once, without waiting for orders. The Hospital fell behind, with its walls and its surrounding wasteland of defenses.

The ramrobot package was floating down on its parachutes.

Other cars were in flight, erratically shifting course as their drivers tried to guess where the white dot would come down. It would be near the Hospital of course. The ramrobot would have aimed for one or another of the ships; and the Hospital had grown like something living, like a growth of architectural coral, between the two former spacecraft.

But the wind was strong today.

Jesus Pietro frowned. The parachute would be blown over the edge of the cliff. It would end not on Alpha plateau, where the crew built their homes and where no colonist could be tolerated, but in the colonist regions beyond.

It did. The cars swooped after it like a flock of geese, following it over the four-hundred-foot cliff that separated Alpha Plateau from Beta Plateau, where forests of fruit trees alternated with fields of grain and vegetables and meadows where cattle grazed. There were no homes on Beta, for the crew did not like colonists so close. But colonists worked there, and often they played there.

Jesus Pietro picked up his phone. "Orders," he said. "Ramrobot package one-forty-three is landing in Beta, sector . . . twenty-two or thereabouts. Send four squads in after us. Do not under any circumstances interfere with cars or crew, but arrest any colonist you find within half a mile of the package. Hold them for questioning only. And get out here fast."

The package skimmed over half an acre of citrus trees and came down at the far edge.

It was a grove of lemon and orange trees. One of the later ramrobot packages had carried the grove's genetically altered ancestors, along with other miracles of terrestrial biological engineering. These trees would not harbor any parasites at all. They would grow anywhere. They would not compete for growth with other similarly altered citrus trees. Their fruit remained precisely ripe for ten months out of the year; and when they dropped the fruit to release the seeds, it was at staggered intervals, so that at any time five trees out of six held ripe fruit.

In their grim need for sunlight the trees had spread their leaves and branches into an opaque curtain, so that being in the grove was like being in a virgin forest. Mushrooms grew here, imported unchanged from Earth.

Polly had already picked a couple of dozen. If anyone had asked, she had gone into the citrus woods to pick mushrooms. By the time her hypothetical questioner arrived, she would have hidden her camera.

Considering that the tending season was a month away, a remarkable number of colonists were abroad on Beta Plateau. In woods, on the plains, climbing cliffs for exercise, hundreds of men and women were on excursions and picnics. An alert Implementation officer would have found their distribution improbably even. Too many would have been recognized as Sons of Earth.

But the ramrobot package chose to land in Polly's area. She was near the edge of the woods when she heard the thump. She moved swiftly but quietly in that direction. With her black hair and darkly tanned skin she was nearly invisible in the forest dusk. She crawled between two tree trunks, moved behind another, and peered out.

A large cylindrical object lay on the grass beyond. A string of five parachutes writhed away before the wind.

So that's what they look like, she thought. It seemed so small to have come so far . . . but it must be only a tiny portion of the total ramrobot. The major portion would be on its way home.

But it was the package that counted. The contents of a ramrobot package were never trivial. For six months, ever since the maser message arrived, the Sons of Earth had been planning to capture ramrobot capsule #143. At worst, they could ransom it to the crew. At best, it might be something to fight with.

She almost stepped out of the woods before she saw the cars. At least thirty of them, landing all around the ramrobot package.

She stayed hidden.

His soldiers would not have recognized Jesus Pietro, but they would have understood. All but two or three of the men and women around him were purebred crew. Their chauffeurs, including his own, had prudently stayed in their cars. Jesus Pietro Castro was obsequious, deferential, and very careful not to joggle an elbow or to step on a toe or even to find himself in somebody's path.

As a result, his vision was blocked when Millard Parlette, a lineal descendant of the first Captain of the *Planck,* opened the capsule and reached in. He did see what the ancient held up to the sunlight, the better to examine it.

It was a rectangular solid with rounded edges, and it had been packed in a resilient material which was now disintegrating. The bottom half was metal. The top was a remote descendant of glass, hard as the cheaper steel alloys, more transparent than a windowpane. And in the top half floated something shapeless.

Jesus Pietro felt his mouth fall open. He looked harder. His eyelids squinted, his pupils dilated. Yes, he knew what this was. It was what the maser message had promised six months ago.

A great gift, and a great danger.

"This must be our most carefully guarded secret," Millard Parlette was saying in a voice like a squeaky door. "No word must ever leak out. If the colonists saw this, they'd blow it out of all proportion. We'll have to tell Castro to—Castro! Where the Mist Demons is Castro?"

"Here I am, sir."

Polly fitted the camera back in its case and began to work her way deeper into the woods. She'd taken several pictures, and two were telescopic shots of the thing in the glass case. Her eyes hadn't seen it clearly, but the film would show it in detail.

She went up a tree with the camera about her neck. The leaves and branches tried to push her back, but she fought through, deeper and deeper into the protecting leaves. When she stopped, there was hardly a square inch of her that didn't feel the gentle pressure. It was dark as the caves of Pluto.

In a few minutes the police would be all through here.

They would wait only until the crew was gone before converging on this area. It was not enough that Polly be invisible. There must be enough leaves to block any infrared light leaving her body.

She could hardly blame herself for losing the capsule. The Sons of Earth had been unable to translate the maser message, but the crew had. They knew the capsule's worth. But so did Polly—now. When the eighteen thousand colonists of Mount Lookitthat knew what was in that capsule . . .

Night came. The Implementation police had collected all the colonists they could find. None had seen the capsule after it came down, and all would be released after questioning. Now the police spread out with infrared detectors. There were several spots of random heat in Polly's grove, and all were sprayed with sonic stunners. Polly never knew she'd been hit. When she woke next morning, she was relieved to find herself still in her perch. She waited until high noon, then moved toward the Beta-Gamma Bridge with her camera hidden under the mushrooms.

CHAPTER II

THE SONS OF EARTH

FROM THE bell tower of Campbelltown came four thunderous ringing notes. The sonic wave-fronts marched out of town in order, crossing fields and roads, diminishing as they came. They overran the mine with hardly a pause. But men looked up, lowering their tools.

Matt smiled for the first time that day. Already he could taste cold beer.

The bicycle ride from the mine was all downhill. He reached Cziller's as the place was beginning to fill up. He ordered a pitcher, as usual, and downed the first glassful without drawing breath. A kind of bliss settled on him, and he poured his second glass carefully down the side to avoid a head. He sat sipping it while more and more freed workmen poured into the taproom.

Tomorrow was Saturday. For two days and three nights he could forget the undependable little beasties who earned him his living.

Presently an elbow hit him in the neck. He ignored it: a habit his ancestors had brought from crowded Earth and retained. But the second time the elbow poked him, he had the glass to his lips. With beer dripping wetly down his neck, he turned to deliver a mild reproof.

"Sorry," said a short dark man with straight black hair. He had a thin, expressionless face and the air of a tired clerk. Matt looked more closely.

"Hood," he said.

"Yes, my name is Hood. But I don't recognize you." The man put a question in his voice.

Matt grinned, for he liked flamboyant gestures. He

wrapped his fingers in his collar and pulled his shirt open to the waist. "Try again," he invited.

The clerkish type shied back, and then his eyes caught the tiny scar on Matt's chest. "Keller."

"Right," said Matt, and zipped his shirt up.

"Keller. I'll be d—damned," said Hood. You could tell somehow that he saved such words for emergencies. "It's been at least seven years. What have you been doing lately?"

"Grab that seat." Hood saw his opportunity and was into the stool next to Matt before the occupant was fully out of it. "I've been playing nursemaid to mining worms. And you?"

Hood's smile suddenly died. "Er—you don't still hold that scar against me, do you?"

"No!" Matt said with explosive sincerity. "That whole thing was my fault. Anyway it was a long time ago."

It was. Matt had been in the eighth grade that fall day when Hood came into Matt's classroom to borrow the pencil sharpener. It was the first time he'd ever seen Hood: a boy about Matt's size, though obviously a year older, an undersized, very nervous upperclassman. Unfortunately the teacher was out of the room. Hood had marched the full length of the room, not looking at anyone, sharpened his pencil, and turned to find his escape blocked by a mob of yelling, bounding eighth graders. To Hood, a new arrival at the school, they must have looked like a horde of cannibals. And in the forefront was Matt, using a chair in the style of an animal trainer.

Exit Hood, running, wild with terror. He had left the sharpened point of his pencil in Matt's chest.

It was one of the few times Matt had acted the bully. To him, the scar was a badge of shame.

"Good," said Hood, his relief showing. "So you're a miner now?"

"Right, and regretting it every waking hour. I rue the day Earth sent us those little snakes."

"It must be better than digging the holes yourself."

"Think so? Are you ready for a lecture?"

"Just a second." Hood drained his glass in a heroic gesture. "Ready."

"A mining worm is five inches long and a quarter inch in diameter, mutated from an earthworm. Its grinding orifice is rimmed with little diamond teeth. It ingests metal ores for pleasure, but for food it has to be supplied with blocks of synthetic stuff which is different for each breed of worm—and there's a breed for every metal. This makes things complicated. We've got six breeds out at the mine site, and I've got to see that each breed always has a food block within reach."

"It doesn't sound too complicated. Can't they find their own food?"

"In theory, sure. In practice, not always. But that's not all. What breaks down the ores is a bacterium in the worm's stomach. Then the worm drops metal grains around its food block, and we sweep them up. Now, that bacterium dies very easily. If the bacterium dies, so does the worm, because there's metal ore blocking his intestines. Then the other worms eat his body to recover the ore. Only, five times out of six it's the wrong ore."

"The worms can't tell each other apart?"

"Flaming right they can't. They eat the wrong metals, they eat the wrong worms, they eat the wrong food blocks; and when they do everything right, they still die in ten days. They were built that way because their teeth wear out so fast. They're supposed to breed like mad to compensate, but the plain truth is they don't have time when they're on the job. We have to keep going back to the crew for more."

"So they've got you by the gonads."

"Sure. They charge what they like."

"Could they be putting the wrong chemical cues in some of the food blocks?"

Matt looked up, startled. "I'll bet that's just what they're doing. Or too little of the right cues; that'd save them money at the same time. They won't let us grow our own, of course. The—" Matt swallowed the word. After all, he hadn't seen Hood in years. The crew didn't like being called names.

"Time for dinner," said Hood.

They finished the beer and went to the town's one restaurant. Hood wanted to know what had happened to his old school friends, or schoolmates; Hood had not made friends easily. Matt, who knew in many cases, obliged. They talked shop, both professions. Hood was teaching school on Delta. To Matt's surprise, the introverted boy had become an entertaining storyteller. He had kept his dry, precise tone, and it only made his jokes funnier. They were both fairly good at their jobs, and both making enough money to live on. There was no real poverty anywhere on the Plateau. It was not the colonists' money the crew wanted, as Hood pointed out over the meat course.

"I know where there's a party," Hood said over coffee.

"Are we invited?"

"Yes."

Matt had nothing planned for the night, but he wanted reassurance. "Party crashers welcome?"

"In your case, party crashers solicited. You'll like Harry Kane. He's the host."

"I'm sold."

The sun dipped below the edge of Gamma Plateau as they rode up. They left their bicycles in back of the house. As they walked around to the front, the sun showed again, a glowing red half-disk above the eternal sea of cloud beyond the void edge. Harry Kane's house was just forty yards from the edge. They stopped a moment to watch the sunset fade, then turned toward the house.

It was a great sprawling bungalow, laid out in a rough cross, with the bulging walls typical of architectural coral. No attempt had been made to disguise its origin. Matt had never before seen a house which was not painted, but he had to admire the effect. The remnants of the shaping balloon, which gave all architectural coral buildings their telltale bulge, had been carefully scraped away. The exposed walls had been polished to a shining pink sheen. Even after sunset the house glowed softly.

As if it were *proud* of its thoroughly colonist origin.

Architectural coral was another gift of the ramrobots. A genetic manipulation of ordinary sea coral, it was the cheapest building material known. The only real cost was in the plastic balloon that guided the growth of the coral and enclosed the coral's special airborne food. All colonists lived in buildings of coral. Not many would have built in stone or wood or brick even were it allowed. But most attempted to make their dwellings look somewhat like those on Alpha plateau. With paint, with wood and metal and false stone-sidings, with powered sandpaper disks to flatten the inevitable bulges, they tried to imitate the crew.

In daylight or darkness Harry Kane's house was flagrantly atypical.

The noise hit them as they opened the door. Matt stood still while his ears adjusted to the noise level—a survival trait his ancestors had developed when Earth's population numbered nineteen billion, even as it did that night, eleven point nine light-years away. During the last four centuries a man of Earth might as well have been stone deaf if he could not carry on a conversation with a thousand drunks bellowing in his ears. Matt's people had kept some of their habits too. The great living room was jammed, and the few chairs were largely being ignored.

The room *was* big, and the bar across from the entrance was enormous. Matt shouted, "Harry Kane must do a lot of entertaining."

"He does! Come with me; we'll meet him!"

Matt caught snatches of conversation as they pushed their way across the room. The party hadn't been going long, he gathered, and several people knew practically nobody; but they all had drinks. They were of all ages, all professions. Hood had spoken true. If a party crasher wasn't welcome, he'd never know it, because no one would recognize him as one.

The walls were like the outside, a glowing coral pink. The floor, covered with a hairy-looking wall-to-wall rug of mutated grass, was flat except at the walls; no doubt it had been sanded flat after the house was finished and the forming balloon removed. But Matt knew that beneath the rug was not tile or hardwood, but the ever-present pink coral.

They reached the bar, no more jostled than need be. Hood leaned across the bar as far as he could, which because of his height was not far, and called, "Harry! Two vodka sodas, and I'd like you to meet—Dammit, Keller, what's your first name?"

"Matt."

"Matt Keller. We've known each other since grade school."

"Pleasure, Matt," said Harry Kane, and reached over to shake hands. "Glad to see you here, Jay." Harry was almost Matt's height, and considerably broader, and his wide face was dominated by a shapeless nose and an even wider grin. He looked exactly like a bartender. He poured the vodka sodas into glasses in which water had been prefrozen. He handed them across. "Enjoy yourselves," he said, and moved down the bar to serve two newcomers.

Hood said, "Harry believes the best way to meet everyone right away is to play bartender for the first couple of hours. Afterward he turns the job over to a volunteer."

"Good thinking," said Matt. "Is your name Jay?"

"Short for Jayhawk. Jayhawk Hood. One of my ancestors was from Kansas. The jayhawk was a symbolic Kansas bird."

"Crazy, isn't it, that we needed eight years to learn each other's first names?"

At that moment a fragment of the crowd noticed Hood and swept down upon them. Hood barely had time to grin in answer before they were in the midst of introductions. Matt was relieved. He was sure he had seen Harry Kane pass something to Jay Hood along with his drink, Manners kept him from asking questions, but it stuck in his curiosity, and he wanted to forget it.

The newcomers were four men and a woman. As an individual, Matt remembered only the woman.

Her name was Laney Mattson. She was around twenty-six years old, five years older than Matt. In bare feet he would have topped her by a scant half-inch. But she was wearing double-spikes, and her piled confection of auburn hair made her even taller. Not merely tall, she was big, with wide pronounced hips and deep breasts behind an "M" neckline. She looked prettier than she was, Matt thought; she used cosmetics well. And there was a booming exuberance in her every act, an enjoyment as big as herself.

The men were her age and over, in their late twenties. Any of the four would have looked normal dancing with Laney. They were huge. Matt retained of them only a composite impression of a resonant voice and an enveloping handclasp and a great handsome face smiling down from the pink ceiling. Yet he liked them all. He just couldn't tell them apart.

Hood surprised him again. Talking along in his dry voice, keeping it raised to an audible bellow, not straining his neck to look anyone in the face, Hood somehow kept control of the conversation. It was he who guided the talk to school days. One of the tall men was moved to speak of a simple trick he'd used to rewire his school's teaching teedee, so that for one day he and his classmates had watched their lessons both upside down and inside out. Matt found himself telling of the specimen bottle of apple juice he'd sneaked into the Gamma medcheck station, and what he did with it. Someone who'd been listening politely from the edge of the circle mentioned that once he'd stolen a car from a picnicking crew family on Beta Plateau. He'd set the autopilot to circle a constant thousand feet beyond the void edge. It had stayed up for five days before dropping into the mist, with scores of Implementation police watching.

Matt watched Jay Hood and Laney as they talked. Laney had a long arm draped over Hood's shoulders, and the top of his head reached just to her chin. They were both talking at once, trampling the tail ends of each other's sentences, racing pell-mell through memories and anecdotes and jokes they'd been saving, sharing them with the group but talking for each other.

It wasn't love, Matt decided, though it was like love. It was an immense satisfaction Hood and Laney felt at knowing each other. Satisfaction and pride. It made Matt feel lonely.

Gradually Matt became aware that Laney was wearing a hearing aid. It was so small and so cunningly colored as to be nearly invisible within her ear. Truthfully, Matt couldn't swear that it was there.

If Laney needed a hearing aid, it was too bad she couldn't hide it better. For centuries more civilized peoples had been wearing specks of laminated plastic buried in the skin above the mastoid bone. Such things did not exist on Mount Lookitthat. A crew, now, would have had his ears replaced from the organ banks . . .

Glasses went empty, and one of Laney's big escorts came back with replacements. The little group grew and shrank and split into other groups with the eternal capriciousness of the cocktail party. For a moment Matt and Jay Hood were left standing alone in a forest of backs and elbows. Hood said, "Want to meet a beautiful girl?"

"Always."

Hood turned to lead the way, and Matt caught a flash of the same odd coloring in his ear that he had noticed in Laney's. Since when had Hood become hard of hearing? It might have been imagination, aided by vodka sodas. For one thing, the tiny instruments seemed too deeply embedded to be removed.

But an item that size could have been just what Harry Kane passed to Jay Hood along with his drink.

"It's the easiest way to conduct a raid, sir." Jesus Pietro sat deferentially forward in his chair, hands folded on his desk, the very image of the highly intelligent man dedicated solely to his work. "We know that members always leave the Kane house by twos and fours. We'll pick them up outside the house. If they stop coming out, we'll know they've caught on. Then we'll go into the house itself."

Behind his mask of deference, Jesus Pietro was annoyed. For the first time in four years he had planned a major raid on the Sons of Earth, and Millard Parlette had picked that night to visit the Hospital. Why tonight? He came only once in two months, thank the Mist Demons. A visit from a crew always upset Jesus Pietro's men.

At least Parlette had come to him. Once Parlette had summoned him to his own house, and that had been bad. Here, Jesus Pietro was in his element. His office was practically an extension of his personality. The desk had the shape of a boomerang, enclosing him in an obtuse angle for more available working space. He had three guests' chairs of varying degrees of comfort, for crew and Hospital personnel and colonist. The office was big and square, but there was a slight curve to the back wall. Where the other walls were cream colored, easy on the eye, the back wall was smoothly polished dark metal.

It was part of the outer hull of the *Planck*. Jesus Pietro's office was right up against the source of half the spiritual strength of Mount Lookitthat, and half the electrical power too: the ship that had brought men to this world. Sitting at his desk, Jesus Pietro felt the power at his back.

"Our only problem," he continued smoothly, "is that not all of Kane's guests are involved in the conspiracy. At least half will be deadheads invited for camouflage. Telling them apart will take time."

"I see that," said the old man. His voice squeaked. He wore the tall, skeletal look of a Don Quixote, but his eyes held no madness. They were sane and alert. For nearly two hundred years the Hospital had kept his body, brain, and mind functioning. Probably even he did not know how much of him had been borrowed from colonists convicted of major crimes. "Why tonight?" he asked.

"Why not, sir?" Jesus Pietro saw what he was driving at, and his mind raced. Millard Parlette was nobody's fool. The ancient was one of the few crew willing to accept any kind of responsibility. Most of the thirty thousand crew on Mount Lookitthat preferred to devise ever more complex forms of playing: sports; styles of dress that changed according to half-a-dozen complex, fluctuating sets of rules; rigid and ridiculous social forms. Parlette preferred to work—sometimes. He had chosen to rule the Hospital. He was competent and quick; though he appeared rarely, he always seemed to know what was happening; and he was difficult to lie to.

Now he said, "Yesterday the ramrobot capsule. Last night your men were scouring the area for spies. Tonight you plan a major raid for the first time in four years. Do you think someone slipped through your fingers?"

"No, sir!" But that would not satisfy Parlette. "But in this instance I can afford to cover my bet even when it's a sure thing. If a colonist had news of the ramrobot package, he'd be at Kane's place tonight though demons bar the way."

"I don't approve of gambling," said Parlette. Jesus Pietro uneasily searched his mind for a suitable answer. "And you have chosen not to gamble. Very good, Castro. Now. What has been done with the ramrobot capsule?"

"I think the organ-bank people have it unpacked, sir. And the . . . contents stored. Would you like to see?"

"Yes."

Jesus Pietro Castro, Head of Implementation, the only armed authority on an entire world, rose hastily to his feet to act as guide. If they hurried, he might get away in time to supervise the raid. But there was no polite way to make a crew hurry.

Hood had spoken true. Polly Tournquist was beautiful.

She was also small and dark and quiet, and Matt definitely wanted to know her better. Polly had long, soft hair the color of a starless night, direct brown eyes, and a smile that came through even when she was trying to look serious. She looked like someone with a secret, Matt thought. She didn't talk; she listened.

"Parapsychological abilities are not a myth," Hood was insisting. "When the *Planck* left Earth, there were all kinds of psionics devices for amplifying them. Telepathy had gotten almost dependable. They—"

"What's 'almost dependable'?"

"Dependable enough so there were specially trained people to read dolphin minds. Enough so telepaths were called as expert witnesses in murder trials. Enough—"

"All right, all right," said Matt. It was the first time tonight that he had seen Hood worked up. Matt gathered from the attitudes of the others that Hood rode this hobbyhorse often. He asked, "Where are they now, these witches of yours?"

"They aren't witches! Look, Kell— Look, Matt. Every one of those psi powers was tied up a little bit with telepathy. They proved that. Now, do you know how they tested our ancestors before they sent them into space for a thirty-year one-way trip?"

Someone played straight man. "They had to orbit Earth for a while."

"Yes. Four candidates in a ferryboat, orbiting for one month. No telepath could take that."

Polly Tournquist was following the debate like a spectator at a tennis match, swinging her shoulders to face whoever was speaking. Her grin widened; her hair swung gently, hypnotically; she was altogether a pleasure to watch. She knew Matt was watching. Occasionally her eyes would flick toward him as if inviting him to share the joke.

"Why not, if he's got company?"

"The wrong company. Anywhere on Earth a latent telepath is surrounded by tens of thousands of minds. In

space he has three. And he can't get away from any of
them for a single hour, for a full month."

"How do you know all this, Jay? Books? You damn
sure don't have anyone to experiment on."

Polly's eyes sparkled as she followed the debate. The
lobes of Hood's ears were turning red. Polly's raven hair
swung wide, and when it uncovered her right ear for an
instant, she was almost certainly wearing a tiny, almost
invisible hearing aid.

So she *did* have a secret. And, finally, Matt thought he
knew what it was.

Three hundred years ago the *Planck* had come to
Mount Lookitthat with six crew members to guard fifty
passengers in suspended animation. The story was in all
the history tapes, of how the circular flying wing had
dipped into the atmosphere and flown for hours above
impenetrable mists which the instruments showed to be
poisonous and deadly hot. And then a great mass had
come over the horizon, a vertical flat-topped mountain
forty miles high and hundreds of miles long. It was like a
new continent rearing over the impalpable white sea. The
crew had gaped, wordless, until Captain Parlette had said,
"Lookitthat!"

Unwritten, but thoroughly known, was the story of the
landing. The passengers had been wakened one at a time
to find themselves living in an instant dictatorship. Those
who fought the idea, and they were few, died. When the
Arthur Clarke came down forty years later, the pattern
was repeated. The situation had not changed but for population growth, not in the last three hundred years.

From the beginning there had been a revolutionary
group. Its name had changed several times, and Matt had
no idea what it was now. He had never known a revolutionary. He had no particular desire to be one. They
accomplished nothing, except to fill the Hospital's organ
banks. How could they, when the crew controlled every
weapon and every watt of power on Mount Lookitthat?

If this was a nest of rebels, then they had worked out a good cover. Many of the merrymakers had no hearing aids, and these seemed to be the ones who didn't know anyone here. Like Matt himself. In the midst of a reasonably genuine open-house brawl, certain people listened to voices only they could hear.

Matt let his imagination play. They'd have an escape hatch somewhere—those of the inner circle—and if the police showed, they would use it during a perfectly genuine panic. Matt and his brethren of the outer circle would be expendable.

"But why should *all* of these occult powers be connected to mind-reading? Does that make sense to you, Jay?"

"Certainly. Don't you see that telepathy is a survival trait? When human beings evolved psi powers, they must have evolved telepathy first. All the others came later, because they're less likely to get you out of a bad situation. . . ."

Matt dismissed the idea of leaving. Safer? Sure. But here he had, for a time, escaped from his persnickety mining worms and their venal crewish growers and the multiple other problems that made his life what it was. And his curiosity bump itched madly. He wanted to know how they thought, how they worked, how they protected themselves, what they had in mind. He wanted to know—

He wanted to know Polly Tournquist. Now more than ever. She was small and lovely and delicate looking, and every man who had ever looked at her must have wanted to protect her. What was such a girl doing throwing her life away? Really, that was all she was doing. Sooner or later the organ banks would run short of healthy livers or live skin or lengths of large intestine at a time when there was a dearth of crime on the Plateau. Then Implementation would throw a raid, and Polly would be stripped down to her component parts.

Matt had a sudden urge to talk her out of it, get her to leave here with him and move to another part of the

Plateau. Would they be able to hide out in a region so limited?

Possibly not, but—

But she didn't even know he'd guessed. If she found out, he could die for his knowledge. He'd have to put a fail-safe on his mouth.

It spoiled things. If Matt could have played the observer, the man who watched and said nothing . . . But he wasn't an observer. He was involved now. He knew Jay and liked him, he'd liked Laney Mattson and Harry Kane at sight, and he could have fallen in love with Polly Tournquist. These people were putting their lives on the line. And his too! And he could do nothing about it.

The middle-aged man with the brush cut was still at it. "Jay," he said with a poor imitation of patience, "you're trying to tell us that Earth had psi powers under good control when the founding fathers left. Well, what have they done since? They've made all *kinds* of progress in biological engineering. Their ships improve constantly. Now the ramrobots go home all by themselves. But what have they done about psi powers? Nothing. Just nothing. And why?"

"Because—"

"Because it's all superstition. Witchcraft. Myths."

Oh, shut up, Matt thought. It was all cover for what was really going on, and he wasn't a part of that. He dropped back out of the circle, hoping nobody would notice him—except Polly. Nobody did. He eased toward the bar for a refill.

Harry Kane was gone, replaced by a kid somewhat younger than Matt, one who wouldn't last another half hour if he kept sampling his own wares. When Matt tasted his drink, it was mostly vodka. And when he turned around, there was Polly, laughing at his puckered face.

The half-dozen suspects were deeply asleep along one wall of the patrol wagon. A white-garbed Implementation medic looked up as Jesus Pietro entered. "Oh, there you are, sir. I think these three must be deadheads. The others had mechanisms in their ears."

The night outside was as black as always on moonless Mount Lookitthat. Jesus Pietro had left Millard Parlette standing before the glass wall of the organ banks, contemplating . . . whatever he might be contemplating. Eternal life? Not likely. Even Millard Parlette, one hundred and ninety years old, would die when his central nervous system wore out. You couldn't transplant brains without transplanting memories. What *had* Parlette been thinking? His expression had been very odd.

Jesus Pietro took a suspect's head in his hands and rolled it to look in the ears. The body rolled too, limply, passively. "I don't see anything."

"When we tried to remove the mechanism, it evaporated. So did the old woman's. This girl still has hers."

"Good." He bent to look. Far down in the left ear, too deep for fingers to reach it, was something colored dead black with a rim of fleshy pink. He said, "Get a microphone."

The man made a call. Jesus Pietro waited impatiently for someone to bring a mike. Someone eventually did. Jesus Pietro held it against the girl's head and turned the sound up high.

Rustling noises came in an amplified crackle.

"Tape it on," said Jesus Pietro. The medic stretched the girl on her side and taped the mike against her head. The thunder of rustling stopped, and the interior of the wagon was full of the deep drumbeat sound of her arteries.

"How long since anybody left the meeting?"

"That was these two, sir. About twenty minutes."

The door in back opened to admit two men and two women, unconscious, on stretchers. One man had a hearing aid.

"Obviously they don't have a signal to show they're clear," said Jesus Pietro. "Foolish." Now, if he'd been running the Sons of Earth . . .

Come to think of it, he might send out decoys, expendable members. If the first few didn't come back, he'd send out more, at random intervals, while the leaders escaped.

Escaped where? His men had found no exit routes; the sonics reported no tunnels underground.

It was seconds before Jesus Pietro noticed that the mike was speaking. The sounds were that low. Quickly he put his ear to the loudspeaker.

"Stay until you feel like leaving, then leave. Remember, this is an ordinary party, open-house style. However, those of you who have nothing important to say should be gone by midnight. Those who wish to speak to me should use the usual channels. Remember not to try to remove the earpieces; they will disintegrate of themselves at six o'clock. Now enjoy yourselves!"

"What'd he say?" asked the medic.

"Nothing important. I wish I could be sure that was Kane." Jesus Pietro nodded briefly at the medic and the two cops. "Keep it up," he said, and stepped out into the night.

"Why'd you leave? It was just getting interesting."

"No it wasn't, and my glass was empty, and anyway I was hoping you'd follow."

Polly laughed. "You must believe in miracles."

"True. Why'd *you* leave?"

Embedded in wall-to-wall humanity, drowned in a waterfall of human voices, Polly and Matt nevertheless had a sort of privacy. Manners and lack of interest would prevent anyone from actually listening to them. Hence nobody could hear them; for how could anyone concentrate on two conversations at once? They might have been in a room by themselves, a room with yielding walls and unyielding elbows, a room as small and private as a phone booth.

"I think Jay's bugs on psi powers," said Polly. She had not answered his question, which was fine by Matt. He'd expected to escape unnoticed from Hood's debate. He was lucky that way. But Polly coming to join him was new and different, and he enjoyed guessing at her motives.

"He talks like that all the time?"

"Yes. He thinks if we could only—" She stopped. Girl with a secret. "Forget Jay. Tell me about yourself."

So he talked of mining worms and home life and the school in sector nine, Gamma Plateau; and he mentioned Uncle Matt, who had died for being a rebel, but she ignored the bait. And Polly talked about growing up a hundred miles away, near the Colony University; and she described her job at the Delta Retransmitting Power Station, but she never mentioned her hearing aid.

"You look like a girl with a secret," Matt said. "I think it must be the smile."

She moved closer to him, which was very close, and lowered her voice. "Can you keep a secret?"

Matt smiled with one side of his mouth to show that he knew what was coming. She said it anyway. "So can I."

And that was that. But she didn't move away. They smiled at each other from a distance of a couple of inches, nose to nose, momentarily content with a silence which, to an earlier man, would have sounded like the center of an air raid. She was lovely, Polly. Her face was a lure and a danger; her figure, small and lithe and woman shaped, rippled with a dancer's grace beneath her loose green jumper. For the moment Matt looked silently into her eyes and felt very good. The moment passed, and they talked small talk.

The flow of the crowd carried them half across the room. Once they pushed back to the bar for refills, then let the crowd carry them again. In the continuous roar there was something hypnotic, something that might have explained why the crowded-room drinking bout was more than half a thousand years old; for monotonous background noise has long been used in hypnosis. Time ceased to exist. But there came a moment when Matt knew that he would ask Polly to go home with him, and she would accept.

He didn't get the chance.

Something changed in Polly's face. She seemed to be listening to something only she could hear. The hearing aid? He was ready to pretend he hadn't noticed, but he didn't get that chance either. For suddenly Polly was moving away, disappearing into the crowd, not as if she were in any hurry, but as if she remembered something she ought to do, some niggling detail she might as well take care of now. Matt tried to follow her, but the sea of humanity closed behind her.

The hearing aid, he told himself. *It called her.* But he stayed by the bar, resisting the pressure that would have borne him away. He was getting very drunk now, and glad of it. He didn't believe it had been the hearing aid. The whole thing was too familiar. Too many girls had lost interest in him just as suddenly as Polly had. He was more than disappointed. It *hurt.* The vodka helped to kill the pain.

About ten-thirty he went around to the other side of the bar. The kid playing bartender was happily drunk and glad to give up his place. Matt was gravely drunk. He dispensed drinks with dignity, being polite but not obsequious. The crowd was thinning now. This was bedtime for most of Mount Lookitthat. By now the sidewalks in most towns would have been rolled up and put away till dawn. These revolutionists must be a late-rising group. Matt served drinks automatically, but he wasn't having any more himself.

The vodka began to run low. And there wasn't anything but vodka, vodka converted from sugar and water and air by one of Earth's educated bacteria. *Let it run out,* Matt thought viciously. He could watch the riot.

He served somebody a vodka grapefruit, as requested. But the hand with the drink did not vanish to make room for someone else. Slowly Matt realized that the hand belonged to Laney Mattson. "Hi," he said.

"Hi. Want a stand-in?"

"Guess so."

Somebody changed places with him—one of Laney's tall escorts—and Laney led him through the thinning ranks to a miraculously unoccupied sofa. Matt sank deep into it. The room would start to whirl if he closed his eyes.

"Do you always get this looped?"

"No. Something bugging me."

"Tell me?"

He turned to look at her. Somehow his vodka-blurred eyes saw past Laney's makeup, saw that her mouth was too wide and her green eyes were strangely large. But she wore a smile of sympathetic curiosity.

"Ever see a twenty-one-year-old virgin male?" He squinted to try to read her reaction.

The corners of Laney's mouth twisted strangely. "No." She was trying not to laugh, he realized. He turned away.

She asked, "Lack of interest?"

"No! Hell, no."

"Then what?"

"She forgets me." Matt felt himself sobering with time and the effort of answering. "All of a sudden the girl I'm chasing just"—he gestured a little wildly—"forgets I'm around. I don't know why."

"Stand up."

"Hmph?"

He felt her hand on his arm, pulling. He stood up. The room spun and he realized that he wasn't sobering; he'd just felt steadier sitting down. He followed the pull of her arm, relieved that he didn't fall down. The next thing he knew, everything was pitch black.

"Where are we?"

No answer. He felt hands pull his shirt apart, hands with small sharp nails which caught in his chest hair. Then his pants dropped. "So this is it," he said, in a tone of vast surprise. It sounded so damn silly that he wanted to cringe.

"Don't panic," said Laney. "Mist Demons, you're nervous! Come here. Don't trip over anything."

He managed to walk out of his pants without falling. His knees bumped something. "Fall face down," Laney commanded, and he did. He was face down on an airfoam mattress, rigidly tense. Hands that were stronger than they ought to be dug into the muscles of his neck and shoulders, kneading them like dough. It felt wonderful. He lay there with his arms out like a swandiver, going utterly limp as knuckles ran down the sides of his vertebrae, as slender fingers pulled each separate tendon into a new shape.

When he was good and ready, he turned over and reached out.

To his left was a stack of photos a foot high. Before him, three photos, obviously candid shots. Jesus Pietro spread them out and looked them over. He wrote a name under one of them. The others rang no bell, so he shuffled them and put them on the big stack. Then he stood up and stretched.

"Match these with the suspects we've already collected," he told an aide. The man saluted, picked up the stack and left the flying office, moving toward the patrol wagons. Jesus Pietro followed him out.

Almost half of Harry Kane's guests were now in patrol wagons. The photographs had been taken as they entered the front door earlier tonight. Jesus Pietro, with his phenomenal memory, had identified a good number of them.

The night was cool and dark. A stiff breeze blew across the Plateau, carrying a smell of rain.

Rain.

Jesus Pietro looked up to see that half the sky was raggedly blotted out. He could imagine trying to conduct a raid in a pouring rainstorm. He didn't like the idea.

Back in his office, he turned the intercom to all-channel. "Now hear this," he said conversationally. "Phase two is on. Now."

"Is everyone that nervous?"

Laney chuckled softly. Now she could laugh all she wanted, if she wanted. "Not that nervous. I think everyone must be a little afraid the first time."

"You?"

"Sure. But Ben handled it right. Good man, Ben."

"Where is he now?" Matt felt a mild gratitude toward Ben.

"He's—he's gone." Her tone told him to *drop* it. Matt guessed he'd been caught wearing a hearing aid or something.

"Mind if I turn on a light?"

"If you can find a switch," said Laney, "you can turn it on.'

She didn't expect him to, not in pitch blackness in a strange room, but he did. He felt incredibly sober, and incredibly peaceful. He ran his eyes over her lying next to him, seeing the tangled ruin of her sculptured hairdo, remembering the touch of smooth warm skin, knowing he could touch her again at will. It was a power he'd never felt before. He said, "Very nice."

"Makeup smeared over forgettable face."

"Unforgettable face." It was true, now. "No makeup over unforgettable body." A body with an infinite capacity for love, a body he'd thought almost too big to be sexy.

"I should wear a mask, no clothes."

"You'd get more attention than you'd like."

She laughed hugely, and he rested his ear over her navel to enjoy the earthquake ripple of abdominal muscles.

The rain came suddenly, beating against the thick coral walls. They stopped talking to listen. Suddenly Laney dug her fingers into his arm and whispered, "Raid."

She means Rain, Matt thought, turning to look at her. She was terrified, her eyes and nostrils and mouth all distended. She meant Raid!

"You've got a way out, don't you?"

Laney shook her head. She was listening to unheard voices through the hearing aid.

"But you must have a way out. Don't worry, I don't want to know about it. I'm in no danger." Laney looked startled, and he said, "Sure, I noticed the hearing aids. But it's none of my business."

"Yes it is, Matt. You were invited here so we could get a look at you. All of us bring outsiders occasionally. Some get invited to join."

"Oh."

"I told the truth. There's no way out. Implementation has ways of finding tunnels. But there is a hiding place."

"Good."

"We can't reach it. Implementation is already in the house. They've filled it with sleepy gas. It should be seeping around the doors any minute."

"The windows?"

"They'll be waiting for us."

"We can *try*."

"Okay." She was on her feet and getting into her dress. Nothing else. Matt wasted not even that much time. He swung a great marble ashtray against a window and followed it through, thanking the Mist Demons that Mount Lookitthat couldn't make unbreakable glass.

Two pairs of hands closed on his arms before his feet cleared the window. Matt kicked out and heard somebody say *Whuff!* In the corner of his eye Laney cleared the window and was running. Good, he'd hold their attention for her. He jerked at the grip on his arms. A meaty hand weighing a full ton smashed across his jaw. His knees buckled. A light shone in his eyes, and he shrank back.

The light passed. Matt made one last frantic attempt to jerk loose, and felt one arm come free. He swung it full around. The elbow smacked solidly into yielding meat and bone: an unmistakable, unforgettable sensation. And he was free, running.

Just once in his life he had hit someone like that. From the feel of it he must have smashed the man's nose all over his face. If Implementation caught him now . . . !

Wet, slippery, treacherous grass underfoot. Once he

stepped on a smooth wet rock and went skidding across the grass on cheek and shoulder. Twice a spotlight found him, and each time he hit the grass and lay where he was, looking back to see where the light went. When it pointed elsewhere, he ran again. The rain must have blurred the lights and the eyes behind him; the rain and the luck of Matt Keller. Lightning flickered about him, but whether it helped or hurt him he couldn't say.

Even when he was sure he was free, he continued to run.

CHAPTER III

THE CAR

—FINISHED.

Millard Parlette pushed his chair back and viewed the typewriter with satisfaction. His speech lay on his desk, last page on top, back-to-front. He picked up the stack of paper with long, knobby fingers and quickly shuffled it into correct order.

—*Record it now?*

—*No. Tomorrow morning. Sleep on it tonight; see if I've left anything out. I don't have to deliver it until day after tomorrow.* Plenty of time to record the speech in his own voice, then play it over and over until he'd learned it by heart.

But it had to go over. The crew had to be made to understand the issues. For too long they had lived the lives of a divinely ordained ruling class. If they couldn't adapt—

Even his own descendants . . . they didn't talk politics often, and when they did, Millard Parlette noticed that they talked in terms not of power but of rights. And the Parlettes were not typical. By now Millard Parlette could claim a veritable army of children, grandchildren, great-grandchildren, and so forth; yet he made every effort to see them all as often as possible. Those who had succumbed to the prevalent crewish tastes—eldritch styles of dress, elegantly worded slander, and all the other games the crew used to cloak their humdrum reality—had done so in spite of Millard Parlette. The average crew was utterly dependent on the fact that he was a crew.

And if the power balance should shift?

They'd be lost. For a time they'd be living in a false

universe, under wrong assumptions; and in that time they would be destroyed.

What chance . . . what chance that they would listen to an old man from a dead generation?

No. He was just tired. Millard Parlette dropped the speech on his desk, stood up, and left the study. At least he would force them to listen. By order of the Council, at two o'clock Sunday every pure-blooded crew on the planet would be in front of his teedee set. If he could put it across . . . he must.

They had to understand the mixed blessing of Ramrobot #143.

Rain filled the coral house with an incessant drumming. Only Implementation police moved within and without. The last unconscious colonist was on his way out the door on a stretcher as Major Jansen entered.

He found Jesus Pietro lounging in an easy chair in the living room. He put the handful of photos beside him.

"What's this supposed to be?"

"These are the ones we haven't caught yet, sir."

Jesus Pietro pulled himself erect, conscious once again of his soaked uniform. "How did they get past you?"

"I can't imagine, sir. Nobody escaped after he was spotted."

"No secret tunnels. The echo sounders would have found them. Mpf." Jesus Pietro shuffled rapidly through the photos. Most had names beneath the faces, names Jesus Pietro had remembered and jotted down earlier that night. "This is the core," he said. "We'll wipe out this branch of the Sons of Earth if we can find these. Where are they?"

The aide was silent. He knew the question was rhetorical. The Head was leaning back with his eyes on the ceiling.

—Where were they?

—There were no tunnels out. They had not left underground.

—They hadn't run away. They would have been stopped, or if not stopped, seen. Unless there were traitors in Implementation. But there weren't. Period.

—Could they have reached the void edge? No, that was better guarded than the rest of the grounds. Rebels had a deplorable tendency to go off the edge when cornered.

—An aircar? Colonists wouldn't have an aircar, not legally, and none had been reported stolen recently. But Jesus Pietro had always been convinced that at least one crew was involved in the Sons of Earth. He had no proof, no suspect; but his studies of history showed that a revolution always moves down from the top of a society's structure.

A crew might have supplied them with an escape car. They'd have been seen but not stopped. No Implementation officer would halt a car— "Jansen, find out if any cars were sighted during the raid. If there were, let me know when, how many, and descriptions."

Major Jansen left without showing his surprise at the peculiar order.

An officer had found the housecleaner nest, a niche in the south wall, near the floor. The man reached in and carefully removed two unconscious adult housecleaners and four pups, put them on the floor, reached in to remove the nest and the food dish. The niche would have to be searched.

Jesus Pietro's clothes dried slowly, in wrinkles. He sat with his eyes closed and his hands folded on his belly. Presently he opened his eyes, sighed, and frowned slightly.

—*Jesus Pietro, this is a very strange house.*

—*Yes. Almost garishly colonist.* (Overtones of disgust.)

Jesus Pietro looked at the pink coral walls, the flat-sanded floor which curved up at the edge of the rug to join the walls. Not a bad effect if a woman were living here. But Harry Kane was a bachelor.

—*How much would you say a house like this cost?*

—Oh, about a thousand stars, not including furnishings. Furnishings would cost twice that. Rugs, ninety stars if you bought one and let it spread. Two housecleaners, mated, fifty stars.

—And how much to put a basement under such a house?

—Mist Demons, what an idea! Basements have to be dug by hand, by human beings! It'd cost twenty thousand stars easily. You could build a school for that. Who would ever think of digging a basement under an architectural coral house?

—Who indeed?

Jesus Pietro stepped briskly to the door. "Major Jansen!"

The sequel was likely to be messy. Jesus Pietro retired to the flying office while a team went in with an echo sounder. Yes, there was a large open space under the house. Major Chin wanted to find the entrance, but that might take all night, and the sounds might warn the colonists. Jesus Pietro sat firmly on his curiosity and ordered explosives.

It was messy. The rebels had put together some ingenious devices from materials anyone would have considered harmless. Two men died before sleepy-gas grenades could be used.

When all was quiet, Jesus Pietro followed the demolition teams into the basement. They found one of the unconscious rebels leaning on a dead-man switch. They traced the leads to a homemade bomb big enough to blow house and basement to bits. While they disconnected the bomb, Jesus Pietro studied the man, making a mental note to ask him if he'd chickened out. He'd found that they often did.

Behind one wall was a car, a three-year-old four-seater model with a bad scrape on the ground-effect skirt. Jesus Pietro could see no way to get it out of the basement, and neither could anyone else. The house must have been formed over it. *Of course,* thought Jesus Pietro; *they dug the basement, then grew the house over it.* He had his men cut away the wall so that the car could be removed later if it was thought worthwhile. They'd practically have to remove the house.

There was a flight of steps with a trapdoor at the top. Jesus Pietro, examining the small bomb under the trapdoor, congratulated himself (pointedly, in Major Chin's hearing) on not allowing Major Chin to search for the entrance. He might have found it. Someone removed the bomb and opened the trapdoor. Above was the living room. An asymmetrical section of mutated grass rug had reluctantly torn away and come up with the door. When the door was lowered, it would grow back within twenty minutes.

After the dead and unconscious had been filed away in patrol wagons, Jesus Pietro walked among them, comparing the faces with his final stack of photos. He was elated. With the exception of one man, he had collected Harry Kane and his entire guest list. The organ banks would be supplied for years. Not only would the crew have a full supply, which they always did anyway, but there would be spare parts for exceptional servants of the regime; i.e., for civil servants such as Jesus Pietro and his men. Even the colonists would benefit. It was not at all unusual for the Hospital to treat a sick but deserving colonist if the medical supplies were sufficient. The Hospital treated everyone they could. It reminded the colonists that the crew ruled in their name and had their interests at heart.

And the Sons of Earth was dead. All but one man, and from his picture he wasn't old enough to be dangerous.

Nonetheless Jesus Pietro had his picture tacked to the Hospital bulletin boards and sent a copy to the newscast station with the warning that he was wanted for questioning.

It was not until dawn, when he was settling down to sleep, that he remembered who belonged to that face.

Matthew Keller's nephew, six years older than when he'd pulled that cider trick.

He looked just like his uncle.

The rain stopped shortly before dawn, but Matt didn't know it. Sheltered from the rain by a cliff and by a thick clump of watershed trees, he slept on.

The cliff was the Beta-Gamma cliff. He'd fetched up against it sometime last night, dizzy and bruised and wet and winded. He could have collapsed there or tried running parallel to the cliff. He had chosen to collapse. If Implementation found him, he'd never awaken, and he had known it as he went to sleep. He had been too exhausted to care.

He woke about ten with a ferocious headache. Every separate muscle hurt from running and from sleeping on bare ground. His tongue felt like the entire Implementation police force had marched over it in sweat socks. He stayed on his back, looking up into the dark trees his ancestors had called pines, and tried to remember.

So much to begin and end in one night.

The people seemed to crowd around him. Hood, Laney, the four tall men, the kid who drank behind the bar, the laughing man who stole crew cars, Polly, Harry Kane, and a forest of anonymous elbows and shouting voices.

All gone. The man whose scar he wore. The woman who'd left him flat. The genial mastermind-bartender. And Laney! How could he have lost Laney?

They were gone. Over the next few years they might reappear in the form of eyes, lengths of artery and vein, grafts of hair-bearing scalp . . .

By now the police would be looking for Matt himself.

He sat up, and every muscle screamed. He was naked. Implementation must have found his clothes in Laney's room. Could they match the clothes to him? And if they couldn't, they'd still wonder how a man came to be wandering stark naked in open countryside. On the pedwalks of

Earth there were licensed nudists, and on Wunderland you didn't need a license; but on the Plateau there was no substitute for clothing.

He couldn't turn himself in. By now he'd never prove he wasn't a rebel. He'd have to get clothes, somehow, and hope they weren't looking for him already.

He surged to his feet, and it hit him again. Laney, Laney in the dark, Laney looking at him in the lamplit bed. Polly, the girl with the secret. Hood, first name Jayhawk. A wave of sickness caught him, and he doubled over, retching. He stopped the spasms by sheer willpower. His skull was a throbbing drum. He straightened and walked to the edge of the watershed forest.

To right and left the watershed trees stretched along the base of the Beta-Gamma cliff. Beta Plateau above him, unreachable except by the bridge, which must be miles to the left. Before him, a wide meadow with a few grazing goats. Beyond that, houses. Houses in all directions, thickly clustered. His own was perhaps four miles away. He'd never reach it without being stopped.

How about Harry's house? Laney had said there was a hiding place. And the ones who left before the raid . . . some of them might have returned. They could help him.

But would they?

He'd have to try it. He might reach Harry's house, crawling through the grass. The luck of Matt Keller might hold that far. He'd never reach his own.

His luck held: the strange luck that seemed to hide Matt Keller when he didn't want to be noticed. He reached the house two hours later. His knees and belly were green and itchy from the grass.

The grounds about the house were solidly spread with wheel tracks. All of Implementation must have been in on the raid. Matt saw no guards, but he went carefully in case they were inside. Implementation guards or rebel guards, he could still be shot. Though a guard might hesitate to shoot him, he'd want to ask questions first. Like: "Where's your pants, buddy?"

Nobody was inside. A dead or sleeping family of housecleaners lay against one wall, beneath their looted nest. Dead, probably, or drugged. Housecleaners hated light; they did their work at night. The rug showed a gaping hole that reached down through indoor grass and architectural coral to a well-furnished hole in the ground. The living-room walls were spotted with explosion marks and mercy-bullet streaks. So was the basement, when Matt climbed down to look.

The basement was empty of men and nearly empty of equipment. Scars showed where heavy machinery had stood, more scars where it had been torn loose or burned loose. There were doors, four of them, all crude looking and all burned open. One led to a kitchen; two opened on empty storerooms. One whole wall lay on its side, but the piece of equipment beyond was intact. The hole left by the fallen wall might have been big enough to remove it, but certainly the hole in the living-room floor was not.

It was a car, a flying car of the type used by all crew families. Matt had never before seen one close up. There it was beyond the broken wall, with no possible way to get it out. What in blazes had Harry Kane wanted with a car that couldn't be flown?

Perhaps this was what had brought on the raid. Cars were strictly denied to colonists. The military uses of a flying car are obvious. But why wasn't its theft noticed earlier? The car must have been here when the house was built.

Dimly Matt remembered a story he'd heard last night. Something about a stolen car set to circle the Plateau until the fuel ran out. No doubt the car had fallen in the mist, watched by furious, impotent crew. But—suppose he'd heard only the official version? Suppose the fuel had not run out; suppose the car had dipped into the mist, circled below the Plateau, and come up where Harry Kane could bury it in a hidden basement?

Probably he'd never know.

The showers were still running. Matt was shivering badly when he stepped in. The hot water thawed him instantly. He let the water pour heavily down on the back of his neck, washing the grass stains and dirt and old sweat from him as it ran in streams to his feet. Life was bearable. With all its horrors and all its failures, life was bearable where there were hot showers.

He thought of something then, and metaphorically his ears pricked up.

The raid had been *so* big. Implementation had grabbed everyone at the party. From the number of tracks, it was likely they had taken even those who had left early, putting them to sleep one-by-one and two-by-two as they turned toward home. They must have returned to the Hospital with close to two hundred prisoners.

Some were innocent. Matt *knew* that. And Implementation was usually fair about convictions. Trials were always closed, and only the results were ever published, but Implementation usually preferred not to convict the innocent. Suspects *had* returned from the Hospital.

—But that wouldn't take long. The police could simply release everyone without a hearing aid, with notations to keep an eye on them in future. He who wore a hearing aid was guilty.

—But it would take time to reduce around a hundred convicted rebels to their component parts. The odds were that Laney, Hood, and Polly were still alive. Certainly they could not *all* be dead by this time.

Matt stepped out of the shower and began looking for clothes. He found a closet which must have belonged to Harry Kane, for the shorts were too wide and the shirts were too short. He dressed anyway, pulling shirt and shorts into a million wrinkles with the belt. At a distance he'd pass.

The clothes problem was as nothing, now. The problem he faced was much worse.

He had no idea how long it took to take a man apart and store him away, though he could guess that it would take a long time to do it right. He didn't know whether Implementation, in the person of the dread Castro, would want to question the rebels first. But he did know that every minute he waited reduced the odds that each of the partygoers was still alive. Right now the odds were good.

Matt Keller would go through life knowing that he had passed up his chance to save them.

But, he reminded himself, it wasn't really a chance. He had no way to reach Alpha Plateau without being shot. He'd have to cross two guarded bridges.

The noonday sun shone through clean air on a clean, ordered world—in contrast to the gutted coral shell behind him. Matt hesitated on the doorstep, then resolutely turned back to the jagged hole in Harry Kane's living room. He must *know* that it was impossible. The basement was the heart of the rebel stronghold—a heart which had failed. If Implementation had overlooked a single weapon . . .

There were no weapons in the car, but he found an interesting assortment of scars. Ripped upholstery showed bolts attached to the exposed metal walls, but the bolts had been cut or torn out. Matt found six places which must have been gun mounts. A bin in back might have held makeshift hand grenades. Or sandwiches; Matt couldn't tell. Implementation had taken anything that might have been a weapon, but they didn't seem to have harmed the car. Presumably they would come back and dig it out someday if they thought it worth the effort.

He got in and looked at the dashboard, but it didn't tell him anything. He'd never seen a car dashboard. There had been a cover over it, padlocked, but the padlock lay broken on the floor and the cover was loose. Harry's padlock? Or the original owner's?

He sat in the unfamiliar vehicle, unwilling to leave because leaving would mean giving up. When he noticed a button labeled Start, he pushed it. He never heard the purr of the motor starting.

The blast made him spasm like a galvanized frog. It came all in one burst, like the sound of a gunshot as heard by a fly sitting in the barrel. Harry must have set something to blow up the house! But no, he was still alive. And there was daylight pouring in on him.

Daylight.

Four feet of earth had disappeared from above him. A wall of the house was in his field of vision. It leaned. Harry Kane must have been a genius with shaped charge explosives. Or known one. Come to that, Matt could have done the job for him. The mining worms didn't do *all* his work.

Daylight. And the motor was running. He could hear an almost soundless hum now that his ears had recovered from the blast. If he flew the car straight up . . .

He'd have had to cross two guarded bridges to reach Alpha Plateau. Now he could fly there—if he could learn to fly before the car killed him.

Or, he could go home. He wouldn't be noticed, despite his ill-fitting clothes. Colonists tended to mind their own business, leaving it to the crew and Implementation to maintain order. He'd change clothes, burn these, and who would know or ask where he'd been over the weekend?

Matt sighed and examined the dashboard again. He couldn't quit now. Later, maybe, when he crashed the car, or when they stopped him in the air. Not now. The blast that had freed his path was an omen, one he couldn't ignore.

Let's see. Four levers set at zero. Fans: 1-2, 1-3, 2-4, 3-4. *Why would those little levers be set to control the fans in pairs?* He pulled one toward him. Nothing.

A small bar with three notches: Neutral. Ground. Air. Set on Neutral. He moved it to Ground. Nothing. If he'd had the Ground Altitude set for the number of inches he wanted, the fans would have started. But he didn't know that. He tried Air.

The car tried to flop over on its back.

He was in the air before he had it quite figured out. In desperation he pulled all the fan throttles full out and tried to keep the car from rolling over by pushing each one in a little at a time. The ground dwindled until the sheep of Beta Plateau were white flecks and the houses of Gamma were tiny squares. Finally the car began to settle down.

Not that he could relax for a moment.

Fans numbers 1, 2, 3, 4 were left front, right front, left rear, right rear. Dropping lever 1-2 dropped the front of the car; 3-4, the back; 1-3, the left side; 2-4, the right side. He had the car upright, and he began to think he had the knack of it.

But how to go forward?

There were Altitude and Rotation dials, but they didn't do anything. He didn't dare touch the switch with the complicated three-syllable word on it. But . . . suppose he tilted the car forward? Depress the 1-2 throttle.

He did, just a little. The car rotated slowly forward. Then faster! He pulled the lever out hard. The rotation slowed and stopped when the Plateau stood before his face like a vertical wall. Before the wall could strike him in the face, he got the car righted, waited until his nerves stopped jumping, then . . . tried it again.

This time he pushed the 1-2 lever in a little, waited three seconds, pulled it out hard. It worked, after a fashion. The car began to move forward with its nose dipped.

Luckily he was facing Alpha Plateau. Otherwise he would have had to fly backwards, and that would have made him conspicuous. He didn't know how to turn around.

He was going pretty fast. He went even faster when he found a knob labeled Slats. The car also started to drop. Matt remembered the venetian-blind arrangements under the four fans. He left the slats where they were, leveled the car's altitude. It must have been right because the car kept moving forward.

It was hardly wobbling at all.

And Matt was faced with the most spectacular view he had ever known.

The fields and woods-orchards of Beta rolled beneath. Alpha Plateau was quite visible at this height. The Alpha-Beta cliff was a crooked line with a wide river following the bottom. The Long Fall. The river showed flashes of blue within the steep channel it had carved for itself. Cliff and river terminated at the void edge to the left, and the murmur of the river's fall came through the cockpit plastic. To the right was a land of endless jagged, tilted plains, softening and blurring in the blue distance.

Soon he would cross the cliff and turn toward the Hospital. Matt didn't know just what it looked like, but he was sure he'd recognize the huge hollow cylinders of the spacecraft. A few cars hovered over Beta, none very close, and a great many more showed like black midges over Alpha. They wouldn't bother him. He hadn't decided how close he would get to the Hospital before landing; even crew might not be permitted within a certain distance. Other than that he should be fairly safe from recognition. A car was a car, and only crew flew cars. Anyone who saw him would assume he was a crew.

It was a natural mistake. Matt never did realize just where he went wrong. He had fine judgment and good balance, and he was flying the car as well as was humanly possible. If someone had told him a ten-year-old crew child could do it better, he would have been hurt.

But a ten-year-old crew child would never have lifted a car without flipping the Gyroscope switch.

As usual, but much later than usual, Jesus Pietro had breakfast in bed. As usual, Major Jansen sat nearby, drinking coffee, ready to run errands and answer questions.

"Did you get the prisoners put away all right?"

"Yes, sir, in the vivarium. All but three. We didn't have room for them all."

"And they're in the organ banks?"

"Yes, sir."

Jesus Pietro swallowed a grapefruit slice. "Let's hope they didn't know anything important. What about the deadheads?"

"We separated out the ones without ear mikes and turned them loose. Fortunately we finished before six o'clock. That's when the ear mikes evaporated."

"Evaporated, forsooth! Nothing left?"

"Doctor Gospin took samples of the air. He may find residues."

"It's not important. A nice trick, though, considering their resources," said Jesus Pietro.

After five minutes of uninterrupted munching and sipping sounds, he abruptly wanted to know, "What about Keller?"

"Who, sir?"

"The one that got away."

And after three phone calls Major Jansen was able to say, "No reports from the colonist areas. Nobody's volunteered to turn him in. He hasn't tried to go home, or to contact any relative or anyone he knows professionally. None of the police in on the raid recognize his face. None will admit that someone got past him."

More silence, while Jesus Pietro finished his coffee. Then, "See to it that the prisoners are brought to my office one at a time. I want to find out if anyone saw the landing yesterday."

"One of the girls was carrying photos, sir. Of package number three. They must have been taken with a scopic lens."

"Oh?" For a moment Jesus Pietro's thoughts showed clear behind a glass skull. Millard Parlette! If he found out—"I don't know why you couldn't tell me that before. Treat it as confidential. Now get on with it. No, wait a minute," he called as Jansen turned to the door. "One more thing. There may be basements that we don't know about. Detail a couple of echo-sounder teams for a house-to-house search on Delta and Eta Plateaus."

"Yes, sir. Priority?"

"No, no, no. The vivarium's two deep already. Tell them to take their time."

The phone stopped Major Jansen from leaving. He picked it up, listened, then demanded, "Well, why call here? Hold on." With a touch of derision he reported, "A car approaching, sir, being flown in a reckless manner. Naturally they had to call you personally."

"Now why the—mph. Could it be the same make as the car in Kane's basement?"

"I'll ask." He did. "It is, sir."

"I should have known there'd be a way to get it out of the basement. Tell them to bring it down."

Geologists (*don't* give me a hard time about that word) believed that Mount Lookitthat was geologically recent. A few hundreds of thousands of years ago, part of the planet's skin had turned molten. Possibly a convection current in the interior had carried more than ordinarily hot magma up to melt the surface; possibly an asteroid had died a violent, fiery death. A slow extrusion had followed, with viscous magma rising and cooling and rising and cooling until a plateau with fluted sides and an approximately flat top stood forty miles above the surface.

It had to be recent. Such a preposterous anomaly could not long resist the erosion of Mount Lookitthat's atmosphere.

And because it was recent, the surface was jagged. Generally the northern end was higher, high enough to hold a permanent sliding glacier, and too high and too cold for comfort. Generally rivers and streams ran south, to join either the Muddy or the Long Fall, both of which had carved deep canyons for themselves through the southland. Both canyons ended in spectacular waterfalls. the tallest in the known universe. Generally the rivers ran south; but there were exceptions, for the surface of Mount Lookitthat was striated, differentiated, a maze of plateaus divided by cliffs and chasms.

Some plateaus were flat; some of the cliffs were straight and vertical. Most of these were in the south. In the north the surface was all tilted blocks and strange lakes with deep, pointed bottoms, and the land would have been cruel to a mountain goat. Nonetheless these regions would be settled someday, just as the Rocky Mountains of Earth were now part of suburbia.

The slowboats had landed in the south, on the highest plateau around. The colonists had been forced to settle lower down. Though they were the more numerous, they covered less territory, for the crew had cars, and flying cars can make a distant mountain-home satisfactory where bicycles will not. Yet Alpha Plateau was Crew Plateau, and for many it was better to live elbow to elbow with one's peers than out in the boondocks in splendid isolation.

So Alpha Plateau was crowded.

What Matt saw below him were all houses. They varied enormously in size, in color, in style, in building material. To Matt, who had lived out his life in architectural coral, the dwellings looked like sheer havoc, like debris from the explosion of a time machine. There was even a clump of deserted, crumbling coral bungalows, each far bigger than a colonist's home. Two or three were as large as Matt's old grade school. When architectural coral first came to the Plateau, the crew had reserved it for their own use. Later it had gone permanently out of style.

None of the nearby buildings seemed to be more than two stories tall. Someday there would be skyscrapers if the crew kept breeding. But in the distance two squat towers rose from a shapeless construction in stone and metal. The Hospital, without a doubt. And straight ahead.

Matt was beginning to feel the strain of flying. He had to divide his attention between the dashboard, the ground, and the Hospital ahead. It was coming closer, and he was beginning to appreciate its size.

Each of the empty slowboats had been built to house six crew in adequate comfort and fifty colonists in stasis.

Each slowboat also included a cargo hold, two water-fueled reaction motors and a water fuel tank. And all of this had to be fitted into a hollow double-walled cylinder the shape of a beer can from which the top and bottom have been removed with a can opener. The slowboats had been circular flying wings. In transit between worlds they had spun on their axes to provide centrifugal gravity; and the empty space inside the inner hull, now occupied only by two intersecting tailfins, had once held two throwaway hydrogen balloons.

They were big. Since Matt could not see the inner emptiness which the crew called the Attic, they looked far bigger. Yet they were swamped by the haphazard-looking stone construction of the Hospital. Most of it was two stories high, but there were towers which climbed halfway up the ships' hulls. Some would be power stations, others—he couldn't guess. Flat, barren rock surrounded the Hospital in a half-mile circle, rock as naked as the Plateau had been before the slowboats brought a carefully selected ecology. From the edge of the perimeter a thin tongue of forest reached across the rock to touch the Hospital.

All else had been cleared away. Why, Matt wondered, had Implementation left that one stretch of trees?

A wave of numbness hit him and passed, followed by a surge of panic. A sonic stun-beam! For the first time he looked behind him. Twenty to thirty Implementation police cars were scattered in his wake.

It hit him again, glancingly. Matt shoved the 1-3 throttle all the way in. The car dipped left, tilted forty-five degrees or more before he moved to steady it. He shot away to the left, gathering speed toward the void edge of Alpha Plateau.

The numbness reached him and locked its teeth. They had been trying to force him to land; now they wanted him to crash before he could go over the edge. His sight blurred; he couldn't move. The car dropped, sliding across space toward the ground and toward the void.

The numbness ebbed. He tried to move his hands and

got nothing but a twitch. Then the sonic found him again, but with lessened intensity. He thought he knew why. He was outracing the police because they did not care to sacrifice altitude for speed, to risk striking the lip of the void edge. That was a game for the desperate.

Through blurred eyes he saw the dark cliff-edge come up at him. He missed it by yards. He could move again, jerkily, and he turned his head to see the cars dropping after him. They must know they'd lost him, but they wanted to see him fall.

How far down was the mist? He'd never known. Miles, certainly. Tens of miles? They'd hover above him until he disappeared behind the mist. He couldn't go back to the Plateau; they'd stun him, wait, and scrape up what was left after the crash. There was only one direction he could go now.

Matt flipped the car over on its back.

The police followed him down until their ears began to pop. Then they hovered, waiting. It was minutes before the fugitive car faded from sight, upside down all the way, a receding blurred dark mote trailing a hairline of shadow through the mist, flickering at the edge of human vision. Gone.

"Hell of a way to go," someone said. It went over the intercom, and there were grunts of agreement.

The police turned for home, which was now far above them. They knew perfectly well that their cars were not airtight. Almost, but not quite. Even in recent years men had taken their cars below the Plateau to prove their courage and to gauge what level they could reach before the air turned poisonous. That level was far above the mist. Someone named Greeley had even tried the daredevil stunt of dropping his car with the fans set to idle, falling as far as he could before the poison mist could leak into his cabin. He had dropped four miles, with the hot, noxious gasses whistling around the door, before he had had to stop. He had been lucky enough to get back up before he passed out. The Hospital had had to replace his lungs. On Alpha Plateau he was still a kind of hero.

Even Greeley would never have flipped his car over and bored for the bottom. Nobody would, not if he knew anything about cars. It might come apart in the air!

But that wouldn't occur to Matt. He knew little about machinery. Earth's strange pets were necessities, but machinery was a luxury. Colonists needed cheap houses and hardy fruit trees and rugs that did not have to be made by hand. They did not need powered dishwashers, refrigerators, razors, or cars. Complex machinery had to be made by other machines, and the crew were wary of passing machines to colonists. Such machinery as they had was publicly owned. The most complex vehicle Matt knew was a bicycle. A car wasn't meant to fly without gyroscopes, but Matt had done it.

He had to get down to the mist to hide himself from the police. The faster he fell, the farther he'd leave them behind.

At first the seat pressed against him with the full force of the fans; about one-and-a-half Mount Lookitthat gravities. The wind rose to a scream, even through the soundproofing. Air held him back, harder and harder, until it compensated for the work of the fans; and then he was in free fall. And still he fell faster! Now the air began to cancel gravity, and Matt tried to fall to the roof. He had suspected that he was making the car do something unusual, but he didn't know how unusual. When the wind resistance started to pull him out of his seat, he snatched at the arms and looked frantically for something to hold him down. He found the seat belts. Not only did they hold him down, once he managed to get them fastened; they reassured him. Obviously they were meant for just this purpose.

It was getting dark. Even the sky beneath his feet was darkening, and the police cars were not to be seen. Very well. Matt pushed the fan throttles down to the Idle notches.

The blood rushing to his head threatened to choke him. He turned the car right side up. Pressure jammed him deep in his seat with a force no man had felt since the brute-force chemical rockets, but he could stand it now. What he couldn't endure was the heat. And the pain in his ears. And the taste of the air.

He pulled the throttles out again. He wanted to stop fast.

Come to that, would he know when he stopped? This around him was not a wispy kind of mist, but a dark blur giving no indication of his velocity. From above, the mist was white; from below, black. Being lost down here would be horrible. At least he knew which way was up. It was fractionally lighter in that direction.

The air tasted like flaming molasses.

He had the throttles all the way out. Still the gas crept in. Matt pulled his shirt over his mouth and tried to breathe through that. No good. Something like a black wall emerged from the mist-blur, and he tilted the car in time to avoid crashing against the side of Mount Lookit-that. He stayed near the black wall, watching it rush past him. He'd be harder to see in the shadow of the void edge.

The mist disappeared. He shot upward through sparkling sunlight. When he thought he was good and clear of the foul mist, and when he couldn't stand to breathe hot poison for another second, he put the window down. The car whipped to the side and tried to turn over. A hurricane roared through the cabin. It was hot and thick and soupy, that hurricane, but it could be breathed.

He saw the edge of the Plateau above him, and he pushed the throttles in a little to slow down. His stomach turned a flip-flop. For the first time since he'd gotten into the car, he had time to be sick. His stomach tried to turn over, his head was splitting from the sudden changes in pressure, and the Implementation sonics were having their revenge in twitching, jerking muscles. He kept the car more or less upright until the edge of the Plateau came level with him. There was a stone wall along the edge here. He eased the car sideways, eased it back when he was over the wall, tilted it by guess and hope until he was motionless in the air, then let it drop.

The car fell about four feet. Matt opened the door but stopped himself from getting out. What he really wanted to do was faint, but he'd left the fans idling. He found the Neutral . . . Ground . . . Air toggle and shoved it forward without much care. He was tired and sick, and he wanted to lie down.

The toggle fell in the Ground slot.

Matt stumbled out the door—stumbled because the car was rising. It rose four inches off the ground and began to slide. During his experimenting Matt must have set the ground altitude, so that the car was now a ground-effect vehicle. It slid away from him as he tried to reach for it. He watched on hands and knees as it glided away across the uneven ground, bounced against the wall and away, against the wall and away. It circled the end of the wall and went over the edge.

Matt flopped on his back and closed his eyes. He didn't care if he never saw a car again.

The motion sickness, the sonic aftereffects, the poisoned air he'd breathed, the pressure changes—they gripped him hard, and he wanted to die. Then, by stages, they began to let go. Nobody found him there. A house was nearby, but it had a vacant look. After some time Matt sat up and took stock of himself.

His throat hurt. There was a strange, unpleasant taste in his mouth.

He was still on Alpha Plateau. Only crew would go to the trouble of building walls along a void edge. So he was committed. Without a car he could no more leave Alpha Plateau than he could have arrived there in the first place.

But the house was architectural coral. Bigger than anything he was used to, it was still coral. Which meant that it should have been deserted about forty years.

He'd have to risk it. He needed cover. There were no trees nearby, and trees were dangerous to hide in; they would probably be fruit trees, and someone might come apple-picking. Matt got up and moved toward the house.

CHAPTER IV

THE QUESTION MAN

THE HOSPITAL was the control nexus of a world. It was not a large world, and the settled region totaled a mere 20,000 square miles; but that region needed a lot of control. It also required considerable electricity, enormous quantities of water to be moved up from the Long Fall River, and a deal of medical attention. The Hospital was big and complex and diversified. Two fifty-six-man spacecraft were its east and west corners. Since the spacecraft were hollow cylinders with the airlocks opening to the inside (to the Attic, as that inner space had been called when the rotating ships were between stars and the ship's axis was Up), the corridors in that region were twisted and mazelike and hard to navigate.

So the young man in Jesus Pietro's office had no idea where he was. Even if he'd managed to leave the office unguarded, he'd have been hopelessly lost. And he knew it. That was all to the good.

"You were on the dead-man switch," said Jesus Pietro.

The man nodded. His sandy hair was cut in the old Belter style, copied from the even older Mohawk. There were shadows under his eyes as if from lack of sleep, and the lie was borne out by a slump of utter depression, though he had been sleeping since his capture in Harry Kane's basement.

"You funked it," Jesus Pietro accused. "You arranged to fall across the switch so that it wouldn't go off."

The man looked up. Naked rage was in his face. He made no move, for there was nothing he could do.

"Don't be ashamed. The dead-man switch is an old trick. It almost never gets used in practice. The man in charge is too likely to change his mind at the last second. It's a—"

"I fully expected to wake up dead!" the man shouted.

"—natural reaction. It takes a psychotic to commit suicide. No, don't tell me all about it. I'm not interested. I want to hear about the car in your basement."

"You think I'm a coward, do you?"

"That's an ugly word."

"*I* stole that car."

"Did you?" The skeptical tone was genuine. Jesus Pietro did not believe him. "Then perhaps you can tell me why the theft went unnoticed."

The man told him. He talked eagerly, demanding that Jesus Pietro recognize his courage. Why not? There was nobody left to betray. He would live as long as Jesus Pietro Castro was interested in him, and for three minutes longer. The organ bank operating room was three minutes' walk away. Jesus Pietro listened politely. Yes, he remembered the car that had tauntingly circled the Plateau for five days. The young crew owner had given him hell for letting it happen. The man had even suggested—demanded—that one of Castro's men drop on the car from above, climb into the cockpit, and bring it back. Jesus Pietro's patience had given out, and he had risked his life by politely offering to help the young man perform the feat.

"So we buried it at the same time we built the basement," the prisoner finished. "Then we let the house grow over it. We had great plans." He sagged into his former position of despair but went on talking, mumbling. "There were gun mounts. Bins for bombs. We stole a sonic stunner and mounted it in the rear window. Now nobody'll ever use them."

"The car was used."

"What?"

"This afternoon. Keller escaped us last night. He returned to Kane's home this morning, took the car, and flew it nearly to the Hospital before we stopped him. The Mist Demons know what he thought he was doing."

"Great! 'The last flight of—' We never got around to naming it. Our air force. Our glorious air force. Who did you say?"

"Keller. Matthew Leigh Keller."

"I don't know him. What would he be doing with my car?"

"Don't play games. You are not protecting anyone. We drove him off the edge. Five ten, age twenty-one, hair brown, eyes blue—"

"I tell you I never met him."

"Good-by." Jesus Pietro pushed a button under his desk. The door opened.

"Wait a minute. Now, wait—"

Lying, Jesus Pietro thought, after the man was gone. *Probably lied about the car too.* Somewhere in the vivarium the man who really took the car waited to be questioned. If it was stolen. It could equally well have been supplied by a crew member, by Jesus Pietro's hypothetical traitor.

He had often wondered why the crew would not supply him with truth drugs. They would have been easy to manufacture from instructions in the ship's libraries. Millard Parlette, in a mellow mood, had once tried to explain. "We own their bodies," he had said. "We take them apart on the slightest pretext; and if they manage to die a natural death, we get them anyway, what we can save. Aren't the poor bastards at least entitled to the privacy of their own minds?"

It seemed a peculiar bleeding-heart attitude, coming from a man whose very life depended on the organ banks. But others apparently felt the same. If Jesus Pietro wanted his questions answered, he must depend on his own empirical brand of psychology.

Polly Tournquist. Age: twenty. Height: five one. Weight: ninety-five. She wore a crumpled party dress in the colonist style. In Jesus Pietro's eyes it did nothing for her. She was small and brown, and compared to most of the women Jesus Pietro met socially, muscular. They were work muscles, not tennis muscles. Traces of callus marred her hands. Her hair, worn straight back, had a slight natural curl to it but no trace of style.

Had she been raised as crew girls were raised, had she access to cosmetics available on Alpha Plateau, she would have known how to be beautiful. Then she wouldn't have been bad at all, once the callus left her hands and cosmetic treatment smoothed her skin. But, like most colonists, she had aged faster than a crew.

She was only a young colonist girl, like a thousand other young colonist girls Jesus Pietro had seen.

She bore his silent stare for a full minute before she snapped, "Well?"

"Well? You're Polly Tournquist, aren't you?"

"Of course."

"You had a handful of films on you when you were picked up last night. How did you get them?"

"I prefer not to say."

"Eventually I think you will. Meanwhile, what would you like to talk about?"

Polly looked bewildered. "Are you serious?"

"I am serious. I've interviewed six people today. The organ banks are full and the day is ending. I'm in no hurry. Do you know what those films of yours imply?"

She nodded warily. "I think so. Especially after the raid."

"Oh, you saw the point, did you?"

"It's clear you have no more use for the Sons of Earth. We've always been some danger to you—"

"You flatter yourselves."

"But you've never had a real try at wiping us out. Not till now. Because we serve as a recruiting center for your damned organ banks!"

"You amaze me. Did you know this when you joined?"

"I was fairly sure of it."

"Then why join?"

She spread her hands. "Why does anybody join? I couldn't stand the way things are now. Castro, what happens to your body when you die?"

"Cremated. I'm an old man."

"You're crew. They'd cremate you anyway. Only colonists go into the banks."

"I'm half crew," said Jesus Pietro. His desire to talk was genuine, and there was no need for reticence with a girl who was, to all intents and purposes, dead. "When my—you might say—pseudo-father reached the age of seventy, he was old enough to need injections of testosterone. Except that he chose a different way to get them."

The girl looked bewildered, then horrified.

"I see you understand. Shortly afterward his wife, my mother, became pregnant. I must admit they raised me almost as a crew. I love them both. I don't know who my father was. He may have been a rebel, or a thief."

"To you there's no difference, I suppose." The girl's tone was savage.

"No. Back to the Sons of Earth," Jesus Pietro said briskly. "You're quite right. We don't need them anymore, not as a recruiting center nor for any other purpose. Yours was the biggest rebel group on Mount Lookitthat. We'll take the others as they come."

"I *don't* understand. The organ banks are obsolete now, aren't they? Why not publish the news? There'd be a worldwide celebration!"

"That's just why we *don't* broadcast the news. Your kind of sloppy thinking! No, the organ banks are not obsolete. It's just that we'll need a smaller supply of raw material. And as a means of punishment for crimes the banks are as important as ever!"

"You son of a bitch," said Polly. Her color was high, and her voice held an icy, half-controlled fury. "So we might get *uppity* if we thought we were being killed to no *purpose!*"

"You will not be dying to no purpose," Jesus Pietro

explained patiently. "That has not been necessary since the first kidney transplant between identical twins. It has not been necessary since Landsteiner classified the primary blood types in 1900. What do you know about the car in Kane's basement?"

"I prefer not to say."

"You're being very difficult."

The girl smiled for the first time. "I've heard that."

His reaction took Jesus Pietro by surprise. A flash of admiration, followed by a hot flood of lust. Suddenly the bedraggled colonist girl was the only girl in the universe. Jesus Pietro held his face like frozen stone while the flood receded. It took several seconds.

"What about Matthew Leigh Keller?"

"Who? I mean—"

"You prefer not to say. Miss Tournquist, you probably know that there are no truth drugs on this world. In the ships' libraries are instructions for making scopolamine, but no crew will authorize me to use them. Hence I have developed different methods." He saw her stiffen. "No, no. There will be no pain. They'd put *me* in the organ banks if I used torture. I'm only going to give you a nice rest."

"I think I know what you mean. Castro, what are you made of? You're half colonist yourself. What makes you side with the crew?"

"There must be law and order, Miss Tournquist. On all of Mount Lookitthat there is only one force for law and order, and that force is the crew." Jesus Pietro pushed the call button.

He did not relax until she was gone, and then he found himself shaken. Had she noticed that flash of desire? What an embarrassing thing to happen! But she must have assumed he was only angry. Of course she had.

Polly was in the maze of corridors when she suddenly remembered Matt Keller. Her regal dignity, assumed for the benefit of the pair of Implementation police who were her escorts, softened in thought. Why would Jesus Pietro be interested in Matt? He wasn't even a member. Did it mean that he had escaped?

Odd, about that night. She'd liked Matt. He'd interested her. And then, suddenly . . . It must have looked to him as if she'd brushed him off. Well, it didn't matter now. But Implementation should have turned him loose. He was nothing but a deadhead.

Castro. Why had he told her all that? Was it part of the coffin cure? Well, she'd hold out as long as possible. Let Castro worry about who might know the truth of Ramrobot #143. She had told nobody. But let him worry.

The girl looked about her in pleased wonder at the curving walls and ceiling with their peeled, discolored paint, at the spiral stairs, at the matted, withered brown rug which had been indoor grass. She watched the dust puff out from her falling feet, and she ran her hands over the coral walls where the paint had fallen away. Her new, brightly dyed falling-jumper seemed to glow in the gloom of the deserted house.

"It's very odd," she said. Her crewish accent was strange and lilting.

The man lifted an arm from around her waist to wave it about him. "They live just like this," he said in the same accent. "Just like this. You can see their houses from your car on the way to the lake."

Matt smiled as he watched them walk up the stairs. He had never seen a two-story coral house; the balloons were too hard to blow, and the second floor tended to sag unless you maintained two distinct pressures. Why didn't they come to Delta Plateau if they wanted to see how colonists lived?

But why should they? Surely their own lives were more interesting.

What strange people they were. It was hard to understand them, not only because of the lilt but because certain words meant the wrong things. Their faces were alien, with flared nostrils and high, prominent cheekbones.

Against the people Matt had known, they seemed fragile, undermuscled, but graceful and beautiful to the point where Matt wondered about the man's manhood. They walked as though they owned the world.

The deserted house had proved a disappointment. He'd thought all was lost when the crew couple came strolling in, pointing and staring as if they were in a museum. But with luck they would be up there for some time.

Matt moved very quietly from the darkness of a now doorless closet, picked up their picnic basket, and ran on tiptoe for the door. There was a place where he could hide, a place he should have thought of before.

He climbed over the low stone wall with the picnic basket in one hand. There was a three-foot granite lip on the void side. Matt settled himself cross-legged against the stone wall, with his head an inch below the top and his toes a foot from the forty-mile drop to hell. He opened the picnic basket.

There was more than enough for two. He ate it all, eggs and sandwiches and squeezebags of custard and a thermos of soup and a handful of olives. Afterward he kicked the basket and the scraps of plastic wrap into the void. His eyes followed them down.

Consider:

Anyone can see infinity by looking up on a clear night. But only on the small world of Mount Lookitthat can you see infinity by looking down.

No, it's not really infinity. Neither is the night sky, really. You can see a few nearby galaxies; but even if the universe turns out to be finite, you see a very little distance into it. Matt could see apparent infinity by looking straight down.

He could see the picnic basket falling. Smaller. Gone.

The plastic wrap. Fluttering down. Gone.

Then, nothing but the white mist.

On a far-distant day they would call the phenomenon *Plateau trance*. It was a form of autohypnosis well known

to Plateau citizens of both social classes, differing from
other forms only in that nearly anyone could fall into such
a state by accident. In this respect Plateau trance com-
pares to ancient, badly authenticated cases of "highway
hypnosis" or to more recent studies of "the far look," a
form of religious trance endemic to the Belt of Sol. The
far look comes to a miner who spends too many minutes
staring at a single star in the background of naked space.
Plateau trance starts with a long, dreamy look down into
the void mist.

For a good eight hours Matt had not had a chance to
relax. He would not get a chance tonight, and he didn't
want to dwell on that now. Here was his chance. He
relaxed.

He came out of it with a niggling suspicion that time
had passed. He was lying on his side, his face over the
edge, staring down into unfathomable darkness. It was
night. And he felt wonderful.

Until he remembered.

He got up and climbed carefully over the wall. It would
not do to slip, three feet from the edge, and he was often
clumsy when he felt this nervous. Now his stomach
seemed to have been replaced by a plastic demonstration
model from a biology class. There was a jerkiness in his
limbs.

He walked a little way from the wall and stopped.
Which way was the Hospital?

Come now, he thought. *This is ridiculous.*

Well, there was a swelling hill to his left. Light glowed
faintly along its rim. He'd try that.

The grass and the earth beneath it ended as he reached
the top. Now there was stone beneath his bare feet, stone
and rock dust untouched by three hundred years of the
colony planting program. He stood at the crest of the hill
looking down on the Hospital. It was half a mile away
and blazed with light. Behind and to either side were other
lights, the lights of houses, none within half a mile of the

Hospital. Against their general glow he saw the black tongue of forest he'd noticed that morning.

In a direction not quite opposite to the dark, sprawling line of trees, a straighter line of light ran from the Hospital to a cluster of buildings at the perimeter of the bare region. A supply road.

He could reach the trees by moving along the edge of town. The trees would give him cover until he reached the wall—but it seemed a poor risk. Why would Implementation leave that one line of cover across a bare, flat protective field? That strip of forest must be loaded with detection equipment.

He started across the rock on his belly.

He stopped frequently. It was tiring, moving like this. Worse than that, what was he going to do when he got inside? The Hospital was big, and he knew nothing about the interior. The lighted windows bothered him. Didn't the Hospital ever sleep? The stars shone bright and cold. Each time he stopped to rest, the Hospital was a little closer.

So was the wall that surrounded it. It leaned outward, and on this side there was no break at all.

He was a hundred yards from the wall when he found the wire. There were big metal pegs to hold it off the ground, pegs a foot high and thirty yards apart, driven into the rock. The wire itself was bare coppery metal strung taut a few inches off the ground. Matt had not touched it. He crossed it very carefully, staying low but not touching the wire at any time.

Faintly there came the sound of alarm bells ringing inside the wall. Matt stopped where he was. Then he turned and was over the wire in one leap. When he hit the ground he didn't move. His eyes were closed tight. He felt the faint touch of numbness which meant a sonic beam. Evidently he was out of range. He risked a look behind him. Four searchlights hunted him across the bare rock. The wall was lousy with police.

He turned away, afraid they'd see his face shining. There were whirring sounds. Mercy-bullets falling all around him, slivers of glassy chemical which dissolved in blood. They weren't as accurate as lead pellets, but one must find him soon.

A light pinned him. And another, and a third.

From the wall came a voice. "Cease fire." The whirr of anesthetic slivers ended. The voice spoke again, bored, authoritative, tremendously amplified. "Stand up, you. You may as well walk, but we'll carry you if we have to."

Matt wanted to burrow like a rabbit. But even a rabbit wouldn't have made headway in the pitted, dusty stone. He stood up with his hands in the air.

There was no sound, no motion.

One of the lights swung away from him. Then the others. They moved in random arcs for a while, crossing the protective-rock field with swooping blobs of light. Then, one by one, they went out.

The amplified voice spoke again. It sounded faintly puzzled. "What set off the alarms?"

Another voice, barely audible in the quiet night. "Don't know, sir."

"Maybe a rabbit. All right, break it up."

The figures on the wall disappeared. Matt was left standing all alone with his hands in the air. After a while he put them down and walked away.

The man was tall and thin, with a long face and a short mouth and no expression. His Implementation-police uniform could not have been cleaner nor better pressed if he'd donned it a moment ago for the first time. He sat beside the door, bored and used to it, a man who had spent half his life sitting and waiting.

Every fifteen minutes or so he would get up to look at the coffin.

Seemingly the coffin had been built for Gilgamesh or Paul Bunyan. It was oak, at least on the outside. The eight gauge dials along one edge appeared to have been pirated from somewhere else and attached to the coffin by a carpenter of only moderate skill. The long-headed man would stand up, go to the coffin, stand over the dials for a minute. Something could go wrong, after all. Then he would have to act in a hurry. But nothing ever did, and he would return to his chair and wait some more.

Problem:

Polly Tournquist's mind holds information you need. How to get at it?

The mind is the body. The body is the mind.

Drugs would interfere with her metabolism. They might harm her. You'd risk it, but you're not allowed drugs anyway.

Torture? You could damage a few fingernails, bend a few bones. But it wouldn't stop there. Pain affects the adrenal glands, and the adrenal glands affect everything. Sustained pain can have a savage, even permanent, effect on a body needed for medical supplies. Besides, torture is unethical.

Friendly persuasion? You could offer her a deal. Her life, and resettlement in some other region of the Plateau, for anything you want to know. You'd like that, and the organ banks are full ... But she won't deal. You've seen them before. You can tell.

So you give her a nice rest.

Polly Tournquist was a soul alone in space. Less than that, for there was nothing around her that could have been identified as "space." No heat, no cold, no pressure, no light, no darkness, no hunger, no thirst, no sound.

She had tried to concentrate on the sound of her heartbeat, but even that had disappeared. It was too regular. Her mind had edited it out. Similarly with the darkness behind her closed, bandaged eyelids: the darkness was uniform, and she no longer sensed it. She could strain her muscles against the soft, swaddling bandages that bound her, but she sensed no result, for the slack was small fractions of an inch. Her mouth was partly open; she could neither open it further nor close it on the foam-rubber mouthpiece. She could not bite her tongue, nor find it. In no way could she produce the sensation of pain.

The ineffable peace of the coffin cure wrapped her in its tender folds and carried her, screaming silently, into nothingness.

What happened?

He sat at the edge of the grass on the hill above the Hospital. His eyes were fixed on its blazing windows. His fist beat softly against his knee.

What happened? They had me. They had me!

He had walked away. Bewildered, helpless, beaten, he had waited for the magnified voice to shout its orders. And nothing happened. It was as if they had forgotten him. He had walked away with the feel of death at his back, waiting for the numbness of a sonic stun-beam or the prick of a mercy-bullet or the roar of the officer's voice.

Gradually, against all reason, he had sensed that they were not going to come for him.

And then he ran.

His lungs had stopped their tortured laboring many minutes ago, but his brain still spun. Perhaps it would never stop. He had run until he collapsed, here at the top of the hill, but the fear that drove him was not the fear of the organ banks. He had fled from an impossible thing, from a universe without reason. How could he have walked away from that plain of death with no eye to watch him? It smacked of magic, and he was afraid.

Something had suspended the ordinary laws of the universe to save his life. He had never heard of anything that could do that . . . except the Mist Demons. And the Mist Demons were a myth. They had told him so when he was old enough. The Mist Demons were a tale to frighten children, like the reverse of a Santa Claus. The old wives who found powerful beings in the mist beyond the edge of the world had followed a tradition older than history, perhaps as old as man. But nobody believed in the Mist Demons. They were like the Belt miners' Church of Finagle, whose prophet was Murphy. A half-bitter joke. Something to swear by.

They had me and they let me go. Why?

Could they have had a purpose? Was there some reason the Hospital should let a colonist sneak to its very walls, then let him go free?

Could the organ banks be full? But there must be *some*place they could keep a prisoner until there was room.

But if they thought he was a crew! Yes, that was it! A human figure on Alpha plateau—of *course* they'd assume he was crew. But so what? Surely someone would have come to question him.

Matt began pacing a tight circle at the top of the low hill. His head whirled. He'd walked to certain death and been turned loose. By whom? Why? And what did he do next? Go back and give them another chance? Walk to the Alpha-Beta Bridge and hope nobody would see him sneaking across? Fly down the cliff, vigorously flapping his arms?

The awful thing was that he didn't know it wouldn't work. Magic, magic. Hood had talked about magic.

No, he hadn't. He'd practically turned purple denying that magic was involved. He'd been talking about . . . psychic powers. And Matt had been so involved in watching Polly that he couldn't remember anything Hood had said.

It was very bad luck. Because this was his only out. He had to assume that he had a psychic power, though he had not the remotest idea what that implied. At least it put a name to what had happened.

"I've got a psychic power," Matt announced. His voice rang with queer precision in the quiet night.

Fine. So? If Hood had gone into detail on the nature of psychic powers, Matt couldn't remember. But he could fairly well drop the idea of flying down the Alpha-Beta cliff. Whatever else was true of man's unexplored mental powers, they must be consistent. Matt could remember the feeling that he wouldn't be noticed if he didn't want to be, but he had never flown, nor even dreamed of flying.

He ought to talk to Hood.

But Hood was in the Hospital. He might be dead already.

Well . . .

Matt had been eleven years old when Ghengis, or Dad, brought two charms home for gifts. They were model cars, just the right size for charm bracelets, and they glowed in the dark. Matt and Jeanne had loved them at sight and forever.

One night they had left the charms in a closet for several hours, thinking they would grow brighter when they "got used to the dark." When Jeanne opened the closet, they had lost all their glow.

Jeanne was near tears. Matt's reaction was different. If darkness robbed the charms of their powers . . .

He hung them next to a light bulb for an hour. When he turned off the light, they glowed like little blue lamps.

A tide of small, loosely packed clouds was spreading across the stars. In all directions the town lights had gone out, all but the lights of the Hospital. The Plateau slept in a profound silence.

Well . . . he'd tried to sneak into the Hospital. He'd been caught. But when he stood up in the glare of spotlights, they couldn't see him. The *why* of it was just as magical as before, but he thought he was beginning to see the *how* of it.

He'd have to risk it. Matt began to walk.

He'd never planned for it to go this far. If only he'd been stopped before it was too late. But it *was* too late, and he had the sense to know it.

Strictly speaking, he should have been wearing something bright. A blue shirt with a tangerine sweater, iridescent green pants, a scarlet cape with an *S* enclosed in a yellow triangle. And . . . rimmed glasses? It had been a long time since grade school. Never mind; he'd have to go as he was.

A good thing he liked flamboyant gestures.

He skirted the edge of the bare region until he reached the houses. Presently he was walking through dark streets. The houses were fascinating and strange. He would have enjoyed seeing them by daylight. What manner of people lived in them? Colorful, idle, happy, eternally young and healthy. He would have liked to be one of them.

But he noticed a peculiar thing about the houses. Heterogeneous as they were in form, color, style, building material, they had one thing in common. Always they faced away from the Hospital.

As if the Hospital inspired them with fear. Or guilt.

There were lights ahead. Matt walked faster. He had been walking for half an hour now. Yes, there was the supply road, lit bright as day by two close-spaced lines of street lamps. A broken white line ran down the curving middle.

Matt stepped out to the white line and began following it toward the Hospital.

Again his shoulders were unnaturally rigid, as with the fear of death from behind. But the danger was all before him. The organ banks were the most humiliating imaginable form of death. Yet Matt feared something worse.

Men had been released from the Hospital to tell of their trials. Not many, but they could talk. Matt could guess a little of what waited for him.

They would see him, they would fire mercy-bullets into him, they would carry him on a stretcher into the Hospital. When he woke, he would be taken to his first and last interview with the dread Castro. The Head's burning eyes would look into his, and he would rumble, "Keller, eh? Yes, we had to take your uncle apart. Well, Keller? You walked up here like you thought you were a crew with an appointment. What did you think you were doing, Keller?"

And what was he going to say to that?

CHAPTER V

THE HOSPITAL

ASLEEP, JESUS PIETRO looked ten years older. His defenses—his straight back, tight muscles, and controlled features—were relaxed. His startling pale eyes were closed. His carefully combed white hair was messy, showing the bare scalp over which it had been carefully combed. He slept alone, separated from his wife by a door which was never locked. Sometimes he thrashed in his sleep, and sometimes, ridden by insomnia, he stared at the ceiling with his arms folded and muttered to himself, which was why Nadia slept next door. But tonight he lay quiet.

He could have looked thirty again, with help. Inside his aging skin he was in good physical shape. He had good wind, thanks partly to his borrowed lung; his muscles were hard beneath loose wrinkles and deposits of fat; and his digestion was good. His teeth, all transplants, were perfect. Give him new skin, new scalp, a new liver; replace a number of sphincter and other autonomic muscles . . .

But that would take a special order from the crew congress. It would be a kind of testimonial, and he would accept it if it were offered, but he wasn't going to fight for it. Transplants and the giving of transplants were the right of the crew and their most powerful reward. And Jesus Pietro was . . . not squeamish, but somehow reluctant to exchange parts of himself for parts of some stranger. It would be like losing part of his ego. Only the fear of death had made him accept a new lung years ago.

He slept quietly.

And things began to add up.

Polly Tournquist's films: Someone *had* slipped through his net night before last. Keller's getaway last night. A gnawing suspicion, only an intuition as yet, that ramrobot package #143 was even more important than anyone had guessed. Wrinkled, uncomfortable sheets. His blankets, which were a trifle too heavy. The fact that he had forgotten to brush his teeth. A mental picture of Keller diving head-down for the mist—it kept coming back to haunt him. Faint noises from outside, from the wall, noises already an hour old, noises which hadn't awakened him but which were still unexplained. His twinges of lust for the girl in the coffin cure, and the guilt that followed. His temptation to use that ancient brainwashing technique for his own private purposes, to make the rebel girl love him for a time. *Adultery!* More guilt.

Temptations. Escaped prisoners. Hot, wrinkled bedclothes.

No use. He was awake.

He lay rigidly on his back, arms folded, glaring into the dark. No use fighting it. Last night had fouled up his internal clock; he'd eaten breakfast at twelve-thirty. *Why did he keep thinking of Keller?*

(Head down over the mist, with the fans pushing hard on the seat of his pants. Hell above and Heaven below, going *up* into the unknown; lost forever, destroyed utterly. The dream of the Hindu, realized in physical form. The peace of total dissolution.)

Jesus Pietro rolled over and turned on the phone.

A strange voice said, "Hospital—sir."

"Who is this?"

"Master Sergeant Leonard V. Watts, sir. Night duty."

"What's happening at the Hospital, Master Sergeant?" It was not an unusual question. Jesus Pietro had asked it scores of times at early morning hours during the last ten years.

Watts' voice was crisp. "Let me see. You left at seven, sir. At seven-thirty Major Jansen ordered the release of the deadheads we picked up last night, the ones without ear mikes. Major Jansen left at nine. At ten-thirty Sergeant Helios reported that all the deadheads had been returned to their homes. Mmmm . . ." Shuffling of papers in the background. "All but two of the prisoners questioned today have been executed and stored away. The medical supplies section informs us that the banks will be unable to handle new material until further notice. Do you want the list of executions, sir?"

"No."

"Coffin cure proceeding satisfactorily. No adverse medical reactions from suspect. Grounds reports a false alarm at twelve-oh-eight, caused by a rabbit blundering into the electric-eye barrier. No evidence of anything moving on the grounds."

"Then how do they know it was a rabbit?"

"Shall I ask, sir?"

"No. They guessed, of course. Good night." Jesus Pietro turned on his back and waited for sleep.

His thoughts drifted . . .

. . . He and Nadia hadn't been getting together much lately. Shouldn't he start taking testosterone shots? A transplant wouldn't be necessary; many glands were not put in suspended animation, but were kept running, as it were, with a complex and exact food/blood supply and a system for extracting the hormones. He could put up with the inconvenience of shots.

. . . Though his father hadn't.

A younger Jesus Pietro had spent much time wondering about his own conception. Why had the old man insisted that the doctors connect the vas deferens during his gonad transplant? An older Jesus Pietro thought he knew. Even sixty years ago, despite the centuries-old tradition of large families, the Plateau had been mostly uninhabited. Breeding must have seemed a duty to Haneth Castro, as it had to all his ancestors. Besides, how must the old man have felt, knowing that at last he could no longer sire children?

An older Jesus Pietro thought he knew.

His thoughts were wandering far, blurred with impending sleep. Jesus Pietro turned on his side, drowsily comfortable.

. . . Rabbit?

Why not? From the woods.

Jesus Pietro turned on his other side.

. . . What was a rabbit doing in the trapped woods?

What was anything bigger than a field mouse doing in the woods?

What was a rabbit doing on Alpha Plateau? What would it eat?

Jesus Pietro cursed and reached for the phone. To Master Sergeant Watts he said, "Take an order. Tomorrow I want the woods searched thoroughly and then deloused. If they find anything as big as a rat, I want to know about it."

"Yes, sir."

"That alarm tonight. What sector?"

"Let me see. Where the—ah. Sector six, sir."

"Six? That's nowhere *near* the woods."

"No, sir."

And that was that. "Good night, Master Sergeant," said Jesus Pietro, and hung up. Tomorrow they'd search the woods. Implementation was becoming decidedly slack, Jesus Pietro decided. He'd have to do something about it.

The wall slanted outward, twelve feet of concrete cross-laced with barbed wire. The gate slanted too, at the same angle, perhaps twelve degrees from vertical. Solid cast-iron it was, built to slide into the concrete wall, which was twelve feet thick. The gate was closed. Lights from inside lit the upper edges of wall and gate, and tinged the sky above.

Matt stood under the wall, looking up. He couldn't climb over. If they saw him, they'd open the gate for him . . . but they *mustn't* see him.

They hadn't yet. The train of logic had worked. If something that glows in the dark stops glowing when it's been in the dark too long, hang it near a light. If a car goes up when it's rightside up, it'll go down *fast* when it's upside down. If the cops see you when you're hiding, but don't when you're not, they'll ignore you completely when you walk up the middle of a lighted road.

But logic ended here.

Whatever had helped him wasn't helping him now.

Matt turned his back on the wall. He stood beneath the overhanging iron gate, his eyes following the straight line of the road to where its lights ended. Most of the houses were dark now. The land was black all the way to the starry horizon. On his right the stars were blurred along that line, and Matt knew he was seeing the top of the void mist.

The impulse that came then was one he never managed to explain, even to himself.

He cleared his throat. "Something is helping me," he said in an almost normal voice. "I know that. I need help to get through this gate. I have to get into the Hospital."

Noises came from inside the wall, the faintest of sounds: regular footsteps, distant voices. They were the business of the Hospital and had nothing to do with Matt.

Outside the wall nothing changed.

"Get me in there," he pleaded, to himself or to something outside himself. He didn't know which. He knew nothing.

On the Plateau there was no religion.

But suddenly Matt knew that there was just one way to get inside. He stepped off the access road and began hunting. Presently he found a discarded chunk of concrete, dirty and uneven. He carried it back and began pounding it against the iron gate.

CLANG! CLANG! CLANG!

A head appeared on the wall. "*Stop* that, you half-witted excuse for a colonist bastard!"

"Let me in."

The head remained. "You *are* a colonist."

"Right."

"Don't move! Don't you move a muscle!" The man

fumbled with something on the other side of the wall.
Both hands appeared, one holding a gun, the other a
telephone receiver. "Hello? Hello? Answer the phone,
dammit! . . . Watts? Hobart. A fool of a colonist just came
walking up to the gate and started pounding on it. *Yes*, a
real colonist! What do I do with him? . . . All right, I'll
ask."

The head looked down. "You want to walk or be
carried?"

"I'll walk," said Matt.

"He says he'll walk. Why should he get his choice?
. . . Oh. I guess it's easier at that. Sorry, Watts, I'm a little
shook. This never happened to me before."

The gateman hung up. His head and gun continued to
peer down at Matt. After a moment the gate slid back into
the wall.

"Come on through," said the gateman. "Fold your
hands behind your neck."

Matt did. A gatehouse had been built against the wall
on the inside. The gateman came down a short flight of
steps. "Stay ahead of me," he ordered. "Start walking.
That's the front entrance, where all the lights are. See?
Walk toward that."

It would have been hard to miss the front entrance. The
great square bronze door topped a flight of broad, shallow
steps flanked by Doric pillars. The steps and the pillars
were either marble or some plastic substitute.

"Stop looking back at me," snapped the gateman. His
voice shook.

When they reached the door, the gateman produced a
whistle and blew into it. There was no sound, but the door
opened. Matt went through.

Once inside, the gateman seemed to relax. "What were
you doing out there?" he asked.

Matt's fear was returning. He was *here*. These corridors
were the Hospital. He hadn't thought past this moment.
Deliberately so; for if he had, he would have run. The
walls around him were concrete, with a few metal grilles

at floor level and four rows of fluorescent tubing in the ceiling. There were doors, all closed. An unfamiliar odor tinged the air, or a combination of odors.

"I said, "What were—"

"Find out at the trial!"

"Don't bite my head off. What trial? I found you on Alpha Plateau. That makes you guilty. They'll put you in the vivarium till they need you, and then they'll pour antifreeze in you and cart you away. You'll never wake up." It sounded as if the gateman was smacking his lips.

Matt's head jerked around, with the terror showing in his eyes. The gateman jumped back at the sudden move. His gun steadied. It was a mercy-bullet pistol, with a tiny aperture in the nose and a CO_2 cartridge doubling as handle. For a frozen moment Matt knew he was about to shoot.

They'd carry his unconscious body to the vivarium, whatever that was. He wouldn't wake up there. They'd take him apart while he was sleeping. His last living moment dragged out and out . . .

The gun lowered. Matt shrank back from the gateman's expression. The gateman had gone mad. His wild eyes looked about him in horror, at the walls, at the doors, at the mercy-bullet gun in his hand, at everything but Matt. Abruptly he turned and ran.

Matt heard his wail drifting back. "Mist Demons! I'm supposed to be on the *gate!*"

At one-thirty another officer came to relieve Polly's guard.

The newcomer's uniform was not as well pressed, but he himself seemed in better condition. His muscles were gymnasium muscles, and he was casually alert at one-thirty in the morning. He waited until the long-headed man had gone, then moved to inspect the dials along the edge of Polly's coffin.

He was more thorough than the other. He moved methodically down the line, in no hurry, jotting the settings in a notebook. Then he opened two big clamps at two corners of the coffin and swung the lid back, careful not to jar it.

The figure within did not move. She was wrapped like a mummy, a mummy with a snout, in soft swaddling cloth. The snout was a bulge over her mouth and nose, the mouth pads and the arrangements for breathing. There were similar protrusions over her ears. Her arms were crossed at her waist, straitjacket fashion.

The Implementation officer looked down at her for long moments. When he turned, he showed his first signs of furtiveness. But he was alone, and no footsteps sounded in the hall.

From the head end of the coffin protruded a padded tube with a cap even more heavily padded in sponge rubber. The officer opened the cap and spoke softly.

"Don't be afraid. I'm a friend. I'm going to put you to sleep."

He peeled the soft bandage from Polly's arm, drew his gun, and fired at the skin. Half a dozen red beads formed there, but the girl did not move. He could not have been sure that she heard him or that she felt the needles.

He closed the lid and the cap of the speaking tube.

He was perspiring freely as he watched the dials change. Presently he produced a screwdriver and went to work at the backs of the dials. When he finished, all eight dials read as they had read when he came in.

They lied. They said that Polly Tournquist was awake but motionless, conscious but deprived of any sensory stimulus. They said she was going mad by increments. Whereas Polly Tournquist was asleep. She would be asleep for the eight hours of Loren's tour of duty.

Loren wiped his face and sat down. He did not enjoy taking such risks, but it was necessary. The girl must know something, else she wouldn't be here. Now she could hold out for eight hours longer.

The man they wheeled into the organ bank operating

room was unconscious. He was the same man Jesus Pietro's squad had found resting on the dead-man switch, one of those he had questioned that afternoon. Jesus Pietro was through with him; he had been tried and condemned, but in law he was still alive. It was a legal point, nothing more.

The operating room was big and busy. Against one long wall were twenty small suspended-animation tanks mounted on wheels, for moving medical supplies to and from the room next door. Doctors and internes worked quietly and skillfully at a multitude of operating tables. There were cold baths: open tanks of fluid kept at a constant 10 degrees Fahrenheit. Beside the door was a twenty-gallon tank half full of a straw-colored fluid.

Two internes wheeled the convict into the operating room, and one immediately injected a full pint of the straw-colored fluid into his arm. They moved the table next to one of the cold baths. A woman moved over to help, carefully fastening a breathing mask over the man's face. The internes tilted the table. The convict slid into the bath without a splash.

"That's the last," said one. "Oh, boy, I'm beat."

The woman looked at him with concern, a concern that might have showed in her mouth behind the mask but that could not show in her eyes. Eyes have no expression. The interne's voice had shown almost total exhaustion. "Take off, the both of you," she said. "Sleep late tomorrow. We won't need you."

When they finished with this convict, the organ banks would be full. In law he was still alive. But his body temperature fell fast, and his heartbeat was slowing. Eventually it stopped. The patient's temperature continued to fall. In two hours it was well below freezing, yet the straw-colored fluid in his veins kept any part of him from freezing.

In law he was still alive. Prisoners had been reprieved at this point and revived without medical ill effects, though they walked in terror for the rest of their days.

Now they lifted the convict onto an operating table. His skull was opened; an incision was made in his neck, cutting the spinal cord just below the brain stem. The brain was lifted out, carefully, for the membranes surrounding it must not be damaged. Though the doctors might deny it, there was a kind of reverence attached to the human brain, and to this moment. At this moment the convict became legally dead.

In a New York hospital a cardiectomy would have been performed first, and the prisoner would have been dead when it was over. On We Made It he would have been dead the moment his body temperature reached 32 degrees Fahrenheit. It was a legal point. You had to draw the line somewhere.

They flash-burned his brain and saved the ashes for urn burial. His skin came next, removed in one piece, still living. Machines did most of the work, but the machines of the Plateau were not advanced enough to work without human control. The doctors proceeded as if they were disassembling a delicate, very valuable, vastly complex jigsaw puzzle. Each unit went into a suspended-animation tank. Someone then took a tiny sample with a hypodermic and tested it for a wide variety of rejection reactions. A transplant operation was never cut-and-dried. A patient's body would reject foreign parts unless each rejection reaction was balanced by complex biochemicals. When the tests were over, each unit was labeled in full detail and wheeled next door, into the organ banks.

Matt was lost. He wandered through the halls looking for a door labeled Vivarium. Some of the doors he passed had labels; some did not. The Hospital was huge. Chances were, he could wander for days without finding the vivarium the gateman had mentioned.

Solitary individuals passed him in the corridors, in police uniforms or in white gowns and white masks pulled down around their necks. If he saw someone coming, Matt shrank against the wall and remained perfectly still until the intruder passed. Nobody noticed him. His strange invisibility protected him well.

But he wasn't getting anywhere.

A map, that's what he needed.

Some of these doors must lead to offices. Some or all offices must have maps in them, perhaps built into wall or desk. After all, the place was *so* complicated. Matt nodded to himself. Here was a door, now, with a strange symbol and some lettering: AUTHORIZED PERSONNEL ONLY. Maybe . . .

He opened the door. And froze halfway through it, shocked to the core.

Glass tanks filled the room like floor-to-ceiling aquarium tanks, each subdivided into compartments. They were arranged like a labyrinth, or like the bookcases in a public library. In the first moments Matt couldn't recognize anything he saw in those tanks; but in their asymmetrical shapes and in their infinite dark shades of red, their nature was unmistakable.

He stepped all the way inside. He had abandoned control of his legs, and they moved of themselves. These flattish dark-red objects, those translucent membranes, the soft-looking blobs of alien shapes, the great transparent cylindrical tanks filled with bright-red fluid . . . Yes, these had been human beings. And there were epitaphs:

Type AB, RH+. Glucose content . . . Rd Corp count . . .

Thyroid gland, male. Rejection classes C, 2, pn, 31. Overactive for body weight less than . . .

Left humerus, live. Marrow type O, Rh−, N, 02. Length . . . IMPORTANT: Test for fit in sockets before using.

Matt closed his eyes and rested his head against one of the tanks. The glass surface was cold. It felt good against his perspiring forehead. He had always had too much empathy. Now there was a grief in him, and he needed time to mourn these strangers. Mist Demons grant they were strangers.

Pancreas. Rejection classes F, 4, pr, 21. DIABETIC TENDENCIES: Use for pancreatic fluid secretion only. DO NOT TRANSPLANT.

A door opened.

Matt slid behind the tank and watched from around the corner. The woman wore gown and mask, and she pushed something on wheels. Matt watched her transfer things from the cart into various of the larger tanks.

Somebody had just died.

And the woman in the mask was a monster. If she'd taken off her mask to reveal foot-long poison-dripping fangs, Matt couldn't have feared her more.

Voices came through the open door.

"We can't use any more muscle tissue." A woman's voice, high and querulous, with a crew lilt. The lilt didn't quite ring true, though Matt couldn't have said where it failed.

A sarcastic male voice answered. "What shall we do, throw it away?"

"Why not?"

Seconds of silence. The woman with the cart finished her work and moved toward the door. Then: "I've never liked the idea. A man *died* to give us healthy, living tissue, and you want to throw it away like—" The closing door cut him off.

Like the remnants of a ghoul's feast, Matt finished for him.

He was turning toward the hall door when his eye caught something else. Four of the tanks were different from the others. They sat near the hall door, on flooring whose scars and shaded color showed where suspended-animation tanks had stood. Unlike the suspended-animation tanks, these did not have heavy machinery-filled bases. Instead, machinery rested in the tanks themselves, behind the transparent walls.

It might have been aerating machinery. The nearest tank contained six small human hearts.

Unmistakably they were hearts. They beat. But they were tiny, no bigger than a child's fist. Matt touched the surface of the tank, and it was blood warm. The tank next to it held five-lobed objects which had to be livers; but they were small, small.

That did it. In what seemed one leap, Matt was out in the hall. He leaned against the wall, gasping, his shoulders heaving, his eyes unable to see anything but those clusters of small hearts and livers.

Someone rounded the corner and came to an abrupt stop.

Matt turned and saw him: a big, soft man in an Implementation-police uniform. Matt tried his voice. It came out blurred but comprehensible: "Where's the vivarium?"

The man stared, then pointed. "Take a right and you'll find a flight of stairs. Up one flight, take a right, then a left, and watch for the sign. It's a big door with an alarm light; you can't miss it."

"Thanks." Mat turned toward the stairs. His stomach hurt, and there was a shivering in his hands. He wished he could drop where he was, but he had to keep going.

Something stung his arm.

Matt turned and raised his arm in the same instant. Already the sting was gone; his arm was as numb as a haunch of meat. Half a dozen tiny red drops bedewed his wrist.

The big, soft man regarded Matt with a puzzled frown. His gun was in his hand.

The galaxy spun madly, receding.

Corporal Halley Fox watched the colonist fall, then holstered his gun. What was the world coming to? First the ridiculous secrecy about the ramrobot. Then, two hundred prisoners swept up in one night, and the whole Hospital going crazy trying to cope. And now! A colonist wandering the Hospital corridors, actually asking for the vivarium!

Well, he'd get it. Halley Fox lifted the man and slung him over his shoulder, grunting with the effort. Only his face was soft. *Report it and forget it.* He shifted his burden and staggered toward the stairs.

CHAPTER VI

THE VIVARIUM

AT DAWN the graded peak of Mount Lookitthat swam beneath a sea of fog. For those few who were already abroad, the sky merely turned from black to gray. This was not the poison mist below the void edge but a continuous cloud of water vapor, thick enough to let a blind man win a shooting match. Crew and colonists, one and all, as they stepped outside their homes, their homes vanished behind them. They walked and worked in a universe ten yards in diameter.

At seven o'clock Implementation police moved into the trapped forest, a squad at each end. Yellow fog lights swept the tongue of forest from the nearest sections of wall. The light barely reached the trees. Since the men who had been on watch that night had gone home, the searchers had no idea what animal they were searching for. Some thought it must be colonists.

At nine they met in the middle, shrugged at each other and left. Nothing human or animal lived in the trapped woods, nothing bigger than a big insect. Four aircars nevertheless rose into the fog and sprayed the wood from end to end.

At nine-thirty . . .

Jesus Pietro cut the grapefruit in half and held one half upside down. The grapefruit meat dropped in sections into his bowl. He asked, "Did they ever find that rabbit?"

Major Jansen stopped with his first sip of coffee half-way to his lips. "No, sir, but they did find a prisoner."

"In the woods?"

"No, sir. He was pounding on the gate with a rock. The

gate man took him inside the Hospital, but from there it becomes a little unclear—"

"Jansen, it's already unclear. What was this man doing pounding on the gate?" A horrible thought struck him. "Was he a crew?"

"No, sir. He was Matthew Keller. Positive identification."

Grapefruit juice spilled on the breakfast rack. "Keller?"

"The same."

"Then who was in the car?"

"I doubt we'll ever know, sir. Shall I ask for volunteers to examine the body?"

Jesus Pietro laughed long and loud. Jansen was pure colonist, though he and his ancestors had been in service so long that their accents and manners were almost pure crew. It would never do for him to joke with his superiors in public. But in private he could be amusing—and he had the sense to know the difference.

"I've been trying to think of a way to shake up Implementation," said Jesus Pietro. "That might do it. Well. Keller came up to the gate and began pounding on it with a rock?"

"Yes, sir. The gateman took him in charge after calling Watts. Watts waited half an hour before he called the gatehouse again. The gateman couldn't remember what happened after he and the prisoner reached the Hospital. He was back on duty, and he couldn't explain that either. He should have reported to Watts, of course. Watts put him under arrest."

"Watts shouldn't have waited half an hour. Where was Keller all this time?"

"A Corporal Fox found him outside the door to the organ banks, shot him, and carted him off to the vivarium."

"Then he and the gateman are both waiting for us. Good. I'll never sleep again until I get this straightened out." Jesus Pietro finished his breakfast in a remarkable hurry.

Then it occurred to him that the mystery was deeper than that. How had Keller reached Alpha Plateau at all? The guards wouldn't have let him past the bridge.

By car? But the only car involved . . .

Hobart was scared. He was as frightened as any suspect Jesus Pietro had seen, and he took no interest in hiding it. "I don't *know!* I took him through the door, the big door. I made him walk ahead so he couldn't jump me—"

"And did he?"

"I can't remember anything like that."

"A bump on the head might have given you amnesia. Sit still." Jesus Pietro walked around the chair to examine Hobart's scalp. His impersonal gentleness was frightening in itself. "No bumps, no bruises. Does your head hurt?"

"I feel fine."

"Now, you walked in the door. Were you talking to him?"

The man bobbed his graying head. "Uh huh. I wanted to know what he was doing banging on the gate. He wouldn't say."

"And then?"

"All of a sudden I—" Hobart stopped, swallowed convulsively.

Jesus Pietro put an edge in his voice. "Go on."

Hobart started to cry.

"Stop that. You started to say something. What was it?"

"All of a sudden I—gulp—remembered I was s'posed t'be at the gate—"

"But what about Keller?"

"Who?"

"What about your prisoner?"

"I can't remember!"

"Oh, get out of here." Jesus Pietro thumbed a button. "Take him back to the vivarium. Get me Keller."

Up a flight of stairs, take a right, then a left . . .

VIVARIUM. Behind the big door were rows of contour couches, skimpily padded. All but two couches had occupants. There were ninety-eight prisoners here, of all ages from fifteen to fifty-eight, and all were asleep. Each was wearing a headset. They slept quietly, more quietly than the usual sleeper, breathing shallowly, their peaceful expressions untroubled by bad dreams. It was a strangely restful place. They slept in rows of ten, some snoring gently, the rest silent.

Even the guard looked sleepy. He sat in a more conventional chair to one side of the door, with his double chin drooping on his chest, his arms folded in his lap.

More than four centuries ago, at some time near the middle of the nineteen hundreds, a group of Russian scientists came up with a gadget that might have made sleep obsolete. In some places it did. By the twenty-fourth century it was a rare corner of the known universe that did not know of the sleepmaker.

Take three electrodes, light electrodes. Now pick a guinea pig, human, and get him to lie down with his eyes closed. Put two electrodes on his eyelids, and tape the third to the nape of his neck. Run a gentle, rhythmic electric current from eyelids to nape, through the brain. Your guinea pig will drop off immediately. Turn the current off in a couple of hours, and he will have had the equivalent of eight hours' sleep.

You'd rather not turn off the current? Fine. It won't hurt him. He'll just go on sleeping. He'll sleep through a hurricane. You'll have to wake him occasionally to eat, drink, evacuate, exercise. If you don't plan to keep him long, you can skip the exercise.

Suspects weren't kept long in the vivarium.

Heavy footsteps sounded outside the door. The vivarium guard jerked alert. When the door opened, he was at attention.

"Sit down there," said one of Hobart's escorts. Hobart sat. Tears had streaked his sunken cheeks. He donned his own headset, dropped his head back, and was asleep.

Peace spread across his face. The bigger guard asked, "Which one is Keller?"

The vivarium guard consulted a chart. "Ninety-eight."

"Okay." Instead of taking off Keller's headset, the man moved to a panel of one hundred buttons. He pushed number ninety-eight. As Keller began to stir, they both moved in to attach handcuffs. Then they lifted the headset.

Matt Keller's eyes opened.

His new escorts lifted him to his feet with a practiced motion. "On our way," one said cheerfully. Bewildered, Matt followed the pull on his arms. In a moment they were in the hall. Matt snatched one look behind him before the door closed.

"Wait a minute," he protested, predictably jerking back against the handcuffs.

"Man wants to ask you a few questions. Look, I'd rather carry you than do this. You want to walk?"

The threat usually quieted them down—as it did now. Matt stopped pulling. He'd expected to wake up dead; these moments of consciousness were a free bonus. Someone must have gotten curious.

"Who wants to see me?"

"A gentleman named Castro," the bigger guard tossed off. The dialogue was following its usual pattern. If Keller was an average suspect, the Head's dread name would paralyze his brain. If he kept his wits, he'd still choose to use this time in preparation for his interview, rather than risk a sonic now. Both guards had been doing this for so long that they'd come to see prisoners as faceless, interchangeable.

Castro. The name echoed between Matt's ears.

What did you think you were doing, Keller? You came in here like you had an engraved invitation. Thought you had a secret weapon, did you, Keller? What did you think you were doing, Keller? WHAT DID YOU THINK YOU—

One instant the suspect was walking between them, lost

in his own fears. The next, he had jerked back like a fish hooked on two lines. The guards instantly pulled apart to string him between them, then regarded him in sheer disgust. One said, "Stupid!" The other pulled out his gun.

They stood there, one with a sonic loose in his hand, looking about them in apparent bewilderment. Matt jerked again, and the smaller guard looked in shocked surprise at his own wrist. He fumbled in his belt, got out a key, and unlocked the handcuff.

Matt threw all his weight on the other steel chain. The bigger guard yelled in anger and pulled back. Matt flew into him, inadvertently butting him in the stomach. The guard hit him across the jaw with a backhand swing of his arm. Momentarily unable to move, Matt watched the guard take a key from his pocket and unlock the remaining handcuff from his own wrist. The guard's eyes were strange.

Matt backed away with two sets of handcuffs dangling from his arms. The guards looked after him, not at him but in his general direction. Something was very wrong with their eyes. Fruitlessly, Matt tried to remember where he'd seen that look before. The gateman last night?

The guards turned and sauntered away.

Matt shook his head, more baffled than relieved, and turned back the way he had come. There was the vivarium door. He'd had only one backward glimpse, but he was sure he'd seen Harry Kane in there.

The door was locked.

Mist Demons, here we go again. Matt raised his hand, changed his mind, changed it again, and slapped the palm three times against the door. It opened at once. A round, expressionless face looked through and suddenly acquired an expression. The door started to close. Matt pulled it open and went in.

The round guard with the round face genuinely didn't know what to do. At least he hadn't forgotten that Matt was here. Matt was grateful. He swung joyfully at the guard's double chin. When the guard didn't fold, Matt hit him again. The man finally reached for his gun, and Matt took a firm grip on the appropriate wrist, holding the gun in its holster, and swung once more. The guard slid to the floor.

Matt took the guard's sonic and put it in his pants pocket. His hand hurt. He rubbed it against his cheek, which also hurt, and ran his eyes down the row of sleepers. There was Laney! Laney, her face pale, with one thin scratch from temple to chin, her auburn hair concealing the three-pronged headset, her deep breasts hardly moving as she slept. And there was Hood, looking like a sleeping child. Something began to unwind inside Matt Keller, a warmth uncoiling to spread through his limbs. For hours he had been all alone with death. There was the tall man who'd spelled him for bartender that night. *Night before last!* There was Harry Kane, a cube of a man, strong even in sleep.

Polly wasn't there.

He looked again, carefully, and she still wasn't there.

Where was she? Instantly the aquarium tanks of the organ bank flashed into his mind's eye. One tank had held skins, whole human skins with barely room between them for the clear conducting nutrient fluid. The scalps had borne hair, short and long, blond and black and red, hair that waved in a cold fluid breeze. *Rejection classes C, 2, nr, 34.* He couldn't remember seeing the space-blackness of Polly's hair. It might or might not have been waving in the aquarium tank. He hadn't been looking for it.

Convulsively he made himself look about him. That bank of buttons? He pushed one. It popped out at the touch of a finger. Nothing else happened.

Oh, well, what the hell . . . He started pushing them all, letting his forefinger run down a row of ten, down the next row, and the next. He had released sixty when he heard motion.

The sleepers were waking.

He released the rest of the buttons. The murmur of awakening grew louder: yawning, confused voices, clatterings, gasps of dismayed shock when prisoners suddenly realized where they were. A clear voice calling, "Matt? Matt!"

"Here, Laney!"

She wove her way toward him through people climbing groggily out of their contour couches. Then she was in his arms, and they clung to each other as if a tornado were trying to pluck them apart and whirl them away. Matt felt suddenly weak, as if he could afford weakness now. "So you didn't make it," he said.

"Matt, where *are* we? I tried to get to the void edge—"

Somebody bellowed, "We are in the Hospital vivarium!" The voice cut like an ax through the rising pandemonium. Harry Kane, Leader, assumed his proper role.

"That's right," Matt said gently.

Her eyes were two inches from his, dead level. "*Oh.* Then you didn't make it either."

"Yes I did. I had to get here on my own."

"What—*how?*"

"Good question. I don't know exactly—"

Laney began to chuckle.

Shouting from the back of the room. Somebody had noticed an Implementation uniform on one of the newly awakened. A scream of pure terror changed to a yell of agony and died abruptly. Matt saw jerking heads, heard sounds he tried to ignore. Laney wasn't laughing anymore. The disturbance subsided.

Harry Kane had mounted a chair. He cupped his hands and bellowed, "Shut up, all of you! Everyone who knows the map of the Hospital, get over here! Gather round me!" There was a shifting in the mass. Laney and Matt still clung to each other, but not desperately now. Their heads turned to watch Harry, acknowledging his leadership. "Take a look, the rest of you!" Harry shouted. "These are the people who can lead you out of here. In a minute we're going to have to make our break. Keep your eyes on . . ." He named eight names. Hood's was one. "Some of us are going to get shot. As long as one of these eight is still moving, follow him! Or her. If all eight are down, and I am too"—he paused for emphasis—"scatter! Make as much trouble as you can! Sometimes the only sensible thing to do is panic!

"Now, who got us out of this? Who woke us up? Anyone?"

"Me," said Matt.

A last buzz of noise died. Suddenly everyone was looking at him. Harry said, "How?"

"I'm not sure how I got in here. I'd like to talk to Hood about it."

"Okay, stick with Jay. Keller, isn't it? We're grateful, Keller. What do those buttons do? I saw you fooling with them."

"They turn off whatever it is that makes you go to sleep."

"Is anyone still in his couch? If so, get out of it *now*. Now, somebody push those buttons back in so it'll look like there was a power failure. Was that it, Keller? Did you just accidentally wake up?"

"No."

Harry Kane looked puzzled, but when Matt didn't elaborate, he shrugged. "Watson, Chek, start pushing those buttons in. Jay, make sure you stick with Keller. The rest of you, are you ready to move?"

There was a shout of assent. As it died, a lone voice asked, "Where to?"

"Good point. If you get free, make for the coral houses around the south void and Alpha-Beta cliffs. Anything else?"

Nobody spoke, including Matt. Why ask questions to which nobody knew the answers? Matt was unutterably relieved to let someone else make the decisions for a while. They might be just as wrong, but ninety-eight rebels could be a mighty force, even moving in the wrong direction. And Harry Kane was a born leader.

Laney moved out of his arms but kept a grip on one hand. Matt became conscious of the handcuffs dangling from his wrists. They might hamper him. Jay Hood moved up beside him, looking rumpled. He shook hands, grinning, but the grin didn't match the fear in his eyes, and he seemed reluctant to let go. Was there one person in this room who wasn't terrified? If there was, it wasn't Matt. He pulled the sonic loose from his pants pocket.

"All out," said Harry Kane, and butted the door open with a wide shoulder. They streamed into the hall.

"I'll take only a minute of your time, Watts." Jesus Pietro relaxed indolently in his chair. He loved mysteries and proposed to enjoy this one. "I want you to describe in detail what happened last night, starting with the call from Hobart."

"But there *aren't* any details, sir." Master Sergeant Watts was tired of repeating himself. His voice was turning querulous. "Five minutes after your call, Hobart called and said he had a prisoner. I told him to bring him to my office. He never came. Finally I called the *gate*. He was *there*, all right, with*out* his prisoner, and he couldn't explain what had happened. I had to put him under arrest."

"His behavior has been puzzling in other ways. That is why I ask, Why didn't you call the gate earlier?"

"Sir?"

"Your behavior is as puzzling as Hobart's, Watts. Why did you assume it would take Hobart half an hour to reach your office?"

"Oh." Watts fidgeted. "Well, Hobart said this bird came right up to the gate and started banging on it with a rock. When Hobart didn't show right away, I thought he must have stopped off to question the prisoner, find out why he did it. After all," he explained hastily, "if he brought the bird straight to me, he'd likely never find out what he was doing banging on the gate."

"Very logical. Did it occur to you at any point that the 'bird' might have overpowered Hobart?"

"But Hobart had a sonic!"

"Watts, have you ever been on a raid?"

"No, sir. How could I?"

"A man came back from the raid of night-before-last with the bones of his nose spread all over his face. He, too, had a sonic."

"Yessir, but that was a *raid,* sir."

Jesus Pietro sighed. "Thank you, Master Sergeant. Will you step outside, please? Your bird should be arriving any minute."

Watts left, his relief showing.

He'd made a good point, thought Jesus Pietro, though not the one he'd intended. Probably all the Hospital guards had the same idea: that a gun was ipso facto invincible. Why not? The Hospital guards had never been on a raid in the colonist regions. Few had ever seen a colonist who wasn't unconscious. Occasionally Jesus Pietro staged mock raids with guards playing the part of colonists. They didn't mind, particularly; mercy-weapons were not unpleasant. But the men with the guns always won. All the guards' experience told them that the gun was king, that a man who had a gun need fear nothing but a gun.

What to do? Interchange guards and raiders long enough to give the guards some experience? No, the elite raiders would never stand for that.

Why was he worrying about Implementation?

Had the Hospital ever been attacked? Never, on Alpha Plateau. A colonist force had no way to get there.

But Keller had.

He used the phone. "Jansen, find out who was on guard at the Alpha-Beta Bridge last night. Wake them up and send them here."

"It will be at least fifteen minutes, sir."

"Fine."

How had Keller gotten past them? There had been one aircar on Gamma Plateau, but it had been destroyed. With the pilot still in it? Had Keller had a chauffeur? Or . . . would a colonist know how to use the autopilot?

Where the Mist Demons was Keller?

Jesus Pietro began to pace the room. He had no cause for worry, yet he worried. Instinct? He didn't believe he had instincts. The phone spoke in his secretary's voice. "Sir, did you order two guards?"

"Bridge guards?"

"No, sir. Intrahospital guards."

"No."

"Thank you." Click.

Something had set off the grounds alarms last night. Not a rabbit. Keller might have tried the wall first. If the grounds guards had let a prisoner escape, then faked a report—he'd have their hides!

"Sir, these guards insist you sent for them."

"Well, I damn well didn't. Tell them—just a minute. Send them in."

They came, two burly men whose submissive countenances unsuccessfully hid their ire at being made to wait.

"When did I send for you?" asked Jesus Pietro.

The big one said, "Twenty minutes ago," daring Jesus Pietro to call him a liar.

"Were you supposed to pick up a prisoner first?"

"No, sir. We took Hobart to the vivarium, put him to beddybye and came straight back."

"You don't remember being—"

The smaller guard went white. "D—Dave! We *were* supposed to p—pick up someone. Keeler. Something Keeler."

Jesus Pietro regarded them for a full twenty seconds. His face was curiously immobile. Then he opened the intercome. "Major Jansen. Sound *'Prisoners Loose.'* "

"Wait a minute," said Matt.

The tail end of the colonist swarm was leaving them behind. Hood brought himself up short. "What are you doing?"

Matt dodged back into the vivarium. One man lay on his face with his headset on. Probably he'd thought he was safe once he was out of the couch. Matt snatched the headset off and slapped him twice, hard; and when his eyelids fluttered, Matt pulled him to his feet and pushed him at the door.

Watson and Chek finished pushing buttons and left, running, shoving around Hood.

"Come on!" Hood yelled from the doorway. Panic was in his voice. But Matt stood rooted by the thing on the floor.

The guard. They'd torn him to pieces!

Matt was back in the organ banks, frozen rigid by horror.

"Keller!"

Matt stooped, picked up something soft and wet. His expression was very strange. He stepped to the door, hesitated a moment, then drew two sweeping arcs and three small closed curves on its gleaming metal surface. He hurled the warm thing backhand, turned, and ran. The two men and Laney charged down the hall, trying to catch the swarm.

The swarm poured down the stairs like a waterfall: a close-packed mass, running and stumbling against each other and brushing against walls and bannisters and generally making a hell of a lot of noise. Harry Kane led. A cold certainty was in his heart, the knowledge that he would be first to fall when they met the first armed guard. But by then the swarm should have unstoppable momentum.

The first armed guard was several yards beyond the first corner. He turned and stared as if his eyes beheld a miracle. He hadn't moved when the mob reached him. Someone actually had the sense to take his gun. A tall blond man got it and immediately forced his way to the front, waving it and yelling for room. The swarm flowed around and over the limp Implementation policeman.

This hallway was long, lined with doors on both sides. Every door seemed to be swinging open at once. The man with the gun closed his fist on the trigger and waved it slowly up and down the hall. Heads peered out the doors, paused, and were followed by falling bodies. The colonist swarm slowed to pick their way around the crewish and half-crewish fallen. Nonetheless, the fallen were all badly or mortally injured when the swarm passed. Implementation used mercy-weapons because they needed their prisoners intact. The swarm had no such motive for mercy.

The swarm was stretching now, dividing the fast from the slow, as Kane reached the end of the hall. He rounded the turn in a clump of six.

Two police were parked indolently against opposite walls, steaming cups in their hands, their heads turned to see where the noise was coming from. For a magic moment they stayed that way . . . and then their cups flew wide, trailing spiral nebulae of brown fluid, and their guns came up like flowing light. Harry Kane fell with a buzzing in his ears. But his last glimpse of the corridor showed him that the police were falling too.

He lay like a broken doll, with his head swimming and his eyes blurring and his body as numb as a frozen plucked chicken. Feet pounded past and over him. Through the blanketing numbness he dimly sensed himself being kicked.

Abruptly four hands gripped his wrists and ankles, and he was off again, swaying and jouncing between his rescuers. Harry Kane was pleased. His opinion of mobs was low. This mob was behaving better than he had expected. Through the buzzing in his ears he heard a siren.

At the bottom of the stairs they reached the tail of the swarm—Laney in the lead, Matt and Jay Hood following. Matt panted, "Stay! Got . . . gun."

Laney saw the point and slowed. Matt could guard the rear. If they tried to reach the front of the swarm, they'd be stuck in the middle, and the sonic would be useless.

But nobody came at them from the rear. There were noises ahead, and they passed sprawled bodies: one policeman, then a string of men and women in lab smocks. Matt found his stomach trying to turn inside out. The rebels' viciousness was apalling. So was Hood's grin: a tight killer's grin, making a lie of his scholar's face.

Ahead, more commotion. Two men stopped to lift a heavy sprawled figure and continued running. Harry Kane was out of the action. "Hope somebody's leading them!" Hood shouted.

A siren blared in the corridors. It was loud enough to wake the Mist Demons, to send them screaming into the sky for a little peace. It jarred the concrete; it shook the very bones of a man. There was a rattling clang, barely heard above the siren. An iron door had dropped into the swarm, cutting it in two. One man was emphatically dead beneath it. The tail of the swarm, including perhaps a dozen men and women, washed against the steel door and rebounded.

Trapped. The other end of the corridor was also blocked. But doors lined both sides. One man took off, running down the hallway toward the far end, swiveling his head back and forth to look briefly through the open doors, ignoring the closed ones. "Here!" he shouted, waving an arm. Wordlessly the others followed.

It was a lounge, a relaxation room, furnished with four wide couches, scattered chairs, two card tables, and a huge coffee dispenser. And a picture window. As Matt reached the door, the window already gaped wide, showing sharp glass teeth. The man who'd found the room was using a chair to clean the glass away.

An almost soundless hum—and Matt felt the numbness of a sonic beamer. From the doorway! He slammed the door and it stopped.

Automatics?

"Benny!" Laney shouted, picking up one end of a couch. The man at the window dropped his chair and ran to take the other end. He'd been one of Laney's escorts the night of the party. Together they dropped the couch across the windowsill, over the broken glass. Colonists began to climb over it.

Hood had found a closet and opened it. It was like opening Pandora's box. Matt saw half-a-dozen men in white smocks swarm over Hood. In seconds they would have torn him to ribbons. Matt used his sonic. They all went down in a lump, including Hood. Matt pulled him out, draped him over a shoulder, and followed the others over the couch. Hood was heavier than he looked.

Matt had to drop him on the grass and follow him down. Far across the lawn was the Hospital wall, leaning outward, the top laced with wires that leaned inward. Very thin wire, just barely visible through the thin fog. Matt picked Hood up, glanced around, saw the others running alongside the building with the tall man named Benny in the lead. He staggered after them.

They reached a corner—the Hospital seemed to have a million corners—stopped sharply, and backed up, milling. Guards coming? Matt put Hood down, hefted his sonic—

A gun and hand emerged questing from the broken picture window. Matt fired and the man slumped. But he knew there must be others in there. Matt ducked beneath the window, rose suddenly, and fired in. Half-a-dozen police fired back. Matt's right side and arm went numb; he dropped the gun, then himself dropped below the sill. In a moment they'd be peering over. The man named Benny was running toward him. Matt threw the first policeman's sonic to him and picked up his own with his left hand.

The men inside hadn't expected Benny. They were trying to fire over the sill at Matt, and to do that they had to lean out. In half a minute it was over.

Benny said, "There's a carport just beyond that corner. Guarded."

"Do they know we're here?"

"I don't think so. The Mist Demons have given us a mist." Benny smiled at his own pun.

"Good. We can use these guns. You'll have to carry Jay; my arm's out."

"Jay's the only one who can fly."

"I can," said Matt.

"Major Jansen. Sound 'Prisoners Loose.' "

The sound of the siren came instantly, even before Jesus Pietro could change his mind. For a moment he was sure, preternaturally sure, that he'd made a fool of himself. This could cost him much face . . .

But no. Keller *must* be freeing the prisoners. Keller wasn't here; therefore Keller was free. His first move would be to free the other Sons of Earth. If the vivarium guard had stopped him, he would then have called here; he hadn't called; hence Keller had succeeded.

But if Keller were harmlessly asleep in the vivarium? Nonsense. Why had the guards forgotten about him? They were behaving too much like Hobart had behaved last night. A miracle had been worked, a miracle of the kind Jesus Pietro was beginning to associate with Keller. There must be some purpose to it.

It must have been used to free Keller.

And the halls must be full of angry rebels.

That was very bad. Implementation had motives for using mercy-weapons. Rebels had none—neither mercy-weapons nor mercy-motives. They'd kill whoever got in their way.

The steel doors would be in place now, vibrating in sleep-producing frequencies. By now the danger would be over—almost certainly. Unless the rebels had first gotten out of the halls.

But what damage had they done already?

"Come with me," Jesus Pietro told the two guards. He marched toward the door. "Keep your guns drawn," he added over his shoulder.

The guards snapped out of their stupor and ran to catch up. They had not the faintest idea what was going on, but

Jesus Pietro was sure they'd recognize a colonist in time to down him. They'd be adequate protection.

One dozen colonists, two stunned. Seven captured guns.

Matt stayed hidden behind the corner, reluctantly obeying Benny's orders. With him were the two women: Laney and a deep-voiced middle-aged tigress named Lydia Hancock, and the two fallen: Jay Hood and Harry Kane.

Matt would have fought the carport guards, but he couldn't fight the logic. Because he was the only one who could fly a car, he had to stay behind while the others charged out onto the field with their sonics going.

The carport was a big, flat expanse of lawn, a variant of mutant grass, which could take an infinite amount of trampling. Lines of near-white crossed the green, outlining landing targets. The white too was grass. Cars rested near the centers of two of the targets. Men moved about the cars, servicing them and removing metal canisters from the underbellies. The mist hung four feet above the grass under diffuse sunlight, curling about the rebels as they ran.

They were halfway to the cars when someone on the Hospital wall swung a spotlight-sized sonic toward them. The rebels dropped immediately, like hay before a scythe. So did the mechanics around the cars. Unconscious men lay scattered across the carport field with the mist curling around them.

Matt pulled his head back as the big sonic swung toward the corner. Even so, he felt the numbness, faint and far-off, matching the deadwood feeling in his right arm. "Shall we wait till they turn it off, then run for it?"

"I think they've got us," said Laney.

"Stop that!" Mrs. Hancock rapped savagely. Matt had first met her fifteen minutes ago and had never seen her without her present enraged expression. She was a fierce one, bulky and homely, a natural for any cause. "They haven't got us until they take us!"

"Something keeps people from seeing me sometimes,"

said Matt. "If you want to risk it, and if you all stay close to me, it may protect us all."

"Crack' unner strain." Hood's voice was slurred, barely comprehensible. Only his eyes moved to watch Matt. Harry, too, was awake, alert, and immobile.

"It's true, Hood. I don't know why, but it's true. I think it must be a psi power."

"Wreebody who blieves in psi things hees psygic."

"The sonic's off us," said Laney.

"My arm's dead. Laney, you and Mrs.—"

"Call me Lydia."

"You and Lydia put Hood over my left shoulder, then pick up Harry. Stay right by me. We'll be *walking*, remember. Don't try to hide. If we get shot, I'll apologize when I get the chance."

" 'Pologise now."

"Okay, Hood. I'm sorry I got us all killed."

" 'Sawrigh'."

"Let's go."

CHAPTER VII

THE BLEEDING HEART

WHEN THEY see this . . . Jesus Pietro shuddered. He watched his own guards shrink back, unwilling to enter, unable to look away. *They'll think a little less of their guns when they see this!*

The vivarium guard had certainly had a gun. Probably he hadn't thought to draw it in time.

He'd get no second chance.

He was like something spilled from an organ-bank conveyor tank.

Hobart, dead near the back of the vivarium, was no prettier. Jesus Pietro felt a stab of guilt. He hadn't meant Hobart for such a fate.

Aside from the bodies, the vivarium was empty. Naturally.

Jesus Pietro looked once more around him—and his eyes found the door and the dark scrawl on its bright steel surface.

It was a symbol of some kind; he was sure of that. But of what? The symbol of the Sons of Earth was a circle containing a streamlined outline of the American supercontinent. This was nothing like it, nor was it like anything he knew of. But it had unmistakably been drawn in human blood.

Two wide arcs, bilaterally symmetrical. Three small closed curves underneath, like circles with tails. Tadpoles? Some microorganism?

Jesus Pietro rubbed the heels of his hands into his eyes. Later he'd ask the prisoners. Best forget it for now.

"Assume they took the fastest route to the main entrance," he said aloud. If the guards were surprised to hear him thus lecture himself, they reacted as Major Jansen had long since learned to react. They said nothing. "Come," said Jesus Pietro.

Left, right, down the stairs . . . a dead policeman sprawled in the hall, his Implementation uniform as torn and ruined as himself. Jesus Pietro passed him without breaking his juggernaut stride. He reached steel emergency doors and used his ultrasonic whistle. As the doors went up, his guards tensed.

Two pitiful rows of maimed and dead, and another steel door at the other end. The dead were like an explosion in the organ banks. That was definitely the way to think of them. It would not do to consider that these had been human beings under Jesus Pietro's protection. Most had not even been police, but civilians: doctors and electricians.

What a valuable lesson the Hospital guards would learn from this! Jesus Pietro felt sick. It showed only in his unusual pallor; but that he could not control. He marched down the corridor with his expression held remotely aloof. The steel doors went up as he approached.

Colonists were piled against the steel doors at both ends, as if trying to escape the trap even while unconscious. One of the policemen spoke into a handphone, asking for stretchers.

Jesus Pietro stood over the piled rebels. "I never really hated them before," he said.

"K'llr, use gyrsco'."

"What?" Matt couldn't spare the attention. He was trying to fly with one hand, the wrong hand; his car bucked and weaved like a frightened stallion.

"Gy—rro—skko'!" Hood enunciated painfully.

"I see it. What do I do with it?"

"Turr' on."

Matt flipped the Gyroscope switch to On. Something hummed below him. The car trembled, then righted itself, going straight up.

"Shlatsh."

Matt used the knob. The car began to accelerate.

"Hel' me see ow', Laney." Hood was propped upright beside the left front window, with Harry Kane in the middle and Matt on the right. Laney reached from the back seat to hold Hood's head out the window.

"Turr' ri'."

"How?"

"Shtee—ring nog."

"Knob? Like this thing?"

"Ye—ss i'iot."

"For the record," Matt said icily, "I flew a car all the way from Harry's basement to Alpha Plateau. It was the first time I'd ever been in a car. Naturally I don't know what all these gadgets do."

"Thass ri'. Now go strray' till I tell you."

Matt released the knob. The car flew on by itself. "We aren't going toward the coral houses," he said.

"No." Harry Kane spoke slowly but understandably. "The coral houses are the first place Implementation will look. I couldn't drag a hundred men where we're going."

"Where's that?"

"A large unoccupied mansion owned by Geoffrey Eustace Parlette and his family."

"And where will Geoffrey Eustace Parlette be all this time?"

"He and his family are swimming and gambling in a small public resort on Iota. I've got contacts on Alpha Plateau, Keller."

"Parlette. Any—"

"His grandson. Millard Parlette was staying with them, but he's making a speech. He should be starting about now. The sending station on Nob Hill is far enough away, and his hosts here are gone, so he'll probably be staying with a relative."

"It still sounds dangerous."

"*You* should talk."

The left-handed compliment hit Matt like six dry martinis. He'd done it! He'd walked into the Hospital, freed prisoners, raised merry hell, left his mark, and walked out free and untouched! "We can hide the car till the furor dies down," he said. "Then, back to Gamma—"

"And leave my men in the vivarium? I can't do that. And there's Polly Tournquist."

Polly. The girl who'd—Yes. "I'm not a rebel, Harry. The grand rescue's over. Frankly, I only came here to get Laney if I could. I can drop this crusade any time."

"You think Castro will just let you go, Keller? He must know you were one of the prisoners. He'll hunt you down wherever you hide. Besides, I can't let you have the car. I'll need it for *my* grand rescue."

Matt grimaced. It was his car, wasn't it? He'd stolen it himself. But they could fight that out later. "Why did you mention Polly?"

"She saw the ramrobot come down. Castro probably found the films on her. He may be questioning her to find out who else knows."

"Knows what?"

"I don't know either. Polly's the only one. But it must be pretty damn important. Polly thought so, and apparently so did Castro. You didn't know there was a ramrobot coming, did you?"

"No."

"They kept it secret. They've never done that before."

Laney said, "Polly acted like she'd found something vastly important. She insisted on telling us all at once, night before last. But Castro didn't give her the chance. Now I'm wondering whether it wasn't the ramrobot that brought on the raid."

"She could be in the organ banks," said Matt.

"Not yet," said Harry. "Not if Castro found the films. She wouldn't have talked yet. He'll be using the coffin cure, and that takes time."

"Coffin cure?"

"It's not important."

Important or not, Matt didn't like the sound of it. "How are you planning to mount your rescue?"

"I don't know yet."

"Angle lef'," said Hood.

Houses and greenery rolled beneath them. Flying a car was infinitely easier with the gyroscopes going. Matt could see no cars around, police or otherwise. Had something grounded them?

"So," said Laney. "You came all the way to the Hospital to get me."

"In a stolen car," said Matt. "With a small detour into the void mist."

Laney's wide mouth formed half a smile and half a grin, half joy and half amusement. "Naturally I'm flattered."

"Naturally."

Mrs. Hancock spoke from the back seat. "I'd like to know why they didn't beam us down, back there at the carport."

"And you knew they wouldn't," said Laney. "How did you know, Matt?"

"Second the motion," said Harry Kane.

"I don't know," said Matt.

"But you knew it might work."

"Yah."

"Why?"

"Okay. Hood, you listening?"

"Ye—ss."

"It's a long story. I'll start with the morning after the party—"

"Start with the party," said Laney.

"Everything?"

"Everything." Laney gave the word undue emphasis. "I think it might be important, Matt."

Matt shrugged an uncomfortable surrender. "It might at that. Okay. I met Hood in a bar for the first time in eight years . . ."

Jesus Pietro and Major Jansen stood well out of the way as a stream of stretchers moved into the vivarium to deposit their charges in contour couches. In another part of the Hospital other stretchers carried dead and wounded into the operating rooms, some to be restored to life and health and usefulness, others to be pirated for undamaged parts.

"What is it?" Jesus Pietro asked.

"I don't know," said Major Jansen. He stepped back from the door to get a better look. "It seems almost familiar."

"That's no help."

"I assume a colonist drew it?"

"You might as well. Nobody else was left alive."

Major Jansen drew even farther back, stood bouncing lightly on his toes, hands on hips. Finally he said, "It's a valentine, sir."

"A valentine." Jesus Pietro glared intense irritation at his aide. He looked back at the door. "I'll be damned. It *is* a valentine."

"With teardrops."

"A valentine with teardrops. Whoever drew that wasn't sane. Valentine, valentine . . . Why would the Sons of Earth leave us a valentine drawn in human blood?"

"Blood. A bleeding—oh, I see. That's what it is, sir. It's a bleeding heart. They're telling us they're against the practice of executing felons for the organ banks."

"A reasonable attitude for them to take." Jesus Pietro looked once more into the vivarium. The bodies of Hobart and the vivarium guard had been removed, but the stains of carnage remained. He said, "They don't act like the usual sort of bleeding heart."

Thirty thousand pairs of eyes waited behind the teedee lenses.

Four teedee cameras circled him. They were blank now, and untended, as cameramen moved casually about the room, doing things and saying things Millard Parlette made no effort to understand. In fifteen minutes those blank teedee lenses would be peepholes for sixty thousand eyes.

Millard Parlette began leafing through his notes. If there were any changes to be made, the time was Now.

I   Lead-in.

    A   Stress genuine emergency.
    B   Mention ramrobot package.
    C   "What follows is background."

How real would an emergency seem to these people? The last emergency session Millard Parlette could recall was the Great Plague of 2290, more than a century ago. Most of his audience would not have been born then.

Hence the lead-in, to grab their attention.

II   The organ-bank problem—exposition.

    A   Earth calls it a problem; we do not. Therefore Earth knows considerably more about it.
    B   Any citizen, with the help of the organ banks, can live as long as it takes his central nervous system to wear out. This can be a very long time if his circulatory system is kept functioning.
    C   But the citizen cannot take more out of the organ banks than goes into them. He must do his utmost to see that they are supplied.
    D   The only feasible method of supplying the organ banks is through execution of criminals. (Demonstrate this; show why other methods are inadequate.)
    E   A criminal's pirated body can save a dozen lives. There is now no valid argument against capital punishment for any given

crime; for all such argument seeks to prove that killing a man does society no good. Hence the citizen, who wants to live as long and as healthily as possible, will vote any crime into a capital crime if the organ banks are short of material.

1) Cite Earth's capital punishment for false advertising, income tax evasion, air pollution, having children without a license.

The wonder was that it had taken so long to pass these laws.

The organ-bank problem could have started in the year 1900, when Karl Landsteiner separated human blood into four types: A, B, AB, and O. Or in 1914, when Albert Hustin found that sodium citrate would prevent blood from clotting. Or in 1940, when Landsteiner and Wiener found the Rh factor. Blood banks could so easily have been supplied by condemned criminals, but apparently nobody had realized it.

And there was Hamburger's work in the 1960's and 1970's, in a Parisian hospital where kidney transplants were made from donors who were not identical twins. There were the antirejection serums discovered by Mostel and Granovich in the 2010's ...

Nobody seemed to have noticed the implications—until the middle of the twenty-first century.

There were organ banks all over the world, inadequately supplied by people kind enough to will their bodies to medical science.

How useful is the body of a man who dies of old age? How fast can you reach a car accident? And in 2043, Arkansas, which had never rescinded the death penalty, made the organ banks the official state method of execution.

The idea had spread like wildfire ... like a moral plague, as one critic of the time had put it. Millard Parlette had researched it very thoroughly, then cut all of the historical matter out of his speech, afraid it would lose him his audience. People, especially crew, did not like to be lectured.

F   Thus the government which controls the organ banks is more powerful than any dictator in history. Many dictators have had the power of death, but organ banks give a government power of life and death.

     1)   Life. The organ banks can cure nearly anything, and the government can regulate which citizens shall benefit, on grounds that materials are running short. Priorities become vital.

     2)   Death. No citizen will protest when the government condemns a man to die, not when his death gives the citizen his chance to live.

Untrue and unfair. There were always altruists. But let it stand.

III   The organ-bank problem—colonies.

A   Alloplasty: the science of putting foreign materials in the human body for medical purposes.

B   Examples:

     1)   Implanted hearing aids
     2)   Heart pacemakers and artificial hearts
     3)   Plastic tubing for veins, arteries

C   Alloplasty in use on Earth for half a thousand years.

D   No alloplasty for a colony world. Alloplasty
    needs a high technology.
E   Every colony world has organ-bank facili-
    ties. The stasis room of a slowboat is de-
    signed to freeze organs. The ships them-
    selves thus become the center of an organ
    bank.
F   Thus the organ-bank "problem" is unre-
    lieved even by the alternative of alloplasty,
    on any colony world.

IV The organ-bank problem—as it relates to the
    power politics of Mount Lookitthat.

A   The Covenant of Planetfall.

Millard Parlette frowned. How would the average crew
react to the truth about the Covenant of Planetfall?

What they were taught in school was true, in the main.
The Covenant of Planetfall, the agreement which gave the
crew authority over the colonists, *had* existed since the
Planck landing. The colonists *had* agreed to it, all of
them.

The rationale held, too. The crew had taken all the
risks, done all the work of decades, suffered and slaved
through years of training, to reach a target which *might* be
habitable. The colonists had slept peacefully through all
those weary years in space. It was right that the crew
should rule.

But—how many crew knew that those first colonists
had signed the Covenant at gunpoint? That eight had died
rather than sign away their freedom?

Was it Millard Parlette's place to tell them?

Yes, it was. They had to understand the nature of
power politics. He left the notation unchanged.

B   The Hospital:

    1) Control of electric power
    2) Control of news media

3) Control of justice: of the police, of trials, of executions

4) Control of medicine and the organ banks: the positive side of justice

C Organ replacement for colonists? Yes!

1) Colonists in good standing are obviously entitled to medical care. Obviously even to themselves.

2) Justice *must* have a positive side.

3) The organ-bank "problem" implies that the colonists who can hope for medical treatment will support the government.

V The ramrobot capsule.

(Show pictures. Give 'em the full tour. Use #1 for visual impact, but concentrate on implications of rotifer.)

There was something he could add to that! Millard Parlette looked down at his right hand. It was coming along nicely. Already the contrast with his untreated left hand was dramatic.

That'd make 'em sit up!

VI The danger of the ramrobot capsule.

A It does not make the organ banks obsolete. The capsule held only four items. To replace the organ banks would require hundreds, or thousands, each a separate project.

B But any colonist report would blow it out of all proportion. Colonists would assume that capital punishment would stop *now*.

Millard Parlette glanced behind him—and shuddered. You couldn't be rational about Ramrobot Capsule #143. The visual impact was too great.

If his speech got dull at any point, he could get their attention back by simply cutting to a shot of the ramrobot packages.

   C   Capital punishment cannot stop in any case.

      1) Decrease the severity of punishment, and crime increases drastically. (Cite examples from Earth history. Unfortunate that Mount Lookitthat has none.)

      2) What punishment to substitute for capital punishment? No prisons on Mount Lookitthat. Warning notes and jottings on one's record hold power only through threat of the organ banks.

VII Conclusion.

Violently or peaceably, the rule of the crew ends when the colonists learn of Ramrobot Capsule #143.

Three minutes to go. No question of changing the speech now.

The question was, and had always been, the speech itself. Should thirty thousand crew be told what had arrived in Ramrobot Capsule #143? Could they be made to understand its importance? And—could such a secret be kept by that many?

Members of the Council had fought bitterly to prevent this event. Only Millard Parlette's sure control, his knowledge of the ways of power and the weaknesses of his fellow Council members, even his own striking authority-figure appearance, which he used ruthlessly—only Millard Parlette's determination had brought the Council to issue their declaration of emergency.

And now every crew on Alpha Plateau, and elsewhere, was before his teedee set. No cars flew above Alpha Plateau; no skiers glided down the snows of the northern glacier; the lake and the hot springs and the gambling halls of Iota were empty.

One minute to go. Too late to call off the speech.

Could thirty thousand people keep such a secret?

Why, no, of course they couldn't.

"That big house with the flat roof," said Harry Kane.

Matt tilted the car to the right. He continued, "I waited till the guards were out of sight, then went back to the vivarium. The man inside opened the door for me. I knocked him down and took his gun, found that bank of buttons and started pushing them."

"Land in the garden, not on the roof. Did you ever figure out what was wrong with their eyes?"

"No." Matt worked the slats and the steering knob, trying to get above the garden. It was big, and it ran to the void edge: a formal garden in a style a thousand years old, a symmetrical maze of right-angle hedges enclosing rectangles of brilliant color. The house too was all rectangles, an oversized version of the small identical-development-houses of the nineteens. Flat-roofed, flat-sided, nearly undecorated, the size of a motel but so wide it seemed low, the house seemed to have been built from prefabricated parts and then added to over the years. Geoffrey Eustace Parlette had evidently imitated ancient bad taste in hopes of getting something new and different.

Matt didn't see it that way, naturally. To him all the houses of Alpha were equally strange.

He brought the car down on the strip of grass at the void edge. The car landed, bounced, landed again. At what he judged was the proper moment, Matt pushed in all four fan levers. The car dropped jarringly. The levers tried to come out again, and Matt held them in with his hand, looking despairingly at Hood for help.

"Gyroscope," said Hood.

Matt forced his numb right arm to cross his torso and flick the Gyroscope switch.

"You need a little training in how to fly," Harry Kane

said with admirable restraint. "You finished your story?" He had insisted that Matt talk without interruption.

"I may have forgotten some things."

"We can save the question-and-answer period until we get established. Matt, Laney, Lydia, get me out of here and move Jay in front of the dashboard. Jay, can you move your arms?"

"Yah. The stunner's pretty well worn off."

They piled out, Matt and the two women. Harry came out on his feet, moving in jerks and twitches but managing to stay upright. He brushed away offers of help and stood watching Hood. Hood had opened a panel in the dash and was doing things inside.

"Matt!" Laney called over her shoulder. She was standing inches from the void.

"Get back from there!"

"No! Come here!"

Matt went. So did Mrs. Hancock. The three of them stood at the edge of the grass, looking down into their shadows.

The sun was at their backs, shining down at forty-five degrees. The water-vapor mist which had covered the southern end of the Plateau that morning now lay just beyond the void edge, almost at their feet. And they looked into their shadows—three shadows reaching down into infinity, three contoured black tunnels growing smaller and narrower as they bored through the lighted mist, until they reached their blurred vanishing points. But for each of the three it seemed that only his own shadow was surrounded by a small, vivid, perfectly circular rainbow.

A fourth shadow joined them, moving slowly and painfully. "Oh, for a camera," mourned Harry Kane.

"I never saw it like that before," said Matt.

"I did, once, a long time ago. It was like I'd had a vision. Myself, the representative of Man, standing at the edge of the world with a rainbow about his head. I joined the Sons of Earth that night."

A muted whirr sounded behind them. Matt turned to see the car slide toward him across the lawn, pause at the edge, go over. It hovered over the mist and then settled into it, fading like a porpoise submerging.

Harry turned and called, "All set?"

Hood knelt on the grass where the car had rested. "Right. It'll come back at midnight, wait fifteen minutes, then go back down. It'll do that for the next three nights. Would someone help me into the house?"

Matt half carried him through the formal garden. Hood was heavy; his legs would move, but they would not carry him. As they walked, he lowered his voice to ask, "Matt, what was that thing you drew on the door?"

"A bleeding heart."

"Oh. Why?"

"I'm not really sure. When I saw what they'd done to the guard, it was like being back in the organ banks. I remembered my Uncle Matt." His grip tightened in reflex on Hood's arm. "They took him away when I was eight. I never found out why. I had to leave something to show I was there—me, Matt Keller, walking in alone and out with an army. One for Uncle Matt! I was a little crazy, Hood; I saw something in the organ banks that would shake anyone's mind. I didn't know your symbol, so I had to make up my own."

"Not a bad one. I'll show you ours later. Was it bad, the organ banks?"

"Horrible. But the worst was those tiny hearts and livers. Children, Jay! I never knew they took children."

Hood looked up questioningly. Then Lydia Hancock pushed the big front door open for them, and they had to concentrate on getting up the steps.

Jesus Pietro was furious.

He'd spent some time in his office, knowing he would be most useful there, but he'd felt cramped. Now he was at the edge of the carport watching the last of the sonic victims being carried away. He wore a beltphone; his secretary could reach him through that.

He'd never hated colonists before.

To Jesus Pietro, human beings came in two varieties: crew and colonist. On other worlds other conditions might apply, but other worlds did not intrude on Mount Lookit-that. The crew were masters, wise and benevolent, at least in the aggregate. The colonists were ordained to serve.

Both groups had exceptions. There were crew who were in no way wise and who did not work at being benevolent, who accepted the benefits of their world and ignored the responsibilities. There were colonists who would overthrow the established order of things and others who preferred to turn criminal rather than serve. When brought into contact with crew he did not admire, Jesus Pietro treated them with the respect due their station. The renegade colonists he hunted down and punished.

But he didn't hate them, any more than Matt Keller really hated mining worms. The renegades were part of his job, part of his working day. They behaved as they did because they were colonists, and Jesus Pietro studied them as biology students studied bacteria. When his working day ended, so did his interest in colonists, unless something unusual was going on.

Now that was over. In running amok through the Hospital, the rebels had spilled over from his working day into his very home. He couldn't have been angrier if they'd been in his house, smashing furniture and killing servants and setting poison for the housecleaners and pouring salt on the rugs.

The intercom buzzed. Jesus Pietro unhooked it from his belt and said, "Castro."

"Jansen, sir. I'm calling from the vivarium."

"Well?"

"There are six rebels missing. Do you want their names?"

Jesus Pietro glanced around him. They'd carried the

last unconscious colonist away ten minutes ago. These last stretcher passengers were carport personnel.

"You should have them all. Have you checked with the operating room? I saw at least one dead under a door."

"I'll check, sir."

The carport was back to normal. The rebels hadn't had time to mess it up as they'd messed up the halls and the electricians' rec room. Jesus Pietro debated whether to return to his office or to trace the rebels' charge back through the rec room. Then he happened to notice two men arguing by the garages. He strolled over.

"You had no right to send Bessie out!" one was shouting. He wore a raider's uniform, and he was tall, very dark, enlistment-poster handsome.

"You bloody raiders think you own these cars," the mechanic said contemptuously.

Jesus Pietro smiled, for the mechanics felt exactly the same. "What's the trouble?" he asked.

"This idiot can't find my car! Sorry, sir."

"And which car is yours, Captain?"

"Bessie. I've been using Bessie for three years, and this morning some idiot took it out to spray the woods. *Now* look! They've lost her, sir!" The man's voice turned plaintive.

Jesus Pietro turned cold blue eyes on the mechanic. "You've lost a car?"

"No sir. I just don't happen to know where they've put it."

"Where are the cars that came back from spraying the woods?"

"That's one of them." The mechanic pointed across the carport. "We were half finished unloading her when those fiends came at us. Matter of fact we were unloading both of them." The mechanic scratched his head. He met Jesus Pietro's eyes with the utmost reluctance. "I haven't seen the other one since."

"There are prisoners missing. You know that?" He didn't wait for the mechanic's answer. "Find Bessie's serial number and description and give them to my secretary. If you find Bessie, call my office. For the moment I'm going to assume the car is stolen."

The mechanic turned and ran toward an office. Jesus Pietro used his handphone to issue instructions regarding a possible stolen car.

Jansen came back on the line. "One rebel dead, sir. That leaves five missing." He listed them.

"All right. It's beginning to look like they took a car. See if the wall guards saw one leaving."

"They'd have reported it, sir."

"I'm not so certain. Find out."

"Sir, the carport was attacked. The guards *had* to report five prisoners stealing an aircar during a mob attack!"

"Jansen, I think they might have forgotten to. You understand me?" There was steel in his voice. Jansen signed off without further protest.

Jesus Pietro looked up at the sky, rubbing his moustache with two fingers. A stolen car would be easy to find. There were no crew pleasure-cars abroad now, not in the middle of Millard Parlette's speech. But they might have landed it. And if a car had been stolen in full view of the wall guards, it had been stolen by ghosts.

That would fit admirably with the other things that had been happening at the Hospital.

CHAPTER VIII

POLLY'S EYES

GEOFFREY EUSTACE PARLETTE'S house was different inside. The rooms were big and comfortable, furnished in soft good taste. They were innumerable. Toward the back were a pool table, a small bowling alley, an auditorium and stage with pull-down movie screen. The kitchen was the size of Harry Kane's living room. Matt and Laney and Lydia Hancock had moved through the entire house with stun guns at the ready. They had found no living thing, barring the rugs and the no-less-than-six housecleaner nests.

Lydia had threatened force to get Matt to return to the living room. He wanted to explore. He'd seen incredible bedrooms. Hobbyists' bedrooms . . .

In a living room two stories tall, before a vast false fireplace whose stone logs showed red electrical heat where they touched, the five survivors dropped into couches. Harry Kane still moved carefully, but he seemed almost recovered from the stunner that had caught him in the Hospital. Hood had his voice back, but not his strength.

Matt slumped in the couch. He wriggled, adjusting his position, and finally put his feet up. It was good to feel safe.

"Tiny hearts and livers," said Hood.

"Yah," said Matt.

"That's impossible."

Harry Kane made a questioning noise.

"I saw them," said Matt. "The rest of it was pretty horrible, but that was the worst."

Harry Kane was sitting upright. "In the organ banks?"

"Yes, dammit, in the organ banks. Don't you believe

134

me? They were in special tanks of their own, makeshift-looking, with the motors sitting in the water next to the organs. The glass was warm."

"Stasis tanks aren't warm," said Hood.

"And Implementation doesn't take children," said Harry Kane. "If they did, I'd know it."

Matt merely glared.

"Hearts and livers," said Harry. "Just those? Nothing else?"

"Nothing I noticed," said Matt. "No, wait. There were a couple of tanks just like them. One was empty. One looked . . . polluted, I think."

"How long were you in there?"

"Just long enough to get sick to my stomach. Mist Demons, I wasn't investigating anything! I was looking for a map!"

"In the organ banks?"

"Lay off," said Laney. "Relax, Matt. It doesn't matter."

Mrs. Hancock had gone to find the kitchen. She returned now, with a pitcher and five glasses. "Found this. No reason we shouldn't mess up the place, is there?"

They assured her there wasn't, and she poured for them.

Hood said, "I'm more interested in your alleged psychic powers. I've never read of anything like you've got. It must be something new."

Matt grunted.

"I should tell you that anyone who believes in the so-called psi powers at all usually thinks he's psychic himself." Hood's tone was dry, professional. "We may find nothing at all."

"Then how did we get here?"

"We may never know. Some new Implementation policy? Or maybe the Mist Demons love you, Matt."

"I thought of that, too."

Mrs. Hancock returned to the kitchen.

"When you tried to sneak up to the Hospital," Hood

continued, "you were spotted right away. You must have run through the electric-eye net. You didn't attempt to run?"

"They had four spotlights on me. I just stood up."

"Then they ignored you? They let you walk away?"

"That's right. I kept looking back, waiting for that loudspeaker to say something. It never did. Then I ran."

"And the man who took you into the Hospital. Did anything happen just before he went insane and ran back to the gatehouse?"

"Like what?"

"Anything involving light."

"No."

Hood looked disappointed. Laney said, "People seem to forget about you."

"Yah. It's been like that all my life. In school the teacher wouldn't call on me unless I knew the answer. Bullies never bothered me."

"I should have been so lucky," said Hood.

Laney wore the abstracted look of one tracing an idea.

"The eyes," said Harry Kane, and paused for thought. He had been listening without comment, in the attitude of The Thinker, jaw on fist, elbow on knee. "You said there was something strange about the guards' eyes."

"Yah. I don't know what. I've seen that look before, I think, but I can't remember—"

"What about the one who finally shot you? Anything odd about his eyes?"

"No."

Laney came out of her abstraction with a startled look. "Matt. Do you think Polly would have gone home with you?"

"What the Mist Demons does *that* have to do with anything?"

"Don't get mad, Matt. I've got a reason for asking."

"I can't imagine—"

"That's why you called in the experts."

"All right, *yes*. I thought she was going home with me."

"Then she suddenly turned and walked away."

"Yah. The bitch just—" Matt swallowed the rest of it. Not until now, when he could feel his pain and rage and humiliation in bearable retrospect, did he realize how badly she'd stung him. "She walked away like she'd remembered something. Something more important than me, but not particularly important for all that. Laney, could it have been her hearing aid?"

"The radio? . . . No, not that early. Harry, did you tell Polly anything by radio that you didn't tell the rest of us?"

"I told her I'd call for her speech at midnight, after everyone had gone home. They could hear it through the radios. Otherwise, nothing."

"So she had no reason to drop me," said Matt. "I still don't see why we have to dig into this."

"It's strange," said Hood. "It can't hurt to look at anything strange in your young life."

Laney said, "Did you resent it?"

"Damn right I did. I hate being left flat like that, toyed with and then dropped."

"You didn't offend her?"

"I don't see how I could have. I didn't get drunk till afterward."

"You told me it's happened before like that."

"Every time. Every damn time, until you. I was virgin until Friday night." Matt looked belligerently around him. Nobody said anything. "That's why I can't see how it helps to talk about it. Dammit, it *isn't* unusual in my young life."

Hood said, "It's unusual in Polly's young life. Polly's not a tease. Am I wrong, Laney?"

"No. She takes her sex seriously. She wouldn't make a play for someone she didn't want. I wonder . . ."

"I don't think I was kidding myself, Laney."

"Neither do I. You keep saying something was strange

about the guards' eyes. Was there anything strange about Polly's eyes?"

"What are you getting at?"

"You claim every time you're getting ready to lose your virginity to a girl, she drops you. Why? You aren't ugly. You probably don't have the habit of being grossly impolite. You weren't with me. You bathe often enough. Was there something about Polly's eyes?"

"Dammit, Laney . . . Eyes." *Something changed in Polly's face. She seemed to be listening to something only she could hear. She certainly wasn't looking at anything; her eyes went past him and through him, and they looked blind . . .*

"She looked abstracted. What do you want me to say? She looked like she was thinking of something else, and then she walked away."

"Was it sudden, this loss of interest? Did she—"

"Laney, what *do* you think? I drove her away deliberately?" Matt jumped to his feet. He couldn't take any more; he was wires stretched on a bone frame, every wire about to break. Nobody had ever so assaulted his privacy! He had never imagined that a woman could share his bed, listen in sympathy to all the agony of the secrets that had shaped his soul, and then spill everything she knew into a detailed, clinical roundtable discussion! He felt like one who has been disassembled for the organ banks, who, still aware, watches a host of doctors probing and prodding his separated innards with none-too-clean hands, hears them making ribald comments about his probable medical and social history.

And he was about to say so, in no mild terms, when he saw that nobody was looking at him.

Nobody was looking at him.

Laney was staring into the artificial fire; Hood was looking at Laney; Harry Kane was in his Thinker position. None of them were really seeing anything, at least not anything there in the room. Each wore an abstracted look.

"One problem," Harry Kane said dreamily. "How the blazes are we going to free the rest of us, when only four of us escaped?" He glanced around at his inattentive audience, then went back to contemplating his navel from the inside.

Matt felt the hair stir on his head. Harry Kane had looked right at him, but he certainly hadn't seen Matt Keller. And there was something very peculiar about his eyes.

Like a man in a wax museum, Matt bent to look into Harry Kane's eyes.

Harry jumped as if he'd been shot. "Where the blazes did you come from?" He stared as if Matt had dropped from the ceiling. Then he said, "Umm . . . oh! You did it."

There wasn't a doubt of it. Matt nodded. "You all suddenly lost interest in me."

"What about our eyes?" Hood seemed about to spring at him, he was so intense.

"Something. I don't know. I was bending down to see, when"—Matt shrugged—"it wore off."

Harry Kane used a word your publisher will cut.

Hood said, "Suddenly? I don't remember its being sudden."

"What do you remember?" Matt asked.

"Well, nothing, really. We were talking about eyes—or was it about Polly? Sure, Polly. Matt, did it bother you to talk about it?"

Matt growled in his throat.

"Then that's why you did whatever you did. You didn't want to be noticed."

"Probably."

Hood rubbed his hands briskly together. "So. We know you've got something, anyway, and it's under your control. Your subconscious control. Well!" Hood became a professor looking around at his not-too-bright class. "What questions are still unanswered?

"For one, what do the eyes have to do with anything?

For another, why was a guard eventually able to shoot you and store you away? For a third, why would you use your ability to drive girls away?"

"Mist Demons, Hood! There's no conceivable reason—"

"Keller."

The voice was a quiet command. Harry Kane was back in Thinker position on the couch, staring off into space. "You said Polly looked abstracted. Did we look abstracted a moment ago?"

"When you forgot about me? Yah."

"Do I look abstracted now?"

"Yah. Wait a minute." Matt stood up and walked around Harry, examining him from different sides. He should have looked like a man deep in thought. Thinker position: chin on fist, elbow on knee; face lowered, almost scowling; motionless; eyes hooded . . . Hooded? But clearly visible.

"No, you don't. There's something wrong."

"What?"

"Your eyes."

"Round and round we go," Harry said disgustedly. "Well, get down and *look* at my eyes, for the Mist Demons' sake!"

Matt knelt on the indoor grass and looked up into Harry's eyes. No inspiration came. A wrongness there, but where? . . . He thought of Polly on Friday night, when they stood immersed in noise and elbows, and talked nose-to-nose. They'd touched from time to time, half accidentally, hands and shoulders brushing . . . He'd felt the warm blood beating in his neck . . . and suddenly—

"Too big," said Matt. "Your pupils are too big. When somebody really isn't interested in what's going on around him, the pupils are smaller."

"What about Polly's eyes?" Hood probed. "Dilated or contracted?"

"Contracted. Very small. And so were the guards' eyes, the ones who came for me this morning." He remembered how surprised they'd been when he yanked on the handcuffs, the handcuffs that still dangled from his wrists. They hadn't been interested in him; they'd merely unlocked the chains from their own wrists. And when they'd looked at him—"That's it. That's why their eyes looked so funny. The pupils were pinpoints."

Hood sighed in relief. "Then that's all of it," he said, and got up. "Well, I think I'll see how Lydia's doing with dinner."

"Come back here." Harry Kane's voice was low and murderous. Hood burst out laughing.

"Stop that cackling," said Harry Kane. "Whatever Keller's got, we need it. Talk!"

Whatever Keller's got, we need it. Matt felt he ought to protest. He didn't intend to be used by the Sons of Earth. But he couldn't interrupt now.

"It's a very limited form of telepathy," said Jay Hood. "And because it is so very limited, it's probably more dependable than more general forms. Its target is so much less ambiguous." He smiled. "We really ought to have a new name for it. Telepathy doesn't apply, not quite."

Three people waited patiently but implacably.

"Matt's mind," said Hood, "is capable of controlling the nerves and muscles which dilate and contract the iris of another man's eye." And he smiled, waiting for their response.

"So what?" asked Harry Kane. "What good is that?"

"You don't understand? No, I suppose you don't. It's more in my field. Do you know anything about motivational research?"

Three heads waggled No.

"The science was banned on Earth long, long ago because its results were being used for immoral advertising purposes. But they found out some interesting things first. One of them involved dilation and contraction of the pupil of the eye.

"It turns out that if you show a man something and measure his pupil with a camera, you can tell whether it interests him. You can show him pictures of his country's political leaders, in places where there are two or more factions, and his eyes will dilate for the leader of his own. Take him aside for an hour and talk to him, persuade him to change his political views, and his pupils will dilate for the other guy. Show him pictures of pretty girls, and the girl he calls prettiest will have dilated pupils. He doesn't know it. He only knows she looks interested. In him.

"I wonder," said Hood, smiling dreamily at himself. Some people love to lecture. Hood was one. "Could that be the reason the most expensive restaurants are always dark? A couple comes in, they look at each other across a dinner table, and they both look interested. What do you think?"

Harry Kane said, "I think you'd better finish telling us about Keller."

"He has," said Laney. "Don't you see? Matt's afraid of being seen by someone. So he reaches out with his mind and contracts the man's pupils whenever he looks at Matt. Naturally the man can't get interested in Matt."

"Exactly." Hood beamed at Laney. "Matt takes a reflex and works it in reverse to make it a conditioned reflex. I *knew* light had something to do with it. You see, Matt? It can't work unless your victim sees you. If he hears you, or if he gets a blip when you cross an electric-eye beam—"

"Or if I'm not concentrating on being scared. That's why the guard shot me."

"I still don't see how it's possible," said Laney. "I helped you do your research on this, Jay. Telepathy is reading minds. It operates on the brain, doesn't it?"

"We don't know. But the optic nerve is brain tissue, not ordinary nerve tissue."

Harry Kane stood up and stretched. "That doesn't matter. It's better than anything the Sons of Earth have put together. It's like a cloak of invisibility. Now we have to figure out how to use it."

The missing car was still missing. It was nowhere in the Implementation garages; it had not been found by the search squad, neither in the air nor on the ground. If a policeman had taken it out for legitimate purposes, it would have been visible; if it had not been visible, it would have been in trouble of some kind, and the pilot would have phoned a Mayday. Apparently it really had been stolen.

To Jesus Pietro, it was disturbing. A stolen car was one thing; an impossible stolen car was another.

He had associated Keller with miracles: with the miracle that had left him unhurt when his car fell into the void mist, with the miracle that had affected Hobart's memory last night. On that assumption he had sounded the "Prisoners Loose." And, lo! there were prisoners running amok in the corridors.

He had associated missing prisoners with a missing car with the miracles of Keller. Thus he had assumed a stolen car where no car could have been stolen. And, lo! a car had indeed been stolen.

Then Major Jansen had called from the vivarium. Nobody had noticed, until that moment, that the sleeper helmets were still running. How, then, had ninety-eight prisoners walked away?

Miracles! What the blazes was he fighting? One man, or many? Had Keller been passenger or driver of that car? Had there been other passengers? Had the Sons of Earth discovered something new, or was it Keller alone?

That was an evil thought. Matthew Keller, come back from the void in the person of his nephew to haunt his murderer . . . Jesus Pietro snorted.

He'd doubled the guard at the Alpha-Beta Bridge. Knowing that the bridge was the only way off the cliff and across the Long Fall River at the bottom, he had nonetheless set guards along the cliff edge. No normal colonist could leave Alpha Plateau without a car. (But could something abnormal walk unseen past the guards?)

And no fugitive would leave in a police car. Jesus Pietro had ordered all police cars to fly in pairs for the duration. The fugitives would be flying alone.

As part colonist, Jesus Pietro had not been allowed to hear Millard Parlette's speech, but he knew it was over. Crew cars were flying again. If the fugitives stole a crew car, they might have a chance. But the Hospital would be informed immediately if a crew car was stolen. (Really? A police car had been stolen, and he'd had to find out for himself.)

Nobody and nothing had been found in the abandoned coral houses. (But would anything important have been seen?)

Most of the escaped prisoners were safe in the vivarium. (From which they had escaped before, without bothering to turn off their sleeper helmets.)

Jesus Pietro wasn't used to dealing with ghosts.

It would require brand new techniques.

Grimly he set out to evolve them.

The arguments began during dinner.

Dinner took place at the unconventional hour of three o'clock. It was good, very good. Lydia Hancock still looked like a sour old harridan, but to Matt, anyone who could cook like her deserved the benefit of the doubt. They had finished the mutton chops when Harry Kane turned to business.

"There are five of us left," he said. "What can we do to get the rest of us loose?"

"We could blow the pumping station," Hood suggested. It developed that the pumping station which supplied Alpha Plateau with water from the Long Fall was the crew's only source of water. It was located at the base of the Alpha-Beta cliff. The Sons of Earth had long ago planted mines to blow it apart. "It would give us a diversion."

"And cut off the power, too," said Matt, remembering that hydrogen for fusion can be taken from water.

"Oh, no. The power plants only use a few bucketfuls of water in a year, Keller. A diversion for what, Jay? Any suggestions?"

"Matt. He got us out once. He can do it again, now that he knows—"

"Oh no you don't. I am not a revolutionary. I told you why I went to the Hospital, and I won't go there again."

Thus, the arguments.

On Matt's side there was little said. He wasn't going back to the Hospital. If he could, he would return to Gamma and live out his life there, trusting his psi power to protect him. If he had to live elsewhere—even if he had to spend the rest of his life in hiding on Alpha Plateau—so be it. His life might be disrupted now, but it was not worthless enough to throw away.

He got no sympathy from anyone, not even from Laney. On their part the arguments ranged from appeals to his patriotism or to his love of admiration, to attacks on his personality, to threats of bodily harm to himself and his family. Jay Hood was the most vituperative. You would have thought he had invented "the luck of Matt Keller," that Matt had stolen it. He seemed genuinely convinced that he held a patent on psi power on the Plateau.

In a way it was ludicrous. They begged him, they browbeat him, they threatened him—and with never a chance of succeeding. Once they actually succeeded in frightening him, and once their personal comments annoyed him beyond the limits of patience. Both times the arguments ended abruptly, and Matt was left alone in his irritation while the Sons of Earth discussed whatever came to mind, their pupils contracting to pinpoints whenever they looked at him.

After the second such episode Harry Kane realized what was happening and ordered the others to lay off. It was interfering with their ability to make plans, he said.

"Go somewhere else," he told Matt. "If you're not going to help us, at least don't listen to our plans. Feeble though they'll probably be, there's no reason we should risk your hearing them. You might use the information to buy your way back into Castro's good graces."

"You're an ungrateful son of a bitch," said Matt, "and I demand an apology."

"Okay, I apologize. Now go somewhere else."

Matt went out into the garden.

The mist was back, but it was an overhanging mist now, turning the sky steel gray, bleaching colors out of the garden, turning the void from a fuzzy flat plain into a dome around the universe. Matt found a stone bench and sat down and put his head in his hands.

He was shaking. A mass verbal attack can do that to a man, can smash his self-respect and set up doubts which remain for hours or days or forever. There are well-developed verbal techniques for many to use against one. You never let the victim speak without interruption; never let him finish a sentence. You interrupt each other so that he can't quite catch the drift of your arguments, and then he can't find the flaws. He forgets his rebuttal points because he's not allowed to put them into words. His only defense is to walk out. If, instead, you throw him out . . .

Gradually his confusion gave way to a kind of sick, curdled anger. The ungrateful . . . ! He'd saved their worthless lives twice, and where was their thanks? Well, he didn't need them. He'd never needed them for a moment.

He knew what he was now. Hood had given him that much. He knew, and he could take advantage of it.

He could become the world's first invulnerable thief. If Implementation would not let him resume his mining career, he would do just that. Weaponless, he could rob storehouses in broad daylight. He could pass guarded bridges unnoticed, be at work on Gamma while they were searching him out in every corner of Eta. Eta, now . . . a nice place to rob if he couldn't return to his old life. The crew gambling-resort must see half the wealth of the Plateau at one time or another.

He'd have a long walk to the Alpha-Beta Bridge, and a longer walk afterward. A car would be useful. Serve the

Sons of Earth right if he took their car—but he'd have to wait till midnight. Did he want to do that?

His daydreams had calmed him still further. His shaking had stopped, and he wasn't as angry now. He could begin to see what had moved the four inside to attack him so, though he saw no justice in it, for there was none. Laney, Hood, Harry Kane, Lydia—they must be fanatics, or why would they sell their lives for a hopeless revolution? Being fanatics, they would have only one ethic: to do anything in their power to advance their cause, no matter whom it might hurt.

He still didn't know where he went from here. One thing he knew: It would not involve the Sons of Earth. Otherwise he had plenty of time for decisions.

A chill thin breeze blew from the north. Gradually the fog was thickening.

The electric fire inside would be welcome.

But the thick hostility would not. He stayed where he was, hunching his back to the wind.

... Why in blazes would Hood assume he drove away women? Did Hood think he was crazy? Or deficient? No; he'd have used that during the arguments. Why, then?

He hadn't driven away Laney.

That memory warmed him. She was lost for good now; their paths would diverge, and someday she'd end in the organ banks. But Friday night had happened; Friday night was permanent ...

... Polly's eyes. Her pupils had contracted, sure enough. Like the gatekeeper's eyes, like Harry's and Hood's and Laney's eyes when Matt had tired of their verbal onslaughts. Why?

Matt nibbled gently at his lower lip.

And if he'd driven Polly away (never mind why; there was no answer), then it was not her fault that she had gone.

But Laney had stayed.

Matt jumped to his feet. They'd have to tell him. He had a lever on them; they couldn't know how sure he was that he'd have nothing to do with their cause. And he had to know.

He turned toward the house and saw the cars—three of them, way up there in the gray sky, disappearing and reappearing around the mist. Dropping.

He stood perfectly still. He wasn't really convinced that they were landing *here,* though they grew bigger and closer every second. Finally they were just overhead and settling. And still he stood. For by then there was no place to run to, and he knew that only "the luck of Matt Keller" could protect him. It should work. He was certainly scared enough.

One of the cars almost landed on him. He was invisible, all right.

A tall, spare man got out of the car, moved his hands briefly inside the dashboard, and stepped back to avoid the wind as the car rose again and settled on the roof. The other cars had landed, and they were Implementation. A man disembarked and moved toward the tall civilian. They spoke briefly. The tall man's voice was high, almost squeaky, and it had the crew lilt. He was thanking the policeman for his escort. The policeman got back into the car, and both Implementation cars rose into the fog.

The tall man sighed and let himself slump. Matt's fear ebbed. This crew was no danger; he was a tired old man, worn out with years and with some recent toil. But what a fool Harry Kane had been to think nobody would come!

The man moved toward the house. Tired he might have been, but he walked straight, like a policeman on parade. Matt cursed softly and moved in behind him.

When the oldster saw the living room, he'd know someone had been there. He'd call for help unless Matt stopped him.

The old man opened the big wooden door and walked in. Matt was right behind him.

He saw the old man go rigid.

The ancient didn't try to scream. If he had a

handphone, he didn't reach for it. His head turned from side to side, studying the living room from where he stood, taking in the abandoned glasses and pitcher and the glowing false fire. When his profile turned to Matt, he looked thoughtful. Not frightened, not angry. Thoughtful.

And when the old man smiled, it was a slow, tense smile, the smile of a chess player who sees victory almost within his grasp—or defeat, for his opponent might have set an unsuspected trap. The old man smiled, but the muscles of his face stood out iron-hard under the loose, wrinkled skin, and his fists tightened at his sides. He cocked his head to one side, listening.

He turned abruptly toward the dining room, and was face to face with Matt.

Matt said, "What are you grinning at?"

The crew batted an eyelash; he was discomposed for just that long. Speaking low, he asked, "Are you one of the Sons of Earth?"

Matt shook his head.

Consternation! And why *that* reaction? Matt held up a hand. "Don't do anything rash," he said. He'd wrapped a handcuff chain around that hand to make it a better weapon. The old man settled back on his heels. Three of him would have been no physical match for Matt.

"I'm going to search you," said Matt. "Raise your hands." He moved behind the old man and ran his hands over various pockets. He found some bulky objects, but no handphone.

He stood back, considering. He had never searched anyone; there might be tricks a man could use to fool him.

"What do you want with the Sons of Earth?"

"I'll tell them when I see them." The baritone lilt was not hard to understand, though Matt could never have imitated it.

"That won't do."

"Something very important has happened." The old

man seemed to make a difficult decision. "I want to tell them about the ramrobot package."

"All right. Go ahead of me. That way."

They moved toward the dining room with Matt trailing.

Matt was about to yell when the door suddenly opened. Lydia Hancock had her nose and a sonic showing around the edge. It took her a second to realize that the man in the lead was not Matt, and then she fired.

Matt caught the old man as he fell. "Stupid," he said. "He wanted to talk to you."

"He can talk to us when he wakes up," said Lydia.

Harry Kane emerged warily, holding the other stolen sonic ready in his hand. "Any others?"

"Just him. He had a police escort, but they left. Better search him; there might be a radio on him somewhere."

"Mist Demons! It's Millard Parlette!"

"Oh!" Matt knew the name, but he hadn't recognized the man. "I think he really wanted to see you. When he realized someone was here, he acted sneaky. He didn't panic until I told him I wasn't one of you. He said he wanted to talk about the ramrobot."

Harry Kane grunted. "He won't wake up for hours. Lydia, you're on guard duty. I'm going for a shower; I'll relieve you when I come down."

He went upstairs. Lydia and Hood picked up Millard Parlette, moved him into the front entrance, and sat him up against a wall. The old man had gone loose, like a puppet without strings.

"A shower sounds wonderful," said Laney.

Matt said, "May I talk to you first? Hood too."

They got Jay Hood and went into the living room. Hood and Laney flopped in front of the fire, but Matt was too restless to sit. "Hood, I've got to know. What makes you think I've been using my psi power to drive away women?"

"You'll recall it was Laney's idea first. But the evidence seems good. Do you doubt that Polly left because you contracted her irises?"

Of course he doubted it. But he couldn't back it up. He looked at Laney, waiting.

"It's important, isn't it, Matt?"

"Yah."

"You remember, just before the raid, when you asked me if everyone was as nervous as you were?"

"Mmm . . . Yah, I remember. You said, 'Not that nervous, but still nervous.' "

"What are you two talking about?"

"Jay, do you remember your first—mmm. Do you remember when you stopped being a virgin?"

Hood threw back his head and laughed. "What a question, Laney! Nobody ever forgets the first time! It was—"

"Right. Were you nervous?"

Hood sobered. "At one point, I was. There was so much I didn't know. I was afraid I'd make a fool of myself."

Laney nodded. "I'll bet everyone's nervous the first time. Including you, Matt. You suddenly realize, This Is It, and you get all tensed up. Then your girl's eyes go funny."

Matt said a bad word. This was exactly what he hadn't wanted to hear. "But what about us? Laney, why didn't I defend myself against you?"

"I don't know."

Hood snapped, "What difference does it make? Whatever you've got, you're not going to use it."

"I have to know!"

Hood shrugged and went to stand before the fire.

"You were pretty sloshed," said Laney. "Could that have had anything to do with it?"

"Maybe."

She couldn't have known why it was important, but she was trying to help. "Maybe it's because I'm older than you. Maybe you decided I knew what I was doing."

"I didn't decide anything. I was too drunk. And too bitter."

She turned restlessly, her wrinkled party dress swirling

out around her. She stopped. "Matt! I remember! It was pitch dark in there!"

Matt closed his eyes. Why, so it was. He'd stumbled unseeing across the bed; he'd had to turn on a light to see Laney at all. "That's it. I didn't even realize what was going on until the door was closed. Oookay," he sighed, letting all his breath rush out with the word, leaving him an empty man.

Hood said, "That's great. Are you finished with us?"

"Yah."

Hood left without looking back. Laney, on the verge of leaving, hesitated. Matt looked half dead, as if every erg of energy had been drained out of him.

She touched his arm. "What's wrong, Matt?"

"I drove her away! It wasn't her fault!"

"Polly?" She grinned into his eyes. "Why let it bother you? You got me the same night!"

"Oh, Laney, Laney. She could be in the organ banks! She could be in the—coffin cure, whateverthehell that is."

"It's not your fault. If you'd found her in the vivarium—"

"Is it my fault that I was glad? She dropped me like a sick housecleaner, and an hour later Implementation took her away! And when I found out, I was glad! I had revenge!" His hands were on her upper arms, squeezing, almost hard enough to hurt.

"It wasn't your fault," she repeated. "You'd have saved her if you could."

"Sure." But he wasn't hearing her. He let go of her arms. "I've got to go after her," he muttered, saying the words aloud, trying the taste of them. "Yah. I've got to go after her."

He turned and made for the entrance.

CHAPTER IX

THE WAY BACK

"COME BACK here, you idiot!"

Matt stopped halfway to the door. "Huh? Isn't this what you all want?"

"Come back here! How are you going to get over the wall? You can't pound on the gate again!"

Matt turned back. He felt feverish, unable to think. "Castro'd be ready for that, wouldn't he? He may not know what happened last night, but he must know *something's* wrong."

"We tried hard enough to tell him! Come here, sit down ... Don't underestimate that man, Matt. We've got to think this through."

"That wall. How am I going to get over? Oh, damn, damn."

"You're tired. Why not wait till Harry comes down? Then we can get things organized."

"Oh, no. I'm not taking help from the Sons of Earth. This has nothing to do with them."

"How about me? Will you take my help?"

"Sure, Laney."

She decided not to question the illogic of this. "All right, let's start at the beginning. How are you going to reach the Hospital?"

"Yah. Too far to walk. Mmm ... Parlette's car. It's on the roof."

"But if Castro gets it, it'll lead him straight here."

"I'd have to wait till midnight to get the other car."

"That may be the only way." Laney wasn't tired; she'd had twice as much sleep as she needed in the vivarium. But she felt used, ready for the laundry. A hot bath would help. She put it out of her mind. "Maybe we can raid a crew house for another car. Then we set the autopilot to take Parlette's car back here."

"That'll take time."

"We'll have to take it. We'll also have to wait till after sunset before we start."

"Will we need darkness that early?"

"It would help. And suppose the fog cleared while we were over the void?"

"Oh." Colonist and crew alike, the people of the Plateau loved to watch the sun setting over the void mist. The colors were never the same twice. Land along the void edge always cost three times as much as land anywhere else.

"Suddenly we'd have a thousand crew looking down at us. It might be a mistake to use the void at all. Castro may have thought of that. We'll be safe if the fog holds. But whatever we do, we'll have to wait till dark."

Matt stood up and stretched muscles that felt knotted. "Okay. So we get to the Hospital. How do we get in?— Laney, what's an electric eye?"

She told him.

"Oh. I didn't see any light. . . . Ultraviolet, of course, or infrared. I should be able to get over that."

"We."

"You're not invisible, Laney."

"I am if I stick close to you."

"Phut."

"I'll have to come that far with you anyway. You can't program an autopilot."

Matt got up to pace. "Leave that a moment. How do we get over the wall?"

"I don't," said Laney, and stopped. "There may be a way," she said. "Leave it to me."

"Tell me."

"I can't."

The cold breeze outside had become a wind, audible through the walls. Laney shivered, though the electric fire was hot enough. The fog beyond the south windows was growing dark.

"We'll need guns," she said.

"I don't want to take one of yours. You've only got the two we picked up on the way to the car."

"Matt, I know more than you do about crew. They all go in for sports of one kind or another."

"So?"

"Some of them hunt. A long time ago Earth sent us some frozen fertilized deer and caribou ova in a cargo ramrobot. The Hospital hatched them out, grew 'em to adulthood and scattered them around the bottom edge of the glacier, north of here. There's enough grass there to keep them happy."

"Then we might find guns here."

"It's a good bet. The richer a crew is, the more sports equipment he buys. Even if he never uses it."

The gun rack was in a room in the upper story, a room lined with paintings of more-or-less wild animals and with heads and hooves of deer and caribou. The rack held half-a-dozen air-powered rifles. They searched the room, and eventually Laney found a drawer containing several boxes of crystal slivers, each sliver two inches long.

"They look like they'd stop a bandersnatch," said Matt. He'd never seen a bandersnatch, except in filmed maser messages from Jinx, but he knew they were big.

"They'll stop an elk cold. But the guns only fire one at a time. You have to be accurate."

"Makes it more sporting?"

"I guess so."

Implementation mercy-guns fired a steady stream of tiny slivers. One would make the victim woozy; it took half a dozen to drop him in his tracks.

Matt closed and pocketed the box of oversized mercy-slivers. "Getting hit with one of these would be like being stabbed with an ice pick, even without the knockout effect. Will they kill a man?"

"I don't know," said Laney. She chose two guns from the rack. "We'll take these."

"Jay!"

Hood stopped halfway to the living room, turned, and made for the entrance hall.

Lydia Hancock was bending over Millard Parlette. She had folded his flaccid hands neatly in his lap. "Come here and have a look at this."

Hood looked down at the stunned crew. Millard Parlette was coming around. His eyes didn't track and wouldn't focus, but they were open. Hood saw something else, and he bent for a closer look.

The crew's hands didn't match. The skin of one was mottled with age. It couldn't be as old as Parlette must be, but he hadn't replaced the skin in a good long time. From fingertips to elbow the arm showed a curious lack of personality, of what Hood decided was artistic continuity. Part of that might have been imagination. Hood knew in advance that Parlette must have used the organ banks continuously during his lifetime. But no imagination was needed to see that the left hand was dry and mottled and faintly callused, with cracked fingernails and receding quick.

Whereas the skin of the right hand was like a baby's, smooth and pink, untanned, almost translucent. The quick of the fingernails ran all the way to the tips of the fingers. Many high school students could not have said the same.

"The old love-child just got a transplant job," said Hood.

"No. Look here." Lydia pointed to the wrist. There was a ragged band of color, something less than an inch wide, running round Parlette's wrist. It was a dead milky-white such as Hood had never seen in human skin.

"Here too." A similar ring circled the first joint of Parlette's thumb. The thumbnail was cracked and dry, with a badly receding quick.

"Right, Lydia. But what is it? An artificial hand?"

"With a gun inside, maybe. Or a radio."

"Not a radio. They'd be all over us by now." Hood took Parlette's right hand and rolled the joints in his fingers. He felt old bone and muscle under the baby skin, and joints that would be arthritic someday soon. "This is a real human hand. But why didn't he get the whole thing replaced?"

"We'll have to let him tell us."

Hood stood up. He felt clean and rested and well fed. If they had to wait for Parlette to talk, they'd picked a nice place to wait.

Lydia asked, "How's Laney doing with Keller?"

"I don't know. I'm not going to try to find out."

"That must be tough, Jay." Lydia laughed a barking laugh. "You've spent half your life trying to find psychic powers on Plateau. Now one finally shows up, and he doesn't want to play with us."

"I'll tell you what really bothers me about Matt Keller. I grew up with him. In school I never noticed him, except one time when he got me mad at him." Absently he rubbed a point on his chest with two fingertips. "He was right under my nose all the time. But I was right, wasn't I? Psi powers exist, and we can use them against the Hospital."

"Can we?"

"Laney's persuasive. If she can't talk him around, I sure can't."

"You're not pretty enough."

"I'm prettier than you."

The barking laugh rang again. "Touché!"

"I knew it," said Laney. "It had to be the basement."

Two walls were covered with various kinds of small tools. Tables held an electric drill and a bandsaw. There were drawers of nails, screws, nuts . . .

Matt said, "Parlette the Younger must have done a lot of building."

"Not necessarily. It may be just a hobby. Come on, Matt, get your wrists down here. I think I see the saw we want."

Twenty minutes later he was rubbing bare wrists,

scratching furiously where he'd been unable to scratch before. His arms felt ten pounds lighter without the handcuffs.

The time of waiting sat heavily on Jesus Pietro.

It was long past quitting time. From the windows of his office he could see the trapped forest as a darker blur in a darkening gray mist. He'd called Nadia and told her not to expect him home that night. The night shift was in charge of the Hospital, reinforced at Jesus Pietro's orders with scores of extra guards.

Soon he'd have to alert them for what he expected. Right now he was trying to decide what to say.

He wasn't about to impress them with the startling news that all of five prisoners were loose somewhere on Alpha Plateau. They would already have heard about the escape. They'd leave the mop-up job to the hunting squads.

Jesus Pietro activated the intercom. "Miss Lauessen, please connect me with all of the Hospital intercoms."

"Will do." She didn't always call him Sir. Miss Lauessen had more crew blood than Jesus Pietro—she was nearly pure—and she had powerful protectors. Fortunately she was a pleasant person and a good worker. If she ever became a disciplinary problem . . .

"You're on, sir."

"This is the Head," said Jesus Pietro. "You all know of the man captured last night infiltrating the Hospital. He and several others escaped this morning. I have information that he was scouting the Hospital defenses in preparation for an attack to take place tonight.

"Sometime between now and dawn the Sons of Earth will almost certainly attack the Hospital. You have all been issued maps of the Hospital showing the locations of automatic protective-devices installed today. Memorize them, and don't stumble into any of the traps. I have issued orders for maximum dosage of anesthetic in these traps, and they can kill. Repeat, they can kill.

"I think it unlikely that the rebels will make any kind

of frontal attack." Unlikely, indeed! Jesus Pietro smiled at the understatement. "You should be alert for attempts to infiltrate the Hospital, possibly by using our own uniforms. Keep your identification handy. If you see someone you do not recognize, ask for his ident. Compare him with the photo. The rebels have not had time to forge idents.

"One last word. Don't be reluctant to shoot each other."

He signed off, waited for Miss Lauessen to clear the lines, then had her contact the Power Sections. "Cut off all power to the colonist regions of the Plateau until dawn," he told them.

The men of Power took pride in their work, and their work was to keep the power running. There were loud protests. "Do it," said Jesus Pietro, and cut them off.

Once again he thought longingly of issuing death darts to his men. But then they *would* be afraid to shoot each other. Worse, they'd fear their own weapons. Never since the Covenant of Planetfall had Implementation used deadly weapons. In any case the poison slivers had been stored so long that they'd probably lost their effectiveness.

He'd raised hell with tradition tonight; there'd be hell to pay if nothing happened. But he knew something would. It wasn't just the fact that this was the last chance for the rebels to get their prisoners out of the vivarium. It was the cold certainty in Jesus Pietro's viscera. *Something would happen.*

A vague red line divided black sky from black land. It faded gradually, and suddenly the Hospital lights came on outside, making the night white. Somebody brought Jesus Pietro dinner, and he ate hurriedly, and kept the coffeepot when the tray was gone.

"Down there," said Laney.

Matt nodded and pushed in the fan levers. They dropped toward a medium-sized dwelling that at first glance looked like a large, flat haystack. There were windows in the haystack, and on one side was a porchlike platform. Under the porch was an oddly curved swimming pool. Lights showed at the windows, and the swimming pool area blazed with light. The water itself was lit from underneath. There was no rooftop landing-zone, but on the other side of the house were two cars.

"I'd have picked an empty house, myself." Matt was commenting, not criticizing. He'd decided hours ago that Laney was the expert in rebellion.

"Then what? Even if you found a car, where would you get the keys? I picked this one because most of them will be out in plain sight by the pool. There, see them? Hover the car and I'll see how many I can pick off."

They'd flown east along the void, flying blind in the fog, staying far from the edge, so that even the sound of their fans would not carry. Finally, miles east of the Parlette mansion, they'd turned inland. Matt flew with the gun balanced beside him on the seat. He'd never owned anything with such power in it. It gave him a warm feeling of security and invulnerability.

Laney was in the back seat, where she could fire from either window. Matt couldn't tell how many people were down around the swimming pool. But the guns had telescopic sights.

There were pops like balloons exploding. "One," said Laney. "Two. Oop, here comes another . . . Three, and out. Okay, Matt, drop her fast. Yeee! Not that fast, Matt."

"Listen, did I get us down or didn't I?"

But she was out and running for the house. Matt followed more slowly. The swimming pool steamed like a huge bathtub. He saw two fallen crew near the pool, and a third near the glass doors to the house, and he blushed, for they were naked. Nobody had ever told him that crew threw nude swimming-parties. Then he noticed blood pooling under a woman's neck, and he stopped blushing. Clothing was trivia here.

From the pool area the house still looked like a haystack, but with more normal solid structures showing through the grassy yellow sides. Inside it was vastly different from Geoffrey Eustace Parlette's house; the walls were all curved, and a conical false fireplace occupied the center of the living room. But there was the same air of luxury.

Matt heard a pop like a balloon exploding, and he ran.

He rounded a door jamb as he heard the second pop. A man stood behind a polished table dialing a handphone. He was beginning to fall as Matt saw him: a brawny middle-aged crew wearing nothing but a few drops of water and an expression of ultimate terror. He was looking straight at Laney. One hand pawed at a blood spot on his ribs. His terror seemed to fade as he fell, but Matt remembered it. Being hunted was bad in itself, but being hunted naked must be far worse. Naked had always been synonymous with "unprotected."

"Try the upstairs,"said Laney. She was reloading the gun. "We'll have to find where they changed. If you find a pair of pants, search the pockets for keys. Hurry; we can't stay here long."

He came down a few minutes later with a bunch of keys dangling from his finger. "They were in the bedroom," he said.

"Good. Throw 'em away."

"Was that a funny?"

"I found these." She too had a key ring. "Think it through. Those clothes upstairs must belong to the owner of the house. If we take his car, Implementation can trace it back here. It may not matter; I can't think of any way they could trace us from here back to Parlette's. But if we take a visitor's car, they can't trace us anywhere. So these are the ones we want. You can ditch yours."

They went back to the pool area for Parlette's car. Laney opened the dash and fiddled inside. "I don't dare send it back," she muttered. "Harry'll have to use the other one. Ah ... So I'll just send it ten miles up and tell it to head south forever. Okay, Matt, let's go."

They found a key to fit one of the cars on the roof. Matt flew east and north, directly toward the Hospital.

The fog had not been abnormally thick on the ground, but at this height it was the edge of Creation. Matt flew for an hour before he saw a faint yellow blur to the left.

"The Hospital." Laney agreed. They turned.

A faint yellow blur on the left ... and white lights forming and clarifying all around them.

Matt dropped the car instantly.

They came down hard on water. As the car bobbed to the surface, they dived out opposite doors. Matt came up gasping with the cold. The fans washed spray over him, and he turned his face to avoid it. Ducks quacked in panic.

The white lights were dropping toward them. Matt called, "Where are we?"

"Parlette Park, I think."

Matt stood up in the water, waist deep, holding his gun high. The car skidded across the duck pond, hesitated at the edge, and then continued on until it nudged into a hedge. The fog was turning yellowish gray as car lights dropped toward the pond.

A thought struck him. "Laney. Got your gun?"

"Yah."

"Test it."

He heard it puff. "Good," he said, and pitched his own gun away. He heard it splash.

Car lights were settling all around them. Matt swam toward the sound of Laney's shot until he bumped into her. He took her arm and whispered, "Stay close." They waded toward shore. He could feel her shivering. The water was cold, but when they stood up, the wind was colder.

"What happened to your gun?"

"I threw it away. My whole purpose in life is being scared, isn't it? Well, I can't get scared with a gun in my hand."

They stumbled onto the grass. White lights surrounded

them at ground level, faintly blurred by the lifting mist. Others hovered overhead, spotlights casting a universal glow over the park. In that light men showed as running black silhouettes. A car settled on the water behind them, gently as a leaf.

"Put me through to the Head," said Major Chin. He rested at ease in the back seat of his car. The car sat a foot above the water on a small duck pond in Parlette Park, supported on its ground-effect air cushion. In such a position it was nearly invulnerable to attack.

"Sir? . . . We've caught a stolen car. . . . Yes, sir, it must have been stolen; it landed the moment we flew over to investigate. Went down like a falling elevator. . . . It was flying straight toward the Hospital. I imagine we're about two miles southwest of you. They must have abandoned the car immediately after landing it on a duck pond. . . . Yes, sir, very professional. The car ran into a hedge and just stayed there, trying to butt its way through on autopilot. . . . License number B—R—G—Y. . . . No, sir, nobody in it, but we've surrounded the area. They won't get through. . . . No, sir, nobody's seen them yet. They may be in the trees. But we'll smoke them out."

A puzzled expression chased itself across his smooth round face. "Yes, sir," he said, and signed off. He thought about directing the search by beltphone, but he had no further orders to give. All around him were the lights of police cars. The search pattern was fixed. When someone found something, he'd call.

But what had the Head meant by that last remark? "Don't be surprised if you don't find anyone."

His eyes narrowed. The car a decoy, on autopilot? But what would that accomplish?

Another car flying in above him. This empty car to hold his attention while the other got through.

He used the beltphone. "Carson, you there? Lift your car out of there. Up to a thousand feet. Turn off your lights and hover and see what you can pick up on in-frared. Stay there until we call off the search."

It was some time before he found out how badly he'd missed the mark.

"Calling Major Chin," said Doheny, hovering one hundred feet above Parlette Park. Controlled excitement tinged his voice with the thrill of the chase.

"Sir? I've got an infrared spot just leaving the pond. . . . Could be two people; this fog is messing up my imagine. . . . Western shore. They're out now, moving toward where all the men are milling around. . . . You don't? They're there; I swear it. . . . Okay, okay, but if they aren't there, then something's wrong with my infrascope—sir. . . . Yes, sir."

Annoyed but obedient, Doheny settled back and watched the dim red spot merge with the bigger spot that was a car motor. That tears it, he thought; that makes them police, whether they're real or not.

He saw the larger infrared source move away, leaving behind a second source smaller than a car but comfortably bigger than one man. That jerked him alert, and he moved to the window to check. It was there, all right, and . . .

He lost interest and returned to the infrascope. The cloverleaf-shaped source was still there, not moving, the right color to be four unconscious men. A man-sized source separated itself from the milling mass around the abandoned car, moving toward the cloverleaf source. Seconds later there was pandemonium.

Gasping, wheezing, running for their lives, they pelted out of Parlette Park and into a wide, well-lighted village walk. Matt gripped Laney's wrist as they ran, so that she couldn't "forget about him" and wander off on her own. As they reached the walk, Laney pulled back on his arm.

"Okay. . . . We can . . . relax now."

"How far . . . to the Hospital?"

" 'Bout . . . two miles."

Ahead of them the white lights of Implementation cars

faded behind a lighted dome of fog as they chased an empty car on autopilot. A yellow glow touched the fading far-end of the walk: the lights of the Hospital.

The walk was a rectangular pattern of red brick, luxuriously wide, with great spreading chestnut trees planted down the middle in a pleasantly uneven row. Street lights along the sides illuminated old and individualistic houses. The chestnuts swayed and sang shrilly in the wind. The wind blew the still-thinning fog into curls and streamers; it cut steel-cold through wet clothes and wet skin to reach meat and marrow.

"We've got to get some clothes," said Matt.

"We'll meet someone. We're bound to. It's only nine."

"How could those crew stand it? Swimming!"

"The water was hot. Probably they had a sauna bath waiting somewhere. I wish we did."

"We should have taken that car."

"Your power wouldn't have hidden us. At night they couldn't see your face in a car window. They'd have seen a stolen car, and they'd have bathed it in sonics, which is just what they must be doing now."

"And why did you insist on stripping that policeman? And having got the damn suit, why did you throw it away?"

"For the Mist Demons' *sake,* Matt! Will you *trust* me?"

"Sorry. We could either of us use that coat."

"It's worth it. Now they'll be looking for one man in an Implementation uniform. Hey! In front of me, quick!"

A square of light had appeared several houses down. Matt stepped in front of her and stooped, hands on knees, so she could use his shoulder as a gun rest.

It had worked on four police in Parlette Park. It worked now. A crew couple appeared in the light. They turned and waved to their hosts, turned again and moved down the steps, hunching slightly against the wind. The closing door cut the light from them and left them as dim moving shadows. As they touched the brick, they crossed the flat trajectories of two hunting slivers.

Matt and Laney stripped them and left them propped against a garden hedge for the sun to find.

"Thank the Mist Demons," said Matt. He was still shivering inside the dry clothes.

Laney was already thinking ahead. "We'll stick with the houses as far as we can. These houses give off a lot of infrared. They'll screen us. Even if a car does spot us, he'll have to drop and question us to be sure we're not crew."

"Good. What happens when we run out of houses?"

Laney didn't answer for a long time. Matt didn't press her. Finally she said, "Matt, there's something I'd better tell you."

Again he didn't press her.

"As soon as we get through the wall—if we get through the wall—I'm going to the vivarium. You don't have to come along, but I've got to go."

"Won't that be the first thing they expect?"

"Probably."

"Then we'd better not. Let's hunt down Polly first. We ought to keep the noise down as long as possible. Once your Sons of Earth come charging out, assuming we get that far, those doors will drop right away. In fact, if we—" At this point he glanced over at her and stopped.

Laney was looking straight ahead. Her face was hard and masklike. So was her voice, deliberately hard.

"That's why I'm telling you now. I'm going to the vivarium. That's why I'm here." She seemed about to break off; then she went on in a rush. "That's why I'm here, because the Sons of Earth are in there and I'm one of them. Not because you need me, but because they need me. I need you to get me in. Otherwise I'd be trying it alone."

"I see," said Matt. He was about to go on, but—no, he couldn't say that. He'd leave himself wide open to be slapped down, and in this mood Laney would do it. Instead he said, "What about Polly's big secret?"

"Millard Parlette knows it too. He seemed eager to talk. If he isn't, Lydia will get it out of him anyway."

"So you don't need Polly anymore."

"That's right. And if you've got the idea I'm here for love of you, you can forget that too. I'm not trying to be boorish, Matt, or cruel either. I just want you to know where you stand. Otherwise you'll be counting on me to make intelligent decisions.

"You're transportation, Matt. We need each other to get in. Once we're inside I'll go straight to the vivarium, and you can do whatever you have to to stay alive."

For some time they walked in silence, arm in arm, a crew couple strolling home along a distance too short to use a car. Other crew appeared from time to time. Mostly they walked quickly, bent against the wind, and they ignored Matt and Laney and each other in their hurry to get out of the cold. Once a good dozen men and women, varying from merely high to falling-down drunk, poured into the street ahead of them, marched four houses down, and began banging on the door. Matt and Laney watched as the door opened and the partygoers poured in. And suddenly Matt felt intensely lonely. He gripped Laney's arm a little tighter, and they went on.

The brick walk swung away to the left, and they followed it around. Now there were no houses on the right. Just trees, high and thick, screening the Hospital from view. The barren defense perimeter must be just the other side.

"Now what?"

"We follow it," said Laney. "I think we ought to go in along the trapped forest."

She waited for him to ask why, but he didn't. She told him anyway. "The Sons of Earth have been planning an attack on the Hospital for decades. We've been waiting for the right time, and it never came. One of the things we planned was to go in along the edge of the trapped woods. The woods themselves are so full of clever widgets that the guards on that side probably never notice it."

"You hope."

"You bet."

"What do you know about the Hospital defenses?"

"Well, you ran into most of them last night. A good thing you had the sense to stay out of the trapped woods. There are two electric-eye rings. You saw the wall; guns and spotlights all over it. Castro probably put extra men on it tonight, and we can bet he closed off the access road. Usually they leave it open, but it's easy enough to close the electric-eye ring and shut off power to the gate."

"And inside the wall?"

"Guards. Matt, we've been assuming that all these men will be badly trained. The Hospital's never been under direct attack. We're outnumbered—"

"Yes, we are, aren't we?"

"But we'll be dealing with guards who don't really believe there's anything to guard against."

"What about traps? We can't fight machinery."

"Practically none in the Hospital—at least, not usually. There are things Castro could set up in an emergency. In the slowboats there could be anything; we just don't know. But we won't be going near the slowboats. Then there are those damn vibrating doors."

Matt nodded, a swift vicious jerk of his chin.

"Those doors surprised us all. We should have been warned."

"By who?"

"Never you mind. Stop a second. . . . Right. This is the place. We go through here."

"Laney."

"Yah? There are pressure wires in the dirt. Step on the roots only as we go through."

"What happened Friday night?"

She turned back to look at his face, trying to read what he meant. She said, "I happened to think you needed me."

Matt nodded slowly. "You happened to think right."

"Okay. That's what I'm there for. The Sons of Earth

are mostly men. Sometimes they get horribly depressed. Always planning, never actually fighting, never winning when they do, and always wondering if they aren't doing just what Implementation wants. They can't even brag except to each other, because not all the colonists are on our side. Then, sometimes, I can make them feel like men again."

"I think I need my ego boosted about now."

"What you need right now, brother, is a good scare. Just keep thinking scared, and you'll be all right. We go through here—"

"I just thought of something."

"What's that?"

"If we'd stayed here this afternoon, we'd have saved all this trouble."

"Will you come on? And don't forget to step on the roots!"

CHAPTER X

PARLETTE'S HAND

DARKNESS COVERED most of Mount Lookitthat.

The crew never knew it. The lights of Alpha Plateau burned undimmed. Even in the houses along the Alpha-Beta cliff, with a view across Beta Plateau toward the distant, clustered town lights of Gamma and Iota, tonight that view was blanked by fog; and who was to know that the clustered lights were dark?

In the colonist regions there was fear and fury, but it couldn't touch Alpha Plateau.

No real danger threatened. On Gamma and Iota there were no hospitals where patients might die in dark operating theaters. No cars would crash without street lights. Spoiling meat in butcher shop freezers would cause no famine; there were the fruit and nut forests, the crops, the herds.

But there was fear and fury. Was something wrong, up there where all power originated? Or was it a prank, a punishment, an experiment—some deliberate act of Implementation?

You couldn't travel without lights. Most people stayed where they were, wherever they were. They bedded down where they could; for colonists it was near bedtime anyway. And they waited for the lights to come back.

They would give no trouble, Jesus Pietro thought. If danger came tonight, it would not come from down there.

Equally certain, the Sons of Earth *would* attack, though they only numbered five. Harry Kane would not leave most of his men to die. Whatever he could do, he would do it, regardless of risk.

And Major Chin's fugitive had escaped, was loose two miles from the Hospital, wearing a police uniform. And because he had escaped, because he was alone, because no man had seen him clearly—it had to be Matt Keller.

Five dossiers to match five fugitives. Harry Kane and Jayhawk Hood: These were old friends, the most dangerous of the Sons of Earth. Elaine Mattson and Lydia Hancock and Matthew Keller: These he had come to know by heart during the long hours following the break this afternoon. He could have recognized any of them a mile away or told them their life stories.

The slimmest dossier was Matt Keller's: two and a half skimpy pages. Mining engineer ... not much of a family man ... few love affairs ... no evidence he had ever joined the Sons of Earth.

Jesus Pietro was worried. The Sons of Earth, if they got this far, would go straight to the vivarium to free their compatriots. But if Matthew Keller was his own agent ...

If the ghost of Alpha Plateau was not a rebel, but a thing with its own unpredictable purpose ...

Jesus Pietro worried. His last sip of coffee suddenly tasted horrible, and he pushed the cup away. He noted with relief that the mist seemed to be clearing. On his desk were a stack of five dossiers and a sixth all alone and a mercy-bullet gun.

In the lights of the Hospital the sky glowed pearl gray. The wall was a monstrous mass above them, a sharp black shadow cutting across the lighted sky. They heard regular footsteps overhead.

They'd crawled here side by side, close enough to get in each other's way. They'd broad-jumped the electric-eye barriers, Matt first, then Laney making her move while Matt stared up at the wall and *willed* nobody to see her. So far nobody had.

"We could get around to the gate," said Matt.

"But if Castro's cut off the power, we can't get it open. No, there's a better way."

"Show me."

"We may have to risk a little excitement. . . . Here it is."

"What?"

"The fuse. I wasn't sure it'd be here."

"Fuse?"

"See, a lot of Implementation is pure colonist. We have to be careful who we approach, and we've lost good men who talked to the wrong person, but it paid off. I hope."

"Someone planted a bomb for you?"

"I hope so. There are only two Sons of Earth in Implementation, and either or both of them could be ringers." She fumbled in the big, loose pockets of her mud-spattered crewish finery. "Bitch didn't carry a lighter. Matt?"

"Lessee. Here."

She took the lighter, then spoke deliberately. "If they see the light, we're done for." She crouched over the wire.

Matt crouched over her, to shield the light with his body. As he did so, he looked up. Two bumps showed on the straight black shadow of the wall. They moved. Matt started to whisper, Stop! Yellow light flared under him, and it was too late.

The heads withdrew.

Laney shook his arm. "Run! Along the wall!" He followed the pull.

"Now flat!" He landed beside her on his belly. There was a tremendous blast. Metal bits sang around them, raising tiny *pings* against the wall. Something bit a piece from Matt's ear, and he slapped at it like a wasp sting.

He didn't have time to curse. Laney jerked him to his feet, and they ran back the way they had come. There was confused shouting on the wall, and Matt looked up to meet a hundred eyes looking down. Then suddenly the area was bright as hell.

"Here!" Laney dropped to her knees, slapped his hand onto her ankle, and crawled. Matt heard mercy-bullets spattering around his ankles as he went in after her.

On the outside the hole was just big enough to crawl through on hands and knees. The bomb must have been a shaped charge. But the wall was thick, and the hole was smaller on the inside. They emerged on their bellies, with scratches. Here too was light, too bright, making Matt's eyes water. Startlingly, there were pits all in a row in the dirt along this side of the wall, and over the cordite stink was the smell of rich, moist new earth.

"Bombs," he said wonderingly. Pressure bombs, set off by the explosion, originally intended to explode under an invader dropping from the top of the wall. Bombs, meant to kill. "I'm flattered," he whispered to himself, and lied.

"Shut up!" Laney turned to glare, and in the lurid artificial light he saw her eyes change. Then she turned and ran. She was beyond reach before Matt had time to react.

Feet pounded all around them, all running at top speed toward the hole in the wall. They were surrounded! Amazingly, nobody tried to stop Laney. But he saw someone jerk to a stop, then go pelting after her.

And nobody tried to stop Matt. He was invisible enough, but he'd lost Laney. Without him, she had nothing but the gun . . . and he didn't know how to reach Polly. He stood there, lost.

Frowning, Harry Kane inspected hands which didn't match. He'd seen transplantees before, but never such a patchwork man as Millard Parlette.

Lydia said, "It isn't artificial, is it?"

"No. But it's not a normal transplant job either."

"He should be coming around."

"I am," said Millard Parlette.

Harry started. "You can talk?"

"Yes." Parlette had a voice like a squeaky door, altered by a would-be musical crew lilt, slurred by the effects of a sonic stunner. He spoke slowly, consciously enunciating. "May I have a glass of water?"

"Lydia, get him some water."

"Here." The stocky virago supported the old man's head with her arm and fed him the water in small sips.

Harry studied the man. They'd propped him against a wall in the vestibule. He hadn't moved since then and probably couldn't, but the muscles of his face, which had been slack and rubbery, now reflected a personality.

"Thank you," he said in a stronger voice. "You shouldn't have shot me, you know."

"You have things to tell us, Mr. Parlette."

"You're Harry Kane. Yes, I have things to tell you. And then I'll want to make a deal of sorts with you."

"I'm open to deals. What kind?"

"You'll understand when I finish. May I start with the recent ramrobot package? This will be somewhat technical—"

"Lydia, get Jay." Lydia Hancock quietly withdrew. "I'll want him to hear anything technical. Jay is our genius."

"Jayhawk Hood? Is he here too?"

"You seem to know a good deal about us."

"I do. I've been studying the Sons of Earth for longer than you've been alive. Jayhawk Hood has a fine mind. By all means, let us wait for him."

"You've been studying us, have you? Why?"

"I'll try to make that clear to you, Kane. It will take time. Has the situation on Mount Lookitthat ever struck you as artificial, fragile?"

"Phut. If you'd been trying to change it as long as I have, you wouldn't think so."

"Seriously, Kane. Our society depends entirely on its technology. Change the technology, and you change the society. Most especially you change the ethics."

"That's ridiculous. Ethics are ethics."

The old man's hand twitched. "Let me speak, Kane."

Harry Kane was silent.

"Consider the cotton gin," said Millard Parlette. "That invention made it economically feasible to grow cotton in quantity in the southern United States, but not in the northern states. It brought slaves in great numbers to one section of that nation while slavery died out in another. The result was a problem in racial tolerance which lasted for centuries.

"Consider feudal armor. The ethics of chivalry were based on the fact that armor was a total defense against anything which wasn't similarly armored. The clothyard arrow, and later gunpowder, ended chivalry and made a new ethic necessary.

"Consider war as a tool of diplomacy." Millard Parlette stopped to gasp for breath. After a moment he went on. "It was, you know. Then came poison gas, and fission bombs, and fission-fusion bombs, and a possible fission-fusion-radiocobalt bomb. Each invention made war less and less useful for imposing one's will, more and more randomly destructive, until nationalism itself became too dangerous to be tolerated, and the United Nations on Earth became more powerful than any possible minority alliance of nations.

"Consider the settling of the Belt. A solely technological development, yet it created the wealthiest population in the system in a region which absolutely required new ethics, where stupidity automatically carries its own death penalty." The old man stopped again, exhausted.

"I'm no historian," said Harry. "But morals are morals. What's unethical here and now is unethical anywhere, anytime."

"Kane, you're wrong. It is ethical to execute a man for theft?"

"Of course."

"Did you know that there was once a vastly detailed science of rehabilitation for criminals? It was a branch of psychology, naturally, but it was by far the largest such branch. By the middle of century twenty-one, nearly two-thirds of all criminals could eventually be released as cured."

"That's silly. Why go to all that trouble when the organ

banks must have been *crying* for—Oh. I see. No organ banks."

The old man was finally smiling, showing perfect new white teeth. Sparkling teeth and keen gray eyes: The real Millard Parlette showed behind the cracked, wrinkled, loose rubber mask of his face.

Except that the teeth couldn't be his, thought Harry. Nuts to that. "Go on," he said.

"One day a long time ago I realized that the ethical situation on Mount Lookitthat was fragile. It was bound to change someday, and *suddenly,* what with Earth constantly bombarding us with new discoveries. I decided to be ready."

There were footsteps on the stairs, running. Lydia and Hood burst in.

Harry Kane introduced Hood to Millard Parlette as if they were already allies. Hood took his cue and shook hands formally, wincing inside himself because Parlette's hand still felt like something dead.

"Keep that hand," said Millard Parlette. "Examine it."

"We already did."

"Your conclusions?"

"Ask you about it."

"Apparently Earth is using biological engineering for medical purposes. There were four gifts in the ramrobot package, along with complete instructions for their care and use. One was a kind of fungus-virus symbiot. I dipped my little finger in it. Now the muck is replacing my skin."

"Replacing—? Sorry," said Hood. It was difficult *not* to interrupt Parlette, his speech was so irritatingly slow.

"That's right. First it dissolves the epidermis, leaving only the living cells beneath. Then it somehow stimulates the DNA memory in the derma. Probably the virus component does that. You may know that a virus does not reproduce; it compells its host to produce more virus, by inserting its own reproductive chains into the host cells."

"You may have a permanent guest," said Hood.

"No. The virus dies after a short time. Any virus does that. Then the fungus starves."

"Wonderful! The muck moves in a ring, leaving new skin behind!" Hood considered. "Earth really came through this time. But what happens when it reaches your eyes?"

"I don't know. But there were no special instructions. I offered myself as a test subject because I could use a new pelt. It's even supposed to get rid of scar tissue. It does."

"That's quite an advance," said Harry.

"But you don't see why it's important. Kane, I showed you this first because I happened to bring it along. The others will jolt you." Parlette let his head droop to relieve the strain on his neck. "I don't know what animal gave birth to the second gift, but it now resembles a human liver. In the proper environment it will behave like a human liver."

Harry's eyes went wide and blank. Lydia made a startled hissing sound. And Millard Parlette added, "The proper environment is, of course, the environment of a human liver. They have not been tested because they are not fully grown. We can expect disadvantages due to the lack of nervous connections—"

"Keller told the truth. Little hearts and livers!" Harry exclaimed. "Parlette, was the third gift an animal to replace the human heart?"

"Yes. Nearly all muscle. It reacts to Adrenalin by speeding up, but once again the lack of nervous—"

"Yee HAH!" Harry Kane began to dance. He grabbed Lydia Hancock, spun her around and around. Hood watched, grinning foolishly. Kane abruptly released her and dropped to his knees in front of Parlette. "What's the fourth?"

"A rotifer."

"A . . . rotifer?"

"It lives as a symbiot in the human bloodstream. It does things the human body will not do for itself. Kane, it has often struck me that evolution as a process leaves something to be desired. Evolution is finished with a man once he is too old to reproduce. Thus there is no genetic program to keep him alive longer than that. Only inertia. It takes enormous medical knowledge to compen—"

"What does it do, this rotifer?"

"It fights disease. It cleans fatty deposits from the veins and arteries. It dissolves blood clots. It is too big to move into the small capillaries, and it dies on contact with air. Thus it will not impede necessary clotting. It secretes a kind of gum to patch weak points in the walls of the arteries and larger capillaries, which is reassuring to a man of my age.

"But it does more than that. It acts as a kind of catch-all gland, a supplementary pituitary. It tends to maintain the same glandular balance a man is supposed to have at around age thirty. It will not produce male and female hormones, and it takes its own good time disposing of excess adrenaline, but otherwise it maintains the balance. Or so say the instructions."

Harry Kane sank back on his heels. "Then the organ banks are done. Obsolete. No wonder you tried to keep it secret."

"Don't be silly."

"What?" Parlette opened his mouth, but Harry rode him down. "I tell you the organ banks are done for! Listen, Parlette. The skin mold replaces skin grafting, and does it better. The heart animal and the liver animal replace heart and liver transplants. And the rotifer keeps everything else from getting sick in the first place! What more do you *want*?"

"Several things. A kidney beast, for example. Or—"

"Quibbling."

"How would you replace a lung? A lung destroyed by nicotine addiction?"

Hood said, "He's right. Those four ramrobot gifts are nothing but a signpost. How do you repair a smashed foot, a bad eye, a baseball finger?" He was pacing now, in short jerky steps. "You'd need several hundred different artifacts of genetic engineering to make the organ banks really obsolete. All the same—"

"All right, cut," said Harry Kane, and Hood was silent. "Parlette, I jumped the gun. You're right. But I'll give you something to think about. Suppose every colonist on Mount Lookitthat knew only the facts about the ramrobot package. Not Hood's analysis, and not yours—just the truth. What then?"

Parlette was smiling. He shouldn't have been, but his white teeth gleamed evenly in the light, and the smile was not forced. "They would assume the organ banks were obsolete. They would confidently expect Implementation to disband."

"And when Implementation showed no sign of disbanding, they'd revolt! Every colonist on Mount Lookitthat! Could the Hospital stand against *that?*"

"You see the point, Kane. I am inclined to think the Hospital could stand against any such attack, though I would not like to gamble on it. But I am *sure* we could lose half the population of this planet in the bloodbath, win *or* lose."

"Then—you've already thought of this."

Parlette's face twisted. His hands fluttered aimlessly and his feet jumped against the floor as the effects of the sonic gave up their hold on him. "Do you think me a fool, Harry Kane? I never made that mistake about you. I first heard of the ramrobot package six months ago, when the ramrobot sent out its maser message. I knew immediately that the present crew rule over the Plateau was doomed."

Laney had vanished around to the left, around the great gentle curve of the *Planck,* while Matt stood gaping. He started after her, then checked himself. She must know of another entrance; he'd never catch her before she reached it. And if he followed her through, he'd be lost in the maze of the Hospital.

But he had to find her. She'd kept him in the dark as much as she could. Probably because she expected Castro

to get him, and didn't want him to spill anything important. She hadn't mentioned the bomb until the fuse was in
her hand, nor the detailed plans for invading the Hospital
until she was already following them.

Eventually she'd have told him how to find Polly. Now
he'd lost both.

Or . . . ?

He ran toward the main entrance, dodging police who
tried to run through his solid bulk. He would meet Laney
at the vivarium—if she got there. But he knew only one
route to reach it.

The great bronze doors swung open as he approached.
Matt hesitated at the bottom of the wide stairs. Electric
eyes? Then three uniformed men trotted through the entrance and down, and Matt trotted up between them. If
there were electric eyes here, and men watching them,
they could never keep track of the last minute's traffic.

The doors swung shut as he went through. They almost
caught him between them. He cursed in a whisper and
stepped aside for a running policeman with a whistle in
his mouth. Like the ultrasonic whistle the gateman had
used to get in last night. He'd need one to get out. But
later. He needn't think about leaving yet.

His legs ached savagely. He slowed to a brisk walk and
tried not to pant.

Right, up a flight, take a right, then a left . . .

VIVARIUM. He saw the door down the corridor, and he
stopped where he was and sagged gratefully against a
wall. He'd beaten her here. And he was horribly tired. His
legs were numb, there was a singing in his head, he
wanted to do nothing but breathe. A taste in his mouth
and throat reminded him of the hot metal taste of the void
mist when he'd bored for the bottom less than thirty-six
plateau hours ago. It seemed he'd been running forever,
terrified forever. His blood had carried adrenaline for too
long. The wall felt soft against his back.

It was good to rest. It was good to breathe. It was good
to be warm, and the Hospital walls were warm, almost too

warm for a cold-weather crewish overjacket. He'd ditch it when it got too hot. Probing idly in his pockets, he found a double handful of unshelled roasted peanuts.

Corporal Halley Fox rounded the corner and stopped. He saw a crew resting against a wall, wearing his overjacket indoors. There was a ragged tear in the crew's ear and a pool of blood below it, soaked into the neck of his overjacket. He was cracking and eating peanuts, dropping the shells on the floor.

It was strange, but not strange enough.

Halley Fox was in the third generation of a family which traditionally produced Implementation police. Naturally he had joined Implementation. His reflexes were not quick enough to make him a raider, and he made a better follower than a leader. For eight years now he had been a competent man in a good position that did not require much responsibility.

Then . . . last night he'd caught a colonist invading the Hospital.

This morning there'd been a break from the vivarium, the first since the vivarium was built. Corporal Fox had seen blood for the first time. Man's blood, not drained into an organ-bank tank but spilled recklessly along a hallway in conscious murderous violence.

This evening the Head had warned of an impending attack on the Hospital. He'd practically warned Corporal Fox to shoot his own fellow guards! And everyone was taking him seriously!

Minutes ago there'd been a hell of a big blast outside the windows . . . and half the guards had deserted their posts to see what had happened.

Corporal Fox was slightly punch-drunk.

He had not deserted his post. Things were confused enough. He stuck to his training as something he knew to be solid. And when he saw a crew resting against a wall eating peanuts, he saluted and said, "Sir."

Matt looked up to see a police officer standing stiff as a

board, holding the short barrel of a mercy-bullet pistol slantwise across his forehead.

Effectively he disappeared. Corporal Fox continued down the hall, stepping wide around the vivarium door. At the end of the corridor he stopped, half turned, and fell.

Matt got unsteadily to his feet. The sight of the guard had damn near stopped his heart.

Laney came around fast. She saw Matt, dodged back, poked the gun around—

"Stop! It's me!"

"Oh, Matt. I thought I'd lost you."

He moved toward her. "I saw someone come after you. Did you get him?"

"Yah." She looked down at Corporal Fox. "They're badly trained. That's something."

"Where'd you learn to shoot like that?"

"Never you mind. Come on." She moved back toward the vivarium.

"Hold it. Where do I find Polly?"

"I really don't know. We've never known where they administer the coffin cure." She reached for the door handle. Matt caught her wrist. "Come now, Matt," she said. "You had fair warning."

"The door's booby-trapped."

"Oh?"

"I saw the way that guy walked around it."

She frowned at the handle. Then, with effort, she tore a strip from the bottom of Matt's jacket. She tied it to the handle, moved back as far as it would reach.

Matt backed away. He said, "Before you do something irrevocable, won't you please tell me where to find Polly?"

"Honestly, Matt, I don't know." She wasn't trying to hide the fact that he was an unneeded distraction.

"Okay, where's Castro's office?"

"You're out of your mind."

"I'm a fanatic. Like you."

That got a grin. "You're crazy, but okay. You go back

the way I came, turn the only way you can, and go up
another flight. Follow the hall until you see signs. The
signs will take you the rest of the way. The office is up
against the hull of the *Planck*. But if you stick with me,
we may find an easier way."

"Pull then."

Laney pulled.

The handle came down and clicked. Immediately something fired from the ceiling: a conical burst of mercy-
bullets spattering the area where anyone would have stood
to pull the handle. And a siren blared in the corridor, loud
and raucous and familiar.

Laney jumped straight back in surprise, fetched up
against the wall. The door swung open a couple of inches.
"In," she cried, and dove through, followed by Matt.

The puffs of mercy-bullets were lost in the sound of the
siren. But Matt saw four men in the room, crouched in
target-shooting position in a line opposite the door. They
were still firing as Laney fell.

"Doomed? Really?" Even to himself Harry sounded
inane. But he'd expected no such easy capitulation.

"How many Sons of Earth are there?"

"I can't tell you that."

"I can tell you," said Millard Parlette. "Less than four
hundred. On all of Mount Lookitthat there are less than
seven hundred active rebels. For three hundred years you
and your kind have been trying to build a rebellion.
You've made no progress at all."

"Precious little."

"You enlist your rebels from the colonists, naturally.
Your trouble is that most colonists don't really want the
crew to lose control of the Plateau. They're happy the way
they are. Yours is an unpopular cause. I tried to explain
why before; let me try again." With obvious effort he
moved his arms enough to fold his hands in his lap.
Random muscles in his shoulders twitched from time to
time.

"It's not that they don't think they could do better than the crew if it came to the point. Everybody always thinks that. They're afraid of Implementation, yes, and they won't risk their good blood and bone to make the change, not when Implementation has all the weapons on the Plateau and controls all the electrical power too.

"But that isn't the point. The point is that they don't really think that the crew rule is *wrong*.

"It all depends on the organ banks. On the one hand, the organ banks are a terrible threat, not only a death penalty, but an ignominious way to die. On the other hand, the banks are a promise. A man who deserves it and can pay for it, even a colonist, can get medical treatment at the Hospital. But without the organ banks there'd be no treatment. He'd die.

"Do you know what your rebels would do if they could beat the crew to their knees? Some would insist that the organ banks be abolished. They'd be killed or ostracized by their own members. The majority would keep the banks just as they are, but use the crew to feed them!"

His neck was stronger now, and he looked up to see patient stares. A good audience. And he had them hooked, finally.

"Up to now," he went on, "you couldn't start a rebellion because you couldn't convince enough fighting men that your cause was just. Now you can. Now you can convince the colonists of Mount Lookitthat that the organ banks are and should be obsolete. Then wait a little. When Implementation doesn't disband, you move."

Harry Kane said, "That's exactly what I was thinking, only you seem to be way ahead of me. Why did you call me silly?"

"You made a silly assumption. You thought I was trying to keep the ramrobot package a secret. Quite the contrary. Just this afternoon I—"

"I've finally got it," said Hood. "You've decided to join the winning side, have you, Parlette?"

"You fool. You bad-mouthed colonist fool."

Jay Hood flushed. He stood perfectly straight with his arms at his sides and his fists clenched. He was no angrier than Parlette. The old man was trying to shift his weight, and every muscle in his body was jumping as a result. He said, "Do you think so little of me, to think I'd follow such motives?"

"Relax, Jay. Parlette, if you have something to say, say it. If we jump to the wrong conclusions, please assume that you're expressing yourself badly, and don't try to shift the blame."

"Why don't you all count to infinity?" Lydia Hancock suggested.

Parlette spoke slowly and evenly. "I am trying to prevent a bloodbath. Is that clear enough for you? I'm trying to prevent a civil war that could kill half the people in this world."

"You can't do it," said Harry Kane. "It's coming."

"Kane, cannot you and I and your associates work out a new . . . constitution for Mount Lookitthat? Obviously the Covenant of Planetfall will no longer work."

"Obviously."

"I made a speech today. In fact, I seem to be spending the whole damn day and night making speeches. This afternoon I called an emergency session—rammed it through the Council. You know what that means?"

"Yah. You were talking to every crew on the Plateau, then."

"I told them what was in ramrobot package one-forty-three. I showed them. I told them about the organ-bank problem and about the relationship between ethics and technology. I told them that if the secret of the ramrobot ever reached the colonists, the colonists would revolt en masse. I did my damndest, Kane, to scare the pants off them.

"I've known from the beginning that we couldn't keep the secret forever. Now that thirty thousand people know it, it'll be out even faster, even if we were all killed this instant. I did all this, Kane, in order to warn them. To scare them. When they realize that the secret is out, they may be scared enough to dicker. The smart ones will.

"I've been planning this a long time, Kane. I didn't even know what it was that Earth would ship us. It might have been a regeneration serum, or designs for cheap alloplasty components, or even a new religion. Anything. But something was coming, and here it is, and, Kane, we've got to try to stop the bloodbath." Gone were Parlette's shortness of breath and his clumsy attempts to make his lips and tongue work against a sonic blast. His voice was smooth and lilting, rising and falling, a little hoarse but terribly earnest. "We've got to try. Maybe we can find something both the crew and the colonists can agree on."

He stopped, and three heads nodded, almost in reflex.

CHAPTER XI

INTERVIEW WITH THE HEAD

HE SAW the four men, and he saw Laney stagger. He tried to turn and run, and in that instant there was a godawful clang, a sound like being inside a church bell. He jumped to the side instead, knowing the hall must be full of sonics.

"Shut the damn door!" a voice yelled. One of the guards jumped to obey. Matt felt the numbness of the sonics, and his knees went watery. He kept his eyes on his four enemies.

One bent over Laney. "All alone," he said. "Crazy. Wonder where she got the clothes?"

"Off a crew, maybe."

Another guard laughed brayingly.

"Shut up, Rick. Come on, lend a hand. Let's get her to a chair."

"A hunting gun. Wouldn't you hate to get shot with this?"

"She came a long way to get to the vivarium. Most of 'em we have to bring."

The braying laugh again.

"Gas bomb didn't go off." One of the guards kicked a metal canister. Immediately the canister began hissing. "Nose plugs, quick!"

They fumbled in their pockets, produced things that looked like large rubber false noses.

"Good. We should have done this before. If we keep the room filled with gas, anyone who comes charging in will drop right away."

Matt had gotten the message. He'd held his breath from the moment he heard the hiss. Now he walked up to the nearest guard and wrenched his false nose away. The man gasped in surprise, looked directly at Matt, and crumpled.

The false nose had a band to fit around the neck, and some kind of adhesive to form a skin-tight lock around the nose. Matt got it on and found himself breathing through it, with difficulty. It was not comfortable.

"Rick? Oh, that idiot. Where the Mist Demons is his nose plug?"

"I'll bet the jerk forgot to bring it."

"Get me Major Jansen, please." One of the guards was using his handphone. "Sir? A girl just tried to crash the vivarium. Yes, a girl, in crew clothing. . . . That's right, just one. . . . She's sleeping in one of the seats, sir. We figured as long as she'd gone to all that trouble getting here . . ."

Matt still felt dizzy, though the door must be blocking the vibrations of the big sonics. Had he been hit by an unnoticed mercy-bullet?

He bent over Laney. She was out of it, for sure. Punctured by far too many anesthetic slivers, her lungs filled with gas, a rhythmic sleep-inducing current playing through her brain . . . ?

He found three wires leading to her headset. He pulled them. Now she was a time bomb. When everything else wore off, she'd wake up. More of a firecracker, actually, with four armed guards in the room.

"One more thing, sir. The place is full of gas. It's just as well, we think.

"No, sir, we haven't. If you'll turn off the sonics, I'll look." He turned from the phone. "Watts, check in the hall and see if anybody dropped dead out there."

"But the sonics are still going!"

"They should be off. Try it."

A ballpoint pen peeped from the shirt pocket of the unconscious guard. Matt saw it, snatched it, and drew rapidly: a heart on the guard's forehead, three drops running down the straight bridge of the nose.

The one called Watts opened the door a crack. No sonic

numbness touched him. He opened it farther. "Hey!" He snaked out and ran down the hall toward Fox's body. Matt was on his heels.

"It's a guard," he called back.

"Check the ident."

Watts began going through Fox's pockets. He looked up once as Matt sidled past him, then continued with his work.

"It's Elaine Mattson," said Jesus Pietro. "Has to be. You're sure she was alone?"

"If there'd been anyone with her, he would have been in the same condition. I think she was alone, sir."

That made sense. Which was hardly a guarantee, Jesus Pietro thought. "Thank you, Major Jansen. How are the hunting squads doing?"

"They've found nothing, sir. They're still quartering Alpha Plateau. Shall I see how far they've gotten?"

"Yes. Call me back." He hung up and tilted back his desk chair, with a frown wrinkling his forehead.

They had to be somewhere on Alpha. And they couldn't *all* be attacking the Hospital.

Elaine Mattson, captured. Well and good. She must have set off that mysterious explosion to cover her entrance. Had she also worn that Implementation uniform? It might be. She'd pass at a distance, long enough to knock out a crew woman and get a better disguise.

Maybe. Maybe.

He picked up the sixth dossier, the one lying alone next to the stunner. Polly Tournquist's life:

Born twenty-two years ago, firstborn in a family with no known connection to the Sons of Earth. *Her father's left eye had come from the organ banks, after he'd lost his own to a fishing fly. A good, loyal colonist. A disciplinarian in his own family.*

Raised on Delta, sector four. Studied at Colony University, with good grades. *She'd met Jayhawk Hood there. Her first love affair. Why? Hood would have made a bad gigolo—small, puny, not good-looking—but some girls like a man with a mind.*

Finished high school and college, went to work at Delta Retransmitting Station. Affair with Hood had cooled to friendship, apparently. But she'd joined the Sons of Earth. *Revolting against authority? Her father would have turned her in, had he known. Look at the lines of disapproval in that ferret face ... hmm? Without those lines, he'd look something like Jayhawk Hood!*

It all helped. By now she'd been in the coffin cure for thirty hours. If a voice came to her now, the only sensory stimulus in her cosmos, she'd listen. And believe. As others had. Especially if the voice appealed to the right incidents in her past.

But for now she'd have to wait. The Sons of Earth came first. One down, four to go ... Jesus Pietro reached for his cup and found the coffee stone cold.

A question touched his mind. He grimaced, pushed it back to wherever it had come from. He opened his desk-phone and said, "Miss Lauessen, will you order me more coffee."

"Are you sure? You'll be awash with the stuff."

"Just get it. And"—the same thought crawled out into the light, and before he could stop himself—"get me Matthew Keller's file. Not the one on my desk, the one in the dead file."

She came in a minute later, slender and blonde and looking coolly remote, carrying a folder and a pot of coffee. He opened the folder at once. She frowned at him, started to ask something, saw that he wasn't listening, and left.

Matthew Keller. Born ... Educated ... Joined Sons of Earth tenth month, 2384, in middle age. *Why so late? Why at all?* Became a professional killer and thief, stealing for the Sons of Earth, killing Implementation officers foolish enough to venture into the colonist regions in insufficient numbers. *Thief? Damn! Could Keller senior have stolen that car? The car Keller junior rode straight down into the void!* Trapped in Sector 28, Beta, fourth month, 2397; captured, convicted of treason, disassembled for the organ banks. *Oh, Jesus Pietro, you clever liar, you. Half the Hospital must know he really went off the edge, forty miles down to Mist Demons and hellfire.*

So? Jesus Pietro dumped his cold coffee into a wastebasket, poured a fresh cup, and sipped.

A flicking shadow somewhere at the corner of his eye. A noise. *Someone was in the room.* The cup jumped in his hand, searing his lip. He put it down fast and looked around.

He went back to the dossier.

Matthew Keller. What idiot whim had made him ask for this? Keller senior was dead. Crippled, crawling, he'd gone off the void edge split seconds before—

"Castro."

Jesus Pietro looked up with a start.

He looked down. Treatment reports . . . Not good, but no disaster. Too many people had been injured in the mass escape, but some could be saved. Luckily the organ banks were full. And could be filled again, from the vivarium, once the Surgery Section found time. Why did everything have to happen at once?

"Castro!"

Jesus Pietro's chin jerked up—and he caught himself before his eyes followed. He'd done this once before, hadn't he? There'd been a noise . . . and someone had called his name . . . and what the Mist Demons was someone doing unannounced in Jesus Pietro's private office? He let his eyes travel to the edge of the desk—

Crew clothing.

But it was rumpled and dirty, and it didn't fit, and the hands that rested flat on his desk had dirty short fingernails. A colonist in crew clothing, for sure. In Jesus Pietro's office. Unannounced. He'd gone past Miss Lauessen, unannounced.

"You."

"That's right. Where is she?"

"You're Matthew Keller."

"Yes."

"How did you get in here?" Somehow he kept the tremor out of his voice, and was proud of it.

"None of your business. *Where is she?*"

"Who?"

"Don't give me that. Where's Polly?"

"I can't tell you that. Or anything else," said Jesus Pietro. He kept his eyes fixed on the man's stolen gold belt buckle.

At the periphery of his vision he saw two big, none-too-clean hands reach down to his own right hand. His visitor leaned heavily on that hand, and when Jesus Pietro belatedly tried to withdraw it, he couldn't. He saw his visitor take hold of his middle finger and bend it back.

The pain was shocking. Jesus Pietro's mouth came wide open, and he looked up to plead . . .

He was reaching for Polly Tournquist's folder when agony struck his hand. He snatched it back as if trying to get it off a hot stove. Reflex. The middle finger stuck out at right angles to the knuckles.

Mist Demons, it *hurt!* How the blazes had he—

"Well, Castro?"

He remembered enough, barely enough, not to look up. Someone or something was in this room, something or someone with the power to make people forget. He made a logical connection and said, "You."

"Right. Where's Polly Tournquist?"

"You. Matthew Keller. So you came for me."

"Let's not play games. Where's Polly?"

"Were you in the car that attacked the Hospital? The one that dove straight down—"

"Yes."

"Then how—"

"Shut up, Castro. Tell me where Polly is. Now. Is she alive?"

"You'll get no information from me. How did you get back from the void?"

"I flew back."

"I mean the first time."

"Castro, I could break every finger in both your hands. Now where's Polly? Is she dead?"

"Would I talk if you did?"

There was hesitation. Then two arms converged on his right hand. Jesus Pietro yelped with the pain and reached with clawed fingers for a pair of eyes . . .

He was halfway through a stack of reports when agony bit into his hand. He found two fingers of his right hand bent back at right angles to the palm. With his teeth clenched hard on a scream, Jesus Pietro turned on the intercom. "Get me the doctor."

"What's wrong?"

"Just get me the—" His eyes caught a flash of movement. Someone in the office with him!

"You're right," said a voice. "I can't torture anything out of you."

Faint, fading memories told him not to look up. He said, "You."

"Go fly a bicycle."

"Matthew Keller?"

Silence.

"Answer me, damn you! How did you get back?"

Two hands slapped together on Jesus Pietro's right hand. His whole face clamped down on the scream, and Jesus Pietro snatched up his stunner and looked wildly for a target.

He looked up again when the doctor entered.

"No point in replacing them," said the doctor. "They're only dislocated." And he deadened Jesus Pietro's arm, set the fingers, and splinted them. "How the Mist Demons did you do it?"

"I don't know."

"You don't know? You dislocated two fingers, and you can't quite recall—"

"Get off my back. I said I can't remember what happened to my hand. But I think that infernal ghost, Matthew Keller, must have had something to do with it."

The doctor gave him a very peculiar look. And left.

Jesus Pietro looked ruefully at his right arm, splinted and dangling from a sling. *Oh, fine.* And he genuinely couldn't remember anything about it.

Which was why he kept thinking about Matthew Keller.

But why did he keep thinking about Polly Tournquist?

It was time and past time for the next phase of her treatment. But surely she could wait? Of course she could.

He tried his coffee. Too cool. He poured it back into the pot and started fresh.

His arm felt like dead meat.

Why did he keep thinking about Polly Tournquist?

"Phut!" He stood up clumsily, because of his bound arm. "Miss Lauessen," he told the intercom, "get me two guards. I'm going over to the *Planck.*"

"Will do."

He was reaching for the stunner on his desk when something caught his eye. It was the dossier for Matthew Keller, senior. A crude drawing defaced its yellow cover.

Two open arcs, joined, in black ink. Three small closed loops beneath.

The bleeding heart. It certainly hadn't been there before.

Jesus Pietro opened the folder. He could smell his own fear, and feel it, in the cool perspiration that soaked his shirt. As if he'd been afraid for hours.

Front and side views. Blue eyes, yellow hair, skin beginning to puff out with age . . .

Something stirred somewhere in Jesus Pietro's mind. For just a moment the face in the folder became younger. Its expression changed slightly, so that it seemed both frightened and angry. There was blood soaking into its collar, and a piece freshly bitten from its ear.

"Your guards are here, sir."

"Thank you," said Jesus Pietro. He took one last look at the dead man and closed the folder. He put the stunner in his pocket before he left.

"I wish we could warn Laney," said Harry Kane. "This changes everything."

"You wouldn't even know what to tell her yet. Here, take this out." Mrs. Hancock put a steaming pitcher of hot cider on a tray, added four mugs.

They were in the kitchen. Hood was in the living room with Millard Parlette. Parlette, leaning on Jay Hood, had managed to stagger into the living room and into an armchair.

It had seemed a good time to call a break.

The wind screamed against black windows. To four conspirators in front of a convincing fire, drinking hot spiced cider against the cold, the living room seemed a haven.

A temporary haven.

"You've been thinking about this longer than we have," said Harry. "We never dreamed the crew might compromise. Just what are you prepared to offer?"

"To start with, amnesty for the Sons of Earth, for you and whoever remains in the vivarium. That comes free. We'll need you. Once the colonists lose faith in the crew, you'll be the only force for law and order in the colony regions."

"That'll be a switch."

"We need to discuss three types of medical care," said Millard Parlette. "Organic transplants, the ramrobot gifts, and minor medical treatment. You already have some access to standard drugs at the medcheck stations. We can expand those. I'm sure we can offer free access to the heartbeasts and liverbeasts and so forth. For a while your colonists will have to come up to the Hospital to get treatment with the ramrobot symbiots, but eventually we can build culture tanks in Gamma and Delta and Eta."

"Very good. What about the organ banks?"

"Right." Millard Parlette wrapped his arms around his narrow rib cage and stared into the fire. "I couldn't plan for that part, because I didn't know just what technological change was coming. What are your ideas?"

"Abolish the organ banks," Mrs. Hancock said firmly.

"Throw away tons of organic transplant material? Dump it on the grass?"

"Yes!"

"Would you also abolish crime? The organ banks are our only way to punish thieves and murderers. There are no prisons on Mount Lookitthat."

"Then build prisons! You've been killing us long enough!"

Parlette shook his head.

Harry Kane intervened. "It wouldn't work. Look, Lydia, I know how you feel, but we couldn't do it. If we dumped all that transplant material out, we'd have the whole Plateau against us. We can't even abolish execution by the organ banks, partly because crime would run rampant without capital punishment, and partly because there are too many crew like Parlette, who need the banks to live. If we did that, we might as well declare war here and now."

Lydia turned appealingly to Hood.

"I pass," said Hood. "I think you're all ignoring something."

Harry said, "Oh?"

"I'm not sure yet. I'll have to wait and see. Keep talking."

"I don't understand," said Lydia. "I don't understand any of you. What have we been fighting for? What have we been dying for? To smash the organ banks!"

"You're overlooking something, Mrs. Hancock," Parlette said gently. "It isn't that the crew wouldn't agree to that, and it isn't that the colonists wouldn't agree to that. They wouldn't, of course. But *I* won't let you kick in the organ banks."

"No." Lydia's words dripped scorn. "You'd have to die then, wouldn't you?"

"Yes, I would. And you need me."

"Why? What have you got for us besides your influence and your good advice?"

"A small army. I have more than one hundred lineal descendants. They've been prepared for this day for a very long time. Not all of them will follow me, but most will obey my orders without question. They all have hunting weapons."

Lydia sighed, raggedly.

"We'll do our best, Mrs. Hancock. We can't eliminate the organ banks, but we can eliminate the injustice."

"What we'll have to do," said Harry, "is establish a first-come, first-serve basis for what's already in the banks. Whoever gets sick first—you see what I mean. Meanwhile we set up a new code of law, so that a crew stands just as much chance of getting into the banks as a colonist."

"Don't push to hard there, Kane. Remember, we have to satisfy both groups."

"Phut!" said Lydia Hancock. It was hard to tell whether she was ready to cry or to start a fistfight.

They were a circle of three, leaning toward each other across the coffeetable, holding forgotten mugs. Hood sat a little back from the coffeetable, ignored, waiting for something.

"The thing is," said Parlette, "We can make everyone equal before the law. We can do that, and get away with it, provided that there is no redistribution of property. Do you agree to that?"

"Not completely."

"Look at the logic. Everyone is equal in the courts. A crime is a crime. But the more property a man has, the less likely he is to want to commit a crime. It gives the crew something to protect, and it gives the colonist something to gain."

"It makes sense, yes. But there are a few things we'll want."

"Go ahead."

"Our own electrical power sources."

"Fine. We'll supply it free until we can build plants on Gamma and Delta. We can put hydraulic plants along the Muddy and Long Fall rivers."

"Good. We want free access to the organ banks guaranteed."

"That's a problem. An organ bank is like any other bank. You can't take out more than you put in. We'll have less condemned criminals and a lot more sick colonists to take care of."

Hood had his chair tilted back on two legs, with his feet on the edge of the table. His eyes were half closed, as if he was dreaming pleasant daydreams.

"Lotteries, then; fair lotteries. And heavy research into alloplasty, financed by the crew."

"Why the crew?"

"You've got all the money."

"We can work out a graduated tax. Anything else?"

"There are a lot of unjust laws. We'll want to build houses as we see fit. No restrictions on the clothes we wear. Free travel. The right to buy machinery, any machinery, at the same price a crew pays. We'll want to put some solid restrictions on Implementation. For—"

"Why? They'll be police. They'll be enforcing *your* laws."

"Parlette, have you ever had a squad of police come crashing through the wall of your house, throwing mercy-bullets and sleepy gas around, dragging housecleaners into the light, tearing up the indoor lawn—"

"I've never been a rebel."

"The hell you say."

Parlette smiled. It made him look too much like a death's head. "I've never been caught."

"Point is, Implementation can do that to anyone. And does, constantly. The householder doesn't even get an apology when they don't find evidence of crime."

"I hate to restrict the police. It's a sure route to chaos." Parlette took a long swallow of cider. "All right, how does this sound? There used to be a thing called a search warrant. It kept the UN police from entering any home unless they had a good and sufficient reason, one they could show to a judge."

"Sounds good."

"I can look up the details in the library."

"Another thing. As things stand now, Implementation has an exclusive monopoly on prisoners. They catch 'em, decide whether they're guilty, and take 'em apart. We ought to split those functions up somehow."

"I've thought about that, Kane. We can establish laws such that no man can be executed until he has been declared guilty by a clear majority of ten men. Five crew, five colonists, in cases where crew and colonists are both involved. Otherwise, trial by five of the prisoner's own social group. All trials to be public, on some special teedee channel."

"That sounds—"

"I knew it." Jay Hood dropped back into the discussion with a thump of chair legs on flooring. "Do you realize that every suggestion either of you has made tonight would take power away from the Hospital?"

Parlette frowned. "Perhaps. What does it matter?"

"You've been talking as if there were two power groups on Mount Lookitthat. There are three! You, us, and the Hospital, and the Hospital is the most powerful. Parlette, you've been studying the Sons of Earth for Mist Demons know how long. Have you spent any time studying Jesus Pietro Castro?"

"I've known him a long time." Millard Parlette considered. "At least, I know he's competent. I don't suppose I really know how he thinks."

"Harry does. Harry, what would Castro do if we tried to put all these restrictions on his police?"

"I don't understand you," said Millard Parlette. "Castro is a good, loyal man. He has never done anything that wasn't in the best interests of the crew. Perhaps I don't know him socially, but I do know that he regards himself as a servant of the crew. Anything the crew accepts, he will accept."

"Dammit, Hood's right," said Harry Kane. "I know Castro better than I knew my father. I just hadn't thought of this."

"Jesus Pietro Castro is a good, loyal—"

"Servant of the crew. Right. Now hold on just a minute, Parlette. Let me speak.

"First of all, what crew? What crew is he loyal to?"

Parlette snorted. He picked up his mug and found it empty.

"He's not loyal to any specific crew," said Harry Kane. "In fact he doesn't respect most crew. He respects you, and there are others who fit his ideals, but what he's loyal to is a sort of ideal crew: a man who does not overspend, is polite to his inferiors and knows exactly how to treat them, and has the best interests of the colonists in his mind at all times. This image is the man he serves.

"Now, let's look for a moment at what we propose to do. Search warrants for the Implementation police. We remove Implementation's power to choose what colonists get the leftover materials from the organ banks. We tell them who they may and may not execute. Anything else, Jay?"

"Power. We're taking the electrical monopoly away from the Hospital. Oh, and with less restrictions on the colonists, the police would have less work to do. Castro would have to fire some of 'em."

"Right. Now, you don't suppose every crew on the Plateau is going to agree with all of that, do you?"

"No, not all. Of course not. We may be able to swing a majority. At least a majority of political power."

"Damn your majority. What crew is Castro going to be loyal to? You can name him."

Parlette was rubbing the back of his neck. "I see your point, of course. Given that you've analyzed Castro correctly, he'll follow the conservative faction."

"He will, believe me. The crew who would rather die than accept our compromise is the man he'll follow. And all of Implementation will follow him. He's their leader."

"And they've got all the weapons," said Hood.

CHAPTER XII

THE SLOWBOAT

BLEEDING HEART. Matthew Keller. Polly Tournquist.

Why Polly Tournquist?

She could have nothing to do with the present trouble. Since Saturday evening she had been suffering sensory deprivation in the coffin cure. Why must he be haunted by the colonist girl? What was her hold on him that she could pull him away from his office at a time like this? He hadn't felt a fascination like this since . . .

He couldn't remember.

The guard in front of him stopped suddenly, pushed a button in the wall, and stepped aside. Jesus Pietro jerked back to reality. They had reached the elevator.

The doors slid back, and Jesus Pietro stepped in, followed by the two guards.

(*Where's Polly?* Deep in his mind something whispered, *Where is she?* Subliminally, he remembered. *Tell me where Polly is!*)

Bleeding heart. Matthew Keller. Polly Tournquist.

Either he'd finally lost his mind—and over a colonist girl!—or there was some connection between Matthew Keller and Polly Tournquist. But he had no evidence of that at all.

Perhaps the girl could tell him.

And if she could, certainly she would.

Matt had trailed them to the end of a blind corridor. When they stopped, Matt stopped too, confused. Was Castro going to Polly, or wasn't he?

Doors slid back in the wall, and Matt's three guides

entered. Matt followed, but stopped at the doors. The room was too small. He'd bump an elbow and get shot—

The doors closed in his face. Matt heard muted mechanical noises, diminishing.

What in blazes was it, an airlock? And why here?

He was at the end of a dead-end corridor, lost in the Hospital. The Head and two guards were on the other side of those doors. Two guards, armed and alert—but they were the only guides he had. Matt pushed the big black button which had opened the doors.

This time they stayed closed.

He pushed it again. Nothing happened.

Was he doing exactly what the guard had done? Had the guard used a whistle, or a key?

Matt looked down the hall to where it bent, wondering if he could make his way back to Castro's office. Probably not. He pushed the button again . . .

A muted mechanical noise, nearly inaudible, but rising.

Presently the doors opened to show a tiny, boxlike room, empty.

He stepped in, crouched slightly, ready for anything. There were no doors in the back. How had the others left? Nothing. Nothing but four buttons labeled One, Two, Door Open, Emergency Stop.

He pushed them in order. One did nothing. He pushed Two, and everything happened at once.

The doors closed.

The room started to move. He felt it, vibration and uncanny pressure against the soles of his feet. He dropped to his hands and knees, choking off a yell.

The pressure was gone, but still the room quivered with motion, and still there was the frightening, unfamiliar sound of machinery. Matt waited, crouching on all fours.

There was a sudden foreign feeling in his belly and gonads, a feel of falling. Matt said, "Wump!" and clutched at himself. The box jarred to a stop.

The doors opened. He came out slowly.

He was on a high narrow bridge. The moving box was

at one end, supported in four vertical girders that dropped straight down into a square hole in the roof of the Hospital. At the other end of the bridge was a similar set of girders, empty.

Matt had never been this high outside a car. All of the Hospital was below him, lit by glare lights: the sprawling amorphous structure of rooms and corridors, the inner grounds, the slanting wall, the defense perimeter, the trapped forest, and the access road. And rising up before him was the vast black hull of the *Planck*.

Matt's end of the bridge was just outside what was obviously the outer hull of the ancient slowboat. The bridge crossed the chisel-sharp ring of the leading edge, so that its other end was over the attic.

The *Planck*. Matt looked down along the smooth black metal flank of the outer hull. For most of its length the ship was cylindrical; but the tail, the trailing edge, flared outward for a little distance, and the leading edge was beveled like a chisel, curving in at a thirty-degree angle to close the twenty-foot gap between outer and inner hulls, the gap that held the guts of the ship. More than halfway down, just below a ring of narrow windows, the roof of the Hospital moved in to grip the hull.

Something hummed behind him. The moving box was on its way down.

Matt watched it go, and then he started across the bridge, sliding his hands along the hip-high handrails. The dropping of the box might mean that someone would be coming up.

At the other end he looked for a black button in one of the four supporting girders. It was there, and he pushed it. Then he looked down.

The attic, the space enclosed by the inner hull, was as perfectly cylindrical as a soup can with both ends removed. Four airfoils formed a cross at the stern, a few yards above the ground, and where they crossed was a bulky, pointed casing. There was a ring of four windows halfway down the inner hull. The airlock was at the same level. Matt could see it by looking between the hull and the moving box, which was rising toward him.

Matt felt a chill as he looked down at that pointed casing between the fins. The ship's center of mass was directly over it. Therefore it had to be the fusion drive.

The *Planck* was rumored to be a dangerous place, and not without reason. A ship that had carried men between the stars, a ship three hundred years old, was bound to inspire awe. But there was real power here. The *Planck*'s landing motors should still be strong enough to hurl her into the sky. Her fusion drive supplied electrical power to all the colonist regions: to teedee stations, homes, smokeless factories—and if that fusion plant ever blew, it would blow Alpha Plateau into the void.

Somewhere in the lifesystem, sandwiched between inner and outer hull, were the controls that could blow the bomb in that casing. The Head was in there too— somewhere.

If Matt could bring them together . . .

The moving box reached the top, and Matt entered.

It dropped a long way. The *Planck* was tall. Even the beveled ring of the leading edge, which had held stored equipment for the founding of a colony, was forty feet high. The ship was one hundred and eighty feet high, including a landing skirt, for the inner hull did not quite reach the ground. The stern and the mouths of the landing motors were supported ten feet above the ground by that flaring skirtlike extension of the outer hull.

This moving box was an open grid. Matt could watch his progress all the way down. Had he been acrophobic, he'd have been insane before the box stopped opposite the airlock.

The airlock was not much bigger than the moving box. Inside, it was all dark metal, with a dial-and-control panel in chipped blue plastic. Already Matt was heartily sick of blinking dials and metal walls. It was strange and discomforting to be surrounded by so much metal, and unnerving to wonder what all those dials were trying to tell him.

Set in the ceiling was something Matt had trouble recognizing. Something simple, almost familiar . . . ah. A ladder. A ladder running uselessly from door to wall across the ceiling of the airlock.

Sure. With the ship spinning in space, the outer door would be a trapdoor down from the attic. Of course you'd need a ladder. Matt grinned and strode through the airlock and nearly ran face on into a policeman.

"The luck of Matt Keller" had no time to work. Matt dodged back into the airlock. He heard a patter of mercy-bullets, like gravel on metal. In a moment the man would be around the corner, firing.

Matt yelled the only thing he could think of. "Stop! It's *me!*"

The guard was around in the same instant. But he didn't fire yet . . . and he didn't fire yet . . . and presently he turned and went, muttering a surly apology. Matt wondered whom he'd been taken for. It wouldn't matter; the man had already forgotten him.

Matt chose to follow him instead of turning the other way. It seemed to him that if a guard saw two men approach, and ignored one and recognized the other, he wouldn't shoot—no matter how trigger-happy he was.

The corridor was narrow, and it curved to the left. Floor and ceiling were green. The left-hand wall was white, set with uncomfortably bright lights; the wall on the right was black, with a roughened rubbery surface, obviously designed as a floor. Worse yet, the doors were all trapdoors leading down into the floor and up into the ceiling. Most of the doors in the floor were closed and covered with walkways. Most of the ceiling doors were open, and ladders led up into these. All the ladders and walkways looked old and crude, colony-built, and all were riveted into place.

It was eerie. Everything was on its side. Walking through this place was like defying gravity.

Matt heard sounds and voices from some of the rooms above. They told him nothing. He couldn't see what was happening above him, and he didn't try. He was listening for Castro's voice.

If he could get the Head to the fusion-drive controls—wherever they were—then he could threaten to blow up the *Planck*. Castro had held out under threat of physical pain, but how would he react to a threat to Alpha Plateau?

And all Matt wanted was to free one prisoner.

... That was Castro's voice. Coming not from the ceiling but from underfoot, from a closed door. Matt bent over the walkway across it and tried the handle. Locked.

Knock? But all of Implementation was on edge tonight, ready to shoot at anything. Under such circumstances Matt could be unconscious and falling long seconds before a gunman could lose interest in him.

No way to steal a key, to identify the right key. And he couldn't stay here forever.

If only Laney were here now.

A voice. Polly jerked to attention—except that she felt no jerk; she did not know if she had moved or not.

A voice. For some timeless interval she had existed with no sensation at all. There were pictures in her memory and games she could play in her mind, and for a time there had been sleep. Some friend had shot her full of mercy-bullets. She remembered the sting, vividly. But she'd wakened. Mental games had failed; she couldn't concentrate. She had begun to doubt the reality of her memories. Friends' faces were blurred. She had clung to the memory of Jay Hood, his sharp-edged, scholarly face, easy to remember. Jay. For two years they had been little more than close friends. But in recent hours she had loved him hopelessly; his was the only visual image that would come clear to her, except for a hated face, wide and expressionless, decorated with a bright snowy moustache: the face of the enemy. But she was trying to make Jay come too clear, to give him texture, expression, meaning. He had blurred, she had reached to bring him back, he had blurred more ...

A voice. It had her complete attention.

"Polly," it said, "you must trust me."

She wanted to answer, to express her gratitude, to tell the voice to keep talking, to beg it to let her *out.* She was voiceless.

"I would like to free you, to bring you back to the world of sense and touch and smell," said the voice. Gently, sympathetically, regretfully, it added, "I cannot do that just yet. There are people making me keep you here."

A voice had become *the voice,* familiar, wholly reassuring. Suddenly she placed it.

"Harry Kane and Jayhawk Hood. They won't let me free you"—Castro's voice. She wanted to scream— "because you failed in your mission. You were to find out about ramrobot number one-forty-three. You failed."

Liar! Liar! I didn't fail! She wanted to scream out the truth, all of the truth. At the same time she knew that that was Castro's aim. But she hadn't talked in so long!

"Are you trying to tell me something? Perhaps I can persuade Harry and Jayhawk to let me free your mouth. Would you like that?"

I'd love that, Polly thought. *I'd tell all the secrets of your ancestry.* Something within her was still rational. The sleep, that was what had done it. How long had she been here? Not years, not even days; she would have been thirsty. Unless they'd given her water intravenously. But however long it had been, she'd slept for some part of the time. Castro didn't know about the mercy-bullets. He'd come hours early.

Where was the voice?

All was silent. Faintly she could hear her pulse beating in her carotid arteries; but as she grasped for the sound, it too was gone.

Where was Castro? Leaving her to rot?

Speak!

Speak to me!

The *Planck* was big, but its lifesystem occupied less than a third of its volume: three rings of pressurized compartments between the cargo holds above and the water fuel tanks and fission-driven landing motors below. Much cargo had been needed to set up a self-sufficient colony. Much fuel had been needed to land the *Planck:* trying to land on the controlled hydrogen bomb of the fusion drive would have been like landing a blowtorch on a featherbed.

So the lifesystem was not large. But neither was it cramped, since the compartments aft of the corridor had been designed for the comfort of just three growing families.

That which was now Jesus Pietro's interrogation room had once been a living room, with sofas, a cardtable, a coffeetable, a reader screen connected to the ship's library, a small refrigerator. The tables and other things were gone now, cut from the outer wall with torches long ago. It had been a big room, luxuriously so for a spacecraft, where room is always at a premium. It had had to be big. Any normal apartment-dweller can step outside for a breath of air.

Now, upended, the room was merely tall. Halfway up the walls were the doors which had led to other parts of the apartment. The door to the corridor had become a trapdoor, and the door just under it, a closet to hold spacesuits in case of emergency, could now be reached only from the ladder. In the crescent of floor space at the bottom of the room were a long, heavy box, two guards in chairs, an empty chair, and Jesus Pietro Castro, closing the padded lip of the speaking tube at one corner of the box.

"Give her ten minutes to think it over," he said. He glanced at his watch, noted the time.

His handphone buzzed.

"I'm in the vivarium," Major Jansen reported. "The girl's a colonist, all right, in stolen crew clothing. We don't know where she got it yet. I doubt we'll like the answer. We had to pump antidotes into her; she was dying from an overdose of mercy-weapons."

"No sign that anyone came with her?"

"I didn't say that, sir. There are two things. One, the wires were pulled on the chair she was sitting in. Her helmet was stone dead. She couldn't have done that herself. Maybe that's why one of the prisoners woke up this afternoon."

"And then he freed the others? I don't believe it. We would have noticed the pulled wires afterward."

"I agree, sir. So somebody pulled those wires after she was in the chair."

"Maybe. What's your second point?"

"When the gas went off in the vivarium, one of the four police wasn't wearing his nose plug. We haven't been able to find it anywhere; his locker's empty, and when I called his wife, she said he took it with him. He's awake now, but he has no idea—"

"Is it worth bothering with? The guards aren't used to gas filters. Or gas."

"There was a mark on the man's forehead, sir. Like the one we found this afternoon, only this one is in ballpoint ink."

"Oh."

"Which means that there must be a traitor in Implementation itself, sir."

"What makes you think so, Major?"

"The bleeding-heart symbol does not represent any known revolutionary organization. Further, only a guard could have made that mark. Nobody else has entered the vivarium tonight."

Jesus Pietro swallowed his impatience. "You may be right, Major. Tomorrow we'll devise ways to smoke them out."

Major Jansen made several suggestions. Jesus Pietro listened, made appropriate comments, and cut him off as soon as he could.

A traitor in Implementation? Jesus Pietro hated to think so. It was possible, and not a thing to be ignored; but the knowledge that the Head suspected such a thing could damage Implementation morale more than any possible traitor.

In any case, Jesus Pietro was not interested. No traitorous guard could have moved invisibly in Jesus Pietro's office. The bleeding heart was something else entirely.

Jesus Pietro called the power room. "You aren't doing anything right now, are you? Good. Would one of you bring us some coffee."

Three minutes more and he could resume interrogation.

Jesus Pietro paced. He walked off balance, with one arm bound immobile against his body: one more annoyance. The numbness was wearing off in his mangled hand.

Yes, the bleeding heart was something else again. A gruesome symbol on a vivarium floor. Fingers that broke without their owner noticing. An ink drawing appearing from nowhere on a dossier cover, like a signature. A signature.

Intuition was tricky. Intuition had told Jesus Pietro that something would happen tonight. And something had; but what? Intuition, or something like it, had brought him here. Surely he'd had no logical reason to keep thinking about Polly Tournquist. Did she really know something? Or did his subconscious mind have other motives for bringing him here?

Jesus Pietro paced, following the arc of the inner wall.

Presently someone knocked on the door overhead. The guards loosened their guns and looked up. Fumbling sounds, and then the door dropped open and a man backed slowly down the ladder. He balanced a tray in one hand. He did not try to close the door after him.

The slowboat had never been a convenient place to work. Ladders everywhere. The man with the tray had to back a long way down—the full length of what had been a large, comfortable living room—before he touched bottom.

Matt poked his head through the doorway, upside down.

There was the lab man, backing down the ladder with

his coffee tray balanced on one hand. On the floor were three more men, and one was Castro. As Matt's head appeared in the doorway each pair of eyes glanced up, held Matt's stare for a moment, then dropped.

Matt started down, looking over his shoulder, trying to hold eight eyes at once.

"Dammit, Hood, help me up."

"Parlette, you can't possibly expect—"

"Help me over to the phone."

"We'd be committing suicide," said Harry Kane. "What would your army of relatives do when they learned we were holding you prisoner in your own house?"

"I'm here of my own free will. You know that."

"But will *they* know that?"

"My family will stand behind me." Parelette set the palms of his hands on the chair arms, and with tremendous effort, stood up. But once up, he was unable to move.

"They won't know what's going on," said Harry Kane. "All they'll know for certain is that you're alone in the house with three escaped vivarium prisoners."

"Kane, they wouldn't understand what's happening if I talked for two hours. But they'll stand behind *me.*"

Harry Kane opened his mouth, closed it again, and began to tremble. He had to fold his hands on the table to keep them from shaking. "Call them," he said.

"No," said Jay Hood.

"Help him, Jay."

"No! If he uses that phone to turn us in, he'll go down as the greatest con man in history. And we'll be finished!"

"Oh, phut." Lydia Hancock stood up and wrapped one of Parlette's arms around her neck. "Be sensible, Jay. Parlette is the best chance we ever had. We've *got* to trust him." And she walked him over to the phone.

Almost time to resume the interrogation. Jesus Pietro waited while the lab man deposited his tray on the "coffin" and started back up.

And he realized that his pulse was racing. There was cold perspiration dribbling wetly down his ribs. His hand throbbed like a heart. His eyes flicked here, there, all about the room, looking for something that wasn't there.

Within seconds, and for no reason at all, the interrogation room had become a trap.

There was a thump, and every muscle in his body jumped. Nothing there, nothing his eyes could find. But he, the nerveless, elephantine Castro, was jumping at shadows. The room was a trap, a trap.

"Back in a moment," said Jesus Pietro. He strode to the ladder, looking every inch the Man in Charge, and went up.

A guard said, "But, sir! What about the prisoner?"

"I'll be right back," said the Head, without slowing.

He pulled himself through the doorway, reached down, and closed the door. And there he stuck.

He'd had no planned destination. Something had screamed at him to *get out,* some intuition so powerful that he had followed it without question—right in the middle of an interrogation.

What was he afraid of? Was he about to learn some unpleasant truth from Polly Tournquist? Or was it guilt? Surely he no longer lusted after the colonist girl. Surely he could control it if he did.

No Implementation man had ever seen him thus: shoulders slumped, face set in wrinkles of fatigue, standing in a hallway because he had no place to go.

In any case, he had to go back. Polly Tournquist was waiting for the sound of his voice. She might or might not know things he needed to know.

He pulled himself together, visibly, and turned to face the door, his eyes sliding automatically around the bright frosted pane in the wall. Men who worked in the slowboats developed such habits. As ceiling lights, the panes would have been just bright enough. As wall lights, they hurt the eyes.

Castro's eyes slid around the pane, caught something,

and came back. There was a blue scrawl on the frosted
pane.

Matt was almost down the ladder when the man in the
lab coat started up.

Matt addressed a subvocal comment to the Mist
Demons, who made no obvious response. Then, because
the lab man was about to bump into him, he swung
around to the underside of the ladder and dropped. He
landed with a thump. Every head in the room jerked
around. Matt backed into a corner, stepping softly, waiting.

He'd known it from the beginning: He couldn't count on
this power of his. At some point he would have enough of
being afraid; the glandular caps over his kidneys would
stop producing adrenaline . . .

The guard turned their eyes back to the ceiling. The lab
man disappeared through the doorway and closed the
door after him. Only Castro himself continued to behave
peculiarly; his eyes kept darting around the room as if
searching for something that wasn't there. Matt began to
breathe more easily.

The man with the coffee had appeared at just the right
time. Matt had been about to leave, to see if he could find
a fusion control room before he got back to Castro. He
had, in fact, discovered that the frosted glass in the hall
light would take ink; and he was marking it to show
which door led to Castro, when someone had rounded the
corner, carrying coffee.

Castro was still behaving oddly. During the interview in
Castro's office, Matt had never ceased to be afraid of him.
Yet now he seemed only a nervous man with a bandaged
arm.

Dangerous thinking, thought Matt. *Be scared!*

Suddenly Castro started up the ladder.

Matt nibbled his lower lip. Some comic chase this was
becoming! Where was the Head going now? And how

could Matt hold six eyes, two above and four below, while climbing a ladder?

He started for the ladder anyway.

"But, sir! What about the prisoner?"

"I'll be right back."

Matt backed into the corner again. Prisoner?

Coffin. The word was nearly obsolete on Mount Lookitthat, where crew and colonist alike cremated their dead. But that box against the wall was easily big enough to hold a prisoner.

He'd have to look inside.

But first, the guards . . .

"It's the Head calling, Major."

"Thank you, Miss Lauessen."

"Jansen, is that you?"

"Yes, sir."

"I've found another bleeding heart."

"In the Planck?"

"Yes. Right above the coffin room, on a light. Now here's what I want done. I want you to close the *Planck*'s airlocks, flood the ship with gas, then come in with a squad. Anyone you can't identify immediately, play a sonic over him to keep him quiet. Got it?"

"Yes, sir. Suppose the traitor is someone we know?"

"Use your own judgment there. I have good reason to assume he's not a policeman, though he may be in uniform. How long will you need?"

"About twenty minutes. I could use cars instead of elevators, but it would take just as long."

"Good. Use the cars. Seal off the elevators first. I want as much surprise effect as possible."

"Yes, sir."

"Execute."

The guards were no trouble at all. Matt stepped up behind one of the men, pulled the gun from his holster, and shot them both.

He kept the gun in his hand. It felt good. He was sick of having to be afraid. It was a situation to drive a man right out of his skull. If he stopped being afraid, even for an instant, he could be killed! But now, at least for the moment, he could stop listening for footsteps, stop trying to look in all directions at once. A sonic stunner was a surer bet than a hypothetical, undependable psi power. It was real, cold and hard in his hand.

The "coffin" was bigger than it had seemed from the doorway. He found clamps, big and easy to operate. The lid was heavy. Foam plastic covered the inside, with a sound-deadening surface of small interlocking conical indentations.

Inside was something packed very carefully in soft, thick white cloth. Its shape was only vaguely human, and its head was not human at all. Matt felt the back hairs stir on his neck. *Coffin*. And the thing inside didn't move. If he had found Polly, then Polly was dead.

He began unwrapping it anyway, starting with what passed for the figure's head. He found ear cups, and underneath, human ears. They were blood-warm to the touch. Matt began to hope.

He unwrapped cloth from a pair of brown eyes. They looked up at him, and then they blinked.

Hoping was over. He had found Polly, and she was alive.

She was more cocoon than girl. Toward the end she was helping to get the wrappings and paddings and sensory wires off her legs. She wasn't much help. Her fingers wouldn't work. Muscles jerked rhythmically in her jaw, her arms, her legs. When she tried to step out of the coffin, Matt had to catch the full weight of her falling body, and they went down in a heap.

"Thanks," she said unsteadily. "Thanks for getting me out of there."

"That's why I'm here."

"I remember you." She got up, clinging to his arm for support. She had not yet smiled. When Matt had uncovered her mouth and removed the clamps and padding, she had looked like a child expecting to be slapped. She still did. "You're Matt something. Aren't you?"

"Matt Keller. Can you stand by yourself now?"

"Where are we?" She did not let go of his arm.

"In the middle of the Hospital. But we have a fair chance to get out, if you do just as I say."

"How did you get in?"

"Jay Hood tells me I have a kind of psychic invisibility. As long as I can stay scared, I can keep people from seeing me. That's what we have to count on. Hey, are you all right?"

"Since you ask, no." She smiled for the first time, a ghost grin, a rictus that vanished in a split second. She was better off without it.

"You don't look it. Come here, sit down." She was clinging to his upper arm with both hands, as if afraid of falling. He led her to one of the chairs. *She's still in shock,* he thought. "Better yet, lie down. On the floor. Easy . . . Now put your feet up on the chair. What the Mist Demons were they doing to you?"

"It's a long story." Her brows puckered, leaving a sudden deep V between her eyes. "I can tell it fast, though. They were doing nothing to me. Nothing and nothing and nothing." She lay on her back with her feet in the air, the way Matt had placed her, and her eyes looked up past the ceiling, looked up at Nothing.

Matt wanted to look away. Polly was no longer pretty. Her hair was a housecleaners' nest, and her makeup had gone every which way; but that wasn't it. Something had gone out of her, and something else had replaced it. Her pale face mirrored the ultimate horror of what she saw, looking up at Nothing.

Presently she said, "How did you get here, Matt?"

"Came to rescue you."

"You're not a Son of Earth."

"No."

"You could be a ringer. Harry's house was raided the night you came."

"That's highly ungrateful for a maiden in distress."

"I'm sorry." But her eyes were watchful and suspicious. She took her feet off the chair and rolled to sitting position on the floor. She was wearing an unfamiliar garment, like a playsuit, but made of soft, flimsy fabric. Her fingers had found a corner of the cloth and were playing with it, kneading it, pulling at it, rolling it, crumpling it. "I can't trust anything. I'm not even sure I'm not dreaming. Maybe I'm still in the box."

"Easy," he said, and squeezed her shoulder reassuringly. "You'll get over—"

She snatched at his hand to hold it there, so quickly that he almost jerked away. Every move she made was exaggerated. "You don't know what it was like! They wrapped me up and put me away, and from then on, it was like being dead!" She was squeezing his hand, feeling the fingers and the nails and the knuckles, as if she'd never touched a human hand before. "I kept trying to remember things, and they were always just out of reach. It was—" She stuck, her larynx bobbing and her lips twitching without sound. Then she jumped at him.

She knocked him flat on his back and wrapped herself around him. It was nothing like affectionate. She clung to him as if she were drowning and he a floating log. "Hey," said Matt. "The gun. You knocked the gun away."

She didn't hear. Matt looked up at the door. It didn't move, and there were no ominous noises.

"It's all right," he said. "It's okay now. You're out." She had her face buried in the hollow of his shoulder, and she was moving against him. Her arms were tight around his chest with a grip of desperation. "You're out now." He massaged her neck and shoulder muscles, trying to do what Laney had done night before last.

The way she kept touching things, kneading them—he understood now. She was making sure they were real. The time in the coffin must have been worse than he could imagine. She must have lost all touch with reality, all her faith in the solidness of things outside that artificial womb. And so she ran her hands along his back, traced the lines of his shoulder blades and vertebrae with her fingertips; and so she moved against him with a sliding motion, with her toes, her thighs, her arms, her body—as if sensing, sensing with every square inch of skin . . .

He felt himself coming alive in response. Trapdoors and curved metal walls, guns and Implementation police, ceased to matter at all. There was only Polly.

"Help me," she said, her voice muffled.

Matt rolled over onto her. The soft, flimsy-looking fabric of her jumper tore like tissue. Fleetingly, Matt wondered why it was there at all. And that didn't matter either.

Presently Polly said, "Well. I'm real after all."

And Matt, drifting peacefully down from some far peak of Nirvana, asked, "Was that what you meant by help?"

"I didn't know what I meant. I needed *help*." She smiled slowly, with her eyes as well as her mouth. "Suppose it wasn't what I meant. Then what?"

"Then I've callously seduced you." He moved his head back a little to look her in the face. The change was incredible. "I was afraid you'd gone off the beam for good."

"So was I."

Matt glanced up at the trapdoor, then stretched to reach for the sonic. Nirvana was over.

"You really came to rescue me?"

"Yah." He didn't mention Laney, not yet. No point in spoiling this moment.

"Thanks."

"You're welcome. We've still got to get out of here."

"You don't have any questions to ask me?"

What was she doing, testing him? Didn't she trust him now? Well, why should she? "No," he said, "no questions. But there are things I've got to tell you—"

She stiffened under him. "Matt. *Where are we?*"

"In the Hospital. Deep in the Hospital. But we *can* get out."

She rolled away and came to her feet in one smooth motion. "We're in one of the slowboats! Which one?"

"The *Planck*. Does it matter?"

She scooped the other guard's sonic stunner from his holster in what looked like a racing dive. "We can set off the fusion plant! Blow the Hospital and the crew into the void mist! Come on, Matt, let's get moving. Are there guards in the corridor? How many?"

"Set off—Are you out of your mind?"

"We'd wipe out the Hospital and most of Alpha Plateau." She picked up her ripped mock-playsuit and threw it down again. "I'll have to depants one of these police. And that'll be *it!* We'll win, Matt! All in one stroke!"

"What win? We'll be *dead!*"

She stood up with her hands on her hips and regarded him with disgust. Now she wore a pair of Implementation uniform pants too big for her. Matt had never seen anyone more thoroughly alive. "I'd forgotten. You aren't a Son of Earth. All right, Matt, see how far you can get. You may be able to get out of range of the blast. Personally, I doubt it."

"I've got a personal interest in you. I didn't come all this way to have you commit suicide. You're coming with me."

Polly donned a guard's shirt, then hurriedly rolled up the pants, which were much too long. "You've done your duty. I'm not ungrateful, Matt, but we just aren't going in the same direction. Our motives aren't the same." She kissed him hard, pushed him back, and whispered, "I can't pass up this chance." She started for the ladder.

Matt blocked her way. "You haven't a prayer of getting anywhere without me. You're coming with me, and we're leaving the Hospital—if we get that far."

Polly hit him.

She hit him with stiffened fingertips just under the

sternum, where the ribs make an inverted V. He doubled up, trying to curl around the pain, not yet trying to breathe, but gaping like a fish. He felt fingers at his throat and realized that she'd seen the gas filter and was taking it.

He saw her as a blur at the corner of his eye, climbing the ladder. He heard the door open, and a moment later, close. Slow fire was spreading through his lungs. He tried to draw air, and it *hurt*.

He'd never learned to fight. "The luck of Matt Keller" had made it unnecessary. Once he'd struck a guard on the point of the jaw. Where else would you hit somebody? And who'd guess that a slightly built girl could hit so hard?

Inch by inch he uncurled, straightened up. He drew his breath in shallow, painful sips. When the pain over his heart would let him move again, he started up the ladder.

CHAPTER XIII

IT ALL HAPPENED AT ONCE

POLLY MOVED at a gliding run. The gas filter was in place over her nose. She held the sonic straight out ahead of her, pointed around the curve of the inner hull. If an enemy appeared, that was where he would be, right in the gunsight. Nobody would come at her from behind. She was moving too fast.

As one of the inner core of the Sons of Earth, Polly knew the *Planck* as well as she knew her own home. The flight control room was a diameter's distance from the airlock. She ticked off the doors as she passed under them. Hydroponics . . . Library . . .

Flight Control. The door was closed. No ladder.

Polly crouched and sprang. She caught the handle at the top of her leap. The door was not locked; it was closed, because nobody ever used the flight control room. Unfortunately the door opened inward, upward. She dropped back, frustrated, landing silently on her toes.

If she'd chosen the fusion room . . . but the fusion room was for fine control. There, the Hospital electricians kept power running to the colonist regions. She'd have run into people, and they might have stopped her.

The guard had carried a wallet.

She leapt again, caught the knob and turned it, pushed the wallet between the door and the jamb, where the catch of the lock ought to be. Again she dropped, and again she leapt. This time she slapped the flat of her hand hard against the door. It flipped upward . . . and over.

Far down the curve of the corridor someone yelled, "What's going on down there?"

Polly's chest heaved, pulling deep lungfuls of air

through her nose, under perfect control. She jumped a last time, caught the jamb, and pulled herself up. Heavy footsteps . . . Before someone could come into sight, she had closed the door.

There was a ladder here, built into what had been the ceiling. Doubtless the *Planck*'s original crew had used it to climb down from those six control chairs after the First Landing. Polly used it now.

She squirmed into the second seat on the left and found the control panel and the bypass. Part of the wall had been pried up, and a simple iron bar had been welded into place between two plates, removing control from the flight control room and giving it directly to the fusion room. In flight both control points had been necessary: the fusion room to keep the drive working and stable, and the flight control room to keep it pointed. Now the fusion drive was used only for making electricity. and Polly's control panel was dead.

She went down the ladder fast. There was a tool closet by the door. If it held a welding arc—

It did.

And if there was no anesthetic gas around—or if it wasn't inflammable . . .

Nothing exploded as she turned on the welder. She began welding the door shut.

Almost immediately she attracted attention. She could hear excited voices, muffled by the door. Then there was the faint numbness of a sonic beamer. The door didn't conduct subsonics well, but she couldn't take this long. Nonetheless she finished the welding job before she went back up the ladder.

She used the welding arc to cut away the bypass. It was slow work. Implementation would surely have barged in on her before she finished. Now they could whistle for entrance. She had all the time in the world. In their world.

Matt reached the corridor and began to walk, leaving the interrogation room open behind him. He walked bent, with his chest half collapsed and his arms folded over the pain. He'd forgotten to take the remaining sonic.

"I'm not the domineering type," he muttered, perversely enjoying the sound of his own voice. And, "Either that, or I'm trying to dominate the wrong woman."

A heavy figure came pounding around the curve. Jesus Pietro Castro, wearing a gas filter and carrying a heavy mercy-sliver gun, looked up in time to avoid a collision. He jerked to a stop, and then his mouth dropped open as he took in blue eyes, brown hair, a bitter and angry colonist's face, an ear with a small piece bitten out of it, and blood soaked into the collar of a crewish overjacket.

"You agree?" Matt said brightly.

Castro raised his gun. The "luck" was off.

And all the rage and humiliation in Matt broke loose. "All right," he yelled, "look at me! Damn you, look at me! I'm Matthew Keller!"

The Head stared. He did not fire. He stared.

"I crashed my way into your crummy Hospital single-handed, twice! I came through walls and void mist and sleepy gas and mercy bullets to rescue that damn woman, and when I got her loose, she punched me in the gut and folded me up like a flower! So go ahead and look!"

Castro looked and looked.

And finally Matt realized that he should have fired.

Castro swiveled his head from side to side in a negative motion. But his eyes never left Matt. And slowly, slowly, as if he were knee deep in hardening cement, he moved one slow step forward.

Abruptly Matt realized what was happening. "Don't look away," he said hastily. "Look at me." The Head was close enough now, and Matt reached out and pushed the barrel of the mercy-gun aside, still striving to hold Castro's eyes. "Keep looking."

They stared eye to eye. Above his bulky false nose, Castro's eyes were remarkable: all white and black, all whites and huge, expanded pupils, with practically no iris showing. His jaw hung loose under the snowy handlebar moustache. He was melting; the perspiration ran in slow streams into his collar. Like a man in an ecstasy of fear, or awe, or worship . . . he stared.

Contract the pupils of eyes not your own, and you got psychic invisibility. Expand them, and you got . . . what? Fascination?

For damn sure, he had the Head's complete attention. Matt drew back his fist, cocked it—and couldn't follow through. It would have been like attacking a cripple. Castro *was* a cripple: one of his arms was in a sling.

There was shouting from down the corridor, from the direction Polly had taken.

The Head moved another gluey step forward.

Too many enemies, before and behind. Matt slapped the gun out of Castro's hand, then turned and ran.

As he dropped through the door to the coffin room, he saw the Head still looking after him, still held in the strange spell. Then he pushed the door closed above him.

Polly cut the last of the bar away, and the control board came alight. She ran her eyes quickly over the lighted dials, then once more, slowly.

According to the control board, the fusion drive was as cold as Pluto's caves.

Polly whistled between her teeth. It was no malfunction of the board. The several dials checked each other too well. Someone had decided to black out the colony regions.

She couldn't start the drive from here. And she'd never reach the fusion room; she'd locked herself in with a vengeance.

If only this had been the *Arthur Clarke!* Castro would never dare cut power to the crew. The *Clark*'s fusion plant must be going full blast.

Well, now, she thought in growing excitement. She slid out onto the ladder. There might be a way to reach the *Clarke*.

Jesus Pietro felt a hand shaking his shoulder. He turned and found Major Jansen. "What is it?"

"We've flooded the *Planck* with gas, sir. Everyone who wasn't warned should be unconscious, unless he's behind doors. I wish there weren't so many filters floating around, though. Whoever we're after has had too good a chance to pick one up."

"Good," said Jesus Pietro. He couldn't concentrate. He wanted to be alone, to think . . . no, he didn't want to be alone . . . "Carry on," he said. "Try the coffin room. He may be in there."

"He isn't. Or if he is, there's more than one traitor. Somebody's in the flight control room, welded in. It's a good thing the fusion plant is off."

"Get him out. But try the coffin room, too."

Major Jansen moved off in the direction of all the commotion. Jesus Pietro wondered what he'd find when he finally looked in the coffin room. Had Keller's ghost really gone in there, or had he faded out while running up the corridor? Jesus Pietro wasn't sure.

But he was sure of the ghost.

He would never in his life forget those eyes. Those binding, blinding, paralyzing eyes. They would haunt him the rest of his life—however many minutes that might be. For surely the ghost didn't intend to let him go now.

His handphone rang. Jesus Pietro picked it off his belt and said, "The Head."

"Sir, we're getting some very strange reports," said the voice of Miss Lauessen. "A large number of cars are converging on the Hospital. Someone claiming to represent the Council is accusing you of treason."

"Me? Of treason?"

"Yes, sir." Miss Lauessen sounded strange. And she kept calling him Sir.

"What grounds?"

"Shall I find out, sir?"

"Yes. And order them to land outside the defense perimeter. If they don't, set patrol cars on them. It's obviously the Sons of Earth." He clicked off and immediately thought, *But where did they all come from? And where did they get the cars?*

And he thought, *Keller?*

His handphone buzzed.

Miss Lauessen's voice had turned plaintive—almost querulous. "Sir, the fleet of cars is led by Millard Parlette. He accuses you of malfeasance and treason, and he orders you to give yourself up for trial."

"He's gone insane." Jesus Pietro tried to think. It was all coming at once. Was this why Keller had appeared to him, shown himself at last? No mysterious symbols, this time; no invisible breaking of fingers. Keller's eyes ... "Try to land the old man without hurting him. The other cars too. Order them to set their cars on autopilot. Tell them they won't be hurt. Give them one minute; then knock them out with sonics."

"I hesitate to remind you, sir, but Millard Parlette is your superior officer. Will you give yourself up?"

Then Jesus Pietro remembered that Miss Lauessen was almost pure crew. Did her veins carry Parlette blood? It was reputedly easy to come by. He said the only thing he could.

"No."

The phone cut off, cut him off from the Hospital switchboard and from the world outside.

He'd gone off half-cocked, and he knew it. Somehow Polly's blow in the belly had made him want to die. He'd stumbled out into the corridor to be captured.

Not this time. He scooped up the remaining sonic and started for the ladder. This time he'd know just what he was doing when he went through that door.

But why go through it at all? The thought stopped him at the foot of the ladder. If Polly was going to blow the drive—

No, she'd never get that far. And she'd had all the

rescuing she was entitled to. It was time to think about escape. He looked up at the exit—and shivered.

Some escape hatch. The moment he poked his head out there, somebody would shoot at it. He had to see his enemy to use the "luck," and he couldn't see in all directions at once.

Yet, this room was no place to stand off a siege. All anyone would have to do would be to fire mercy-needles down toward the floor. If he looked before he fired, the "luck" would get him; but that statement applied to an ordinary sonic stunner. And so he wouldn't look.

He had to get out.

But—Castro's nose piece. It meant Implementation was using gas. The corridor must be already full of it.

Too many things to think about! Matt cursed and began going through a guard's pockets. The guard stirred and tried to strangle Matt with limp fingers. Matt played the sonic over them both, then finished his search. Neither guard had a gas filter.

Matt looked up at the door. He could chance it, of course, but if there was gas in the corridor, only that airtight door was protecting him now. It had to be airtight, of course.

Get to another room? There were the doors leading to what must be bedrooms. But they were halfway up the walls and too far from the ladder.

And there, just under the exit, was a small door placed where any good apartment would have a coat closet. He might be able to reach it.

It wasn't a coat closet, of course. It held two spacesuits.

And it wasn't easy to reach. Matt had to lean far out from the ladder to turn the knob, let the door fall open, and then jump for the opening. Leaving the cubbyhole would be just as bad when the time came.

Spacesuits. They had hung on hooks; now they sprawled on the floor like empty men. Thick rubbery fabric, with a heavy metal neck-ring set with clamps to hold the separate helmet. Metal struts in the fabric braced the rocket backpack and the control unit under the chin.

Would the air converter still work? Ridiculous, after three hundred years. But there might still be air in the tank. Matt found a knob in the control panel of one suit, twisted it, and got a hiss.

So there was still stored air. The suit would protect him against gas. And the big fishbowl of a helmet would not interefere with his vision, nor his "luck."

He snatched up the gun when the door to the corridor dropped open. A long moment later two legs came into sight of the ladder. Matt played the sonic over them. A man grunted in surprise and toppled into view, and down.

A voice of infinite authority spoke. "You! Come out of there!"

Matt grinned to himself. Quietly he put the gun aside and reached for the suit. A wave of dizziness made the world go dreamy. He'd been right about the gas.

He turned the air knob on full and put his head through the neck ring. He took several deep breaths, then held his breath while he slid feet first into the suit.

"You haven't got a chance! Come on out or we'll come in after you!"

Do that. Matt pulled the helmet over his head and resumed breathing. The dizziness was passing, but he had to move carefully. Especially since the suit was a size too small for him.

The door dropped open suddenly, and there was a spattering of mercy-slivers. A snarling face and a hand came into view, the hand firing a mercy-gun. Matt shot at the face. The man slumped, head down, but he didn't fall; someone pulled him up out of sight by his ankles.

The air in the suit had a metallic smell thick enough to cut. Matt wrinkled his nose. Anyone else would have been satisfied with one escape from the Hospital. Who but Lucky Matt Keller would have—

There was a roar like a distant, continuous explosion.

What, Matt wondered, *are they trying now?* He raised the gun.

The ship shook, and shook again. Matt found himself bouncing about like a toy in a box. Somehow he managed to brace his feet and shoulders against walls. *I thought the son of a bitch was bluffing!* He snatched at the stunner as it threatened to slide out into space.

The ship jumped, slapping hard against his cheekbone, as one whole wall of the ship ripped away. The roar was suddenly louder, much louder.

"We're too close," said Parlette.

Hood, in the driver's seat, said, "We have to be close enough to give orders."

"Nonsense. You're afraid someone will call you a coward. Hang back, I tell you. Let my men do the fighting; they know what they're doing. We've practiced enough."

Hood shrugged and eased back on the 3–4 throttle. Already theirs was the last car in a swarm of more than forty, an armada of floating red taillights against the starry night. Each car carried two of Parlette's line, a driver and a gunman.

Parlette, hovering like a vulture over the car's phone, suddenly crowed, "I've got Deirdre Lauessen! All of you, be quiet. Listen, Deirdre, this is an emergency . . ."

And the others, Harry Kane and Lydia Hancock and Jay Hood, listened while Parlette talked.

It took him several minutes, but at last he leaned back, smiling with carnivorous white teeth. "I've done it. She'll put our accusation on the intercom. Now we'll have Implementation fighting each other."

"You'll have a tough time justifying that accusation," Harry Kane warned him.

"Not at all. By the time I finished, I could convince Castro himself that he was guilty of treason, malfeasance of duty, and augmented incest. Provided—" He paused for effect. "Provided we can take the Hospital. If I control the Hospital, they'll believe me. Because I'll be the only one talking.

"The main point is this. In law I am the man in charge of the Hospital, and have been since Castro was the size of Hood. If it weren't me, it would be some other crew of course. In practice, it's Castro's Hospital, and I have to take it away from him. We have to have control before we can begin changing the government of Mount Lookitthat. But once I've got control, I can keep it."

"Look ahead."

"Police cars. Not many."

"Tight formation. I wonder if that's good? None of us ever had any training in dogfights."

"Why didn't you fight each other?"

"We expected to fight," said Parlette. "We never expected to fight the Hospital. So we—"

"What the Mist Demons is that?"

Parlette was leaning far forward in his seat, his mismatched hands bracing him against the dashboard. He didn't answer.

Harry shook his shoulder. "What is it? It looks like fire all around one end of the Hospital." Parlette seemed rigid with shock.

And then one whole end of the Hospital detached itself from the main structure and moved sedately away. Orange flame bloomed all around its base.

"That," said Millard Parlette, "is the *Planck* taking off on its landing motors."

Polly was in the upper-left-hand seat. She manipulated the controls in front of her with extreme delicacy, but still the knobs turned in short jumps. Minute flakes of rust must be coming loose somewhere in the chain of command that led from this control chair to the fission piles.

Finally the piles were hot.

And Polly tried the water valves.

It seemed to her that long ago someone had decided to keep the slowboats ready for a fast takeoff. It must have been during the first years of the colony, when nobody—crew or colonist—had been sure that an interstellar colony was possible. Then, others had forgotten, and the only changes made since then had been the necessary ones.

Until the slowboats themselves were part of the structure of the Hospital, and the interiors of the lifesystems were a maze of ladders and jury-rigs. Until the organ banks were moved entirely out of the ships, and the suspended animation rooms were closed off for good. Until the ships were nothing more than electrical generating plants—if one turned a blind eye to the interrogation room and perhaps to other secrets.

And still the tool closets were undisturbed. And still there were spacesuits in the upended rooms, behind doors which hadn't been opened for centuries.

And still there was water in the landing fuel tanks and uranium in the landing motors. Nobody had bothered to remove them. The water had not evaporated, not from tanks made to hold water for thirty years against interstellar vacuum. The uranium . . .

Polly valved water into the hot motors, and the ship roared. She yipped in triumph. The ship shuddered and shook along her whole length. From beneath the welded door there were muffled screams.

There was more than one way to tell a joke! The *Planck*'s fusion drive was dead, but the *Arthur Clarke*'s drive must be running hot. And when Polly dived the *Planck* on it from the edge of atmosphere, the explosion would tear the top from Alpha Plateau!

"Come loose," she whispered.

The *Planck* pulled loose from the rock around it, rose several feet, and settled, mushily. The huge ship seemed to be bouncing, ponderously, on something soft. Polly twisted the water fuel valve to no effect. Water and pile were running at peak.

Polly snarled low in her throat. The pile must be nearly dead; it couldn't even manage to lift the ship against Mount Lookitthat's point eight gee. If it weren't for the landing skirt guiding the blast for a ground effect, they wouldn't be moving at all!

Polly reached far across to the seat on her right. A bar moved under her hand, and at the aft end of the *Planck*, two fins moved in response. The ship listed to the side and drifted back to nudge the Hospital, almost gently—once, twice.

Live flame roared through the Hospital. It was water vapor heated beyond incandescence, to the point where oxygen dissociated itself from hydrogen, and it cut where it hit. Like death's hurricane it roared through the corridors, cutting its way through walls where there were no corridors. It killed men before they knew what was killing them, for the first touch of the superheated steam made them blind.

The drive flame spread its fiery death through a third of the ground floor.

To men inside and outside the Hospital, to men who had never met and never would, this was the night everything happened at once. Sane men locked their doors and found something to hide under while they waited for things to stop happening.

"Laney. It must be Laney," said Jay Hood. "She got through."

"Elaine Mattson?"

"Right. And she got to the *Planck*. Can you imagine?"

"She must have a wonderful sense of timing. Do you know what will happen when she blows the drive?"

"Oh, my God. What'll we do?"

"Keep flying," said Parlette. "We'd never get out of range now. We might just as well bull through with this and hope Miss Mattson realizes the colonists are winning."

"More police cars," said Harry Kane. "Left and right, both."

Polly touched the bar again. The ship tilted to the other side and began to drift ponderously away from the Hospital.

She dared tilt the ship no farther. How much clearance did she have under the landing skirt? A foot? A yard? Ten? If the skirt touched the ground, the ship would go over on its side.

That was not part of Polly's plan.

Behind her the door had turned red hot. Polly glanced back with bared teeth. She moved her hands over the board, but in the end left the settings just the way they were. She'd have to circle all the way around the Hospital, but then she'd have a gliding run at the *Arthur Clarke*.

And she'd hit it again and again until one ship failed.

She never noticed when the red spot on the door turned white and burned through.

The ship jumped three feet upward, and Matt's head snapped down against the closet floor. When he looked up, the outer hull side of the room was tearing away like tissue paper, except for the agonized scream of old metal dying. And Matt was looking straight into Castro's office.

He couldn't think; he couldn't move. The scene had a quality of nightmare; it was beyond the rational. *Magic!* he thought, and, *Not again!*

The Hospital was drifting away, dreamlike. His ears had gone dead, so that it all took place in an eerie silence. The ship was taking off . . .

And there was no air in his helmet. The tank had held only one last wheeze. He was suffocating. He pulled the clamps up with fingers gone limp and tingly, tossed the helmet away, and gulped air. Then he remembered the gas.

But it was clean hot air, air from outside, howling through the gaping hole in the outer hull. He sucked at it, pulling it to him. There were spots before his eyes.

The ship was going up and down in a seasick manner. *Wavering in the drive,* Matt thought, and tried to ignore it. But one thing he couldn't ignore:

Polly had reached the controls. Apparently she was taking the ship up. No telling how high they were already; the lights of the Hospital had dwindled to the point where everything outside was uniformly black against the lighted room. They were going up, and the room was wide open to naked space, and Matt had no helmet.

The room seemed steadier. He jumped for the ladder. The suit was awkward, but he caught the ladder and made his way down, fighting the imbalance caused by his backpack. It wasn't until he touched bottom that the backpack caught his conscious attention.

After all, if the *Planck*'s landing motors still worked, why not a spacesuit's backpack?

He peered down at a control panel meant to be read by fingertips. With the helmet on, he couldn't have done it. The backpack was studded with small rocket motors; he wanted the ones on the bottom, of course.

How high was he now?

He tried the two buttons on the bottom, and something exploded on his back. It felt about right, as if it were trying to lift him. There was only one throttle knob. Doubtless it controlled all the jets at once, or all that were turned on at a given time.

Well, what else did he need to know? *How high was he?*

He took one last deep breath and went out the hole in the wall. He saw blackness around him, and he twisted the throttle hard over. It didn't move. It was already on full. Matt had something like one second to realize that the backpack was for use in space, that it probably wouldn't have lifted its own weight against gravity.

He hit.

Moving carefully, so as not to interfere with the men using welding torches, Major Jansen peered up into the hole in the flight-control-room door.

They had pushed a platform into position under the door, so that two men could work at once. The platform rose and settled, rose and settled, so that the major had to brace himself with his hands flat on the ceiling. He could see raven hair over the top of a control chair, and one slender brown arm hanging down.

Jesus Pietro, standing below, called, "How long?"

"A few seconds," said one of the men with cutting torches. "Unless she welded the hinge side too."

"Do you know where we're going?" called the Head. "I do."

Major Jansen looked down, surprised. The Head sounded so odd! And he looked like an old man in poor health. He seemed unable to concentrate on what was going on. *He's ready for retirement,* Major Jansen thought with compassion. *If we live through this . . .*

"I do," Jesus Pietro repeated, and nodded to himself.

Major Jansen turned away. He had no time to feel sympathy for the Head, not while this was going on.

"She welded the hinge side," said one of the cutters.

"How long?"

"Three minutes if we work from both ends."

The ship continued to move, drifting along on its cushion of fire.

Fire swept along the edge of the trapped forest, leaving a line of licking red and orange flame, ignored by the embattled aircars above. Presently there were explosions among the trees, and then the whole tongue of forest was aflame.

Now the *Planck* had left the defense perimeter and moved into a place of shops and houses. The crew who lived in those houses were awake, of course; nobody could have slept through that continuous roar. Some stayed where they were; some made for the street and tried to run for it. The ones who reached their basements were the ones who lived. A block-wide path of exploded, burning houses was the wake of the *Planck*.

But now the houses were empty, and they didn't burn.

They were of architectural coral, and they had been deserted, most of them, for upwards of thirty years.

"We're through, sir." The words were hardly necessary. The cutters were pushing the door aside, their hands protected by thick gloves. Major Jansen shoved through and went up the ladder with panic at his back.

Polly's control board bewildered him. Knowing that he knew as much about flying spacecraft as anyone behind him, he continued to search for the dial or wheel or lever that would change the *Planck*'s direction. Finally, puzzled, he looked up; and that was his undoing.

The flight control room was long. It projected through the cargo section to where the outer and inner hulls met, and most of it was transparent. Major Jansen looked out through the outer hull, and he saw what was happening outside.

He saw the glow of the drive flames near the bottom of his view. To the right, a coral house exploding: the last house. Not far ahead, the black line of the void edge, coming closer.

And he froze.

"We're going over," said Jesus Pietro, standing under him on the ladder. He showed neither surprise nor fear.

Major Jansen screamed and buried his face in his arms.

Jesus Pietro squeezed past him and into the left-hand seat. His decision was based on logic alone. If Major Jansen had not found the right control, then he was looking at the wrong panel; and this was the only other control panel the colonist girl could reach from where she was sitting. He found the fin controls and tried them.

The ship tilted back and began to slow.

Still slowing, it drifted over the edge.

Jesus Pietro leaned back in his seat and watched. The *Planck* was no longer supported by the ground effect. Jesus Pietro felt a sensation like an elevator starting down. He watched the cliff go by, faster and faster, a black shadow. Presently it was half the sky, and the other half was stars.

Presently the stars went out.

The ship began to grow hot. It was hot and dark outside, and the ancient walls of the *Planck* creaked and groaned as the pressure rose. Jesus Pietro watched, waiting.

Waiting for Matthew Keller.

CHAPTER XIV

BALANCE OF POWER

HE STRUGGLED half awake, desperate to escape the terror of sleep. *What a wild nightmare that was!*

Then he felt fingers probing him.

Agony! He braced and tried to draw away, putting his whole body into it. His whole body barely twitched, but he heard himself whimper. A cool hand touched his forehead, and a voice—Laney's?—said, "Lie back, Matt."

He remembered it later, the next time he woke. He woke slowly this time, with the images of his memory forming around him. Again he thought, *What a nightmare.* But the images came clearer, too clear for a dream, and:

His right leg and most of his right side were as numb as frozen pork. Parts of him were not numb; they ached and stung and throbbed. Again he tried to withdraw from the pain, but this time he was tied down. He opened his eyes to find himself surrounded.

Harry Kane, Mrs. Hancock, Laney, and several others he didn't recognize all crowded around his strange bed. One was a big woman with red hands and somewhat crewish features, wearing a white smock. Matt disliked her at once. He'd seen such smocks in the organ banks.

"He's awake." The woman in white spoke with a throaty lilt. "Don't try to move, Keller. You're all splinted up. These people want to talk to you. If you get tired, tell me right away and I'll get them out of here."

"Who are you?"

Harry Kane stepped forward. "She's your doctor, Keller. How do you feel?"

How did he feel? A moment ago he'd realized, too late,

that his backpack wouldn't lift him. But he couldn't remember the mile-long fall. "Am I going to die?"

"No, you'll live," said the woman doctor. "You won't even be crippled. The suit must have braced you against the fall. You broke a leg and some ribs, but they'll heal if you follow orders."

"All right," said Matt. Nothing seemed to matter much. Was he doped? He saw that he was on his back, with one leg in the air and something bulky around his rib cage, interfering with his breathing. "Did they put transplants in me?"

"Never mind that now, Keller. You just rest and get well."

"How's Polly?"

"We couldn't find her."

"She was on the *Planck*. She must have reached the drive controls."

"Oh!" Laney exclaimed. She started to say something, then changed her mind.

Harry said, "The *Planck* went over the edge."

"I see."

"You got her loose?"

"I got her loose once," Matt said. The faces were growing hazy. "She was a fanatic. All of you, fanatics. She had all the rescuing I could give her."

The room drifted away, dreamlike, and he knew the *Planck* was taking off. From a distance a woman's authoritarian crew lilt ordered, "Out, now, all of you."

The doctor escorted them to the door, and Harry Kane put a hand on her elbow and took her with them into the corridor. There he asked, "How long before he's well?"

"Let go of me, Mr. Kane."

Harry did. "How long?"

"Don't worry, he'll be no invalid. In a week we'll put him in a walking cast. In a month we'll see."

"How long before he's back at work?"

"Two months, with luck. Why so eager, Mr. Kane?"

"Top secret."

The woman scowled. "Whatever you're planning for him, you can bear in mind that he's my patient. He won't be ready for anything else until I tell you so."

"All right. I suggest you don't tell him about the transplants. He wouldn't like that."

"They're in his records. I can't do anything about that. I won't tell him anything."

When she had left them, Laney asked, "Why so eager?"

"I have an idea about Matt. I'll tell you about it later."

"Don't you think we've used him enough?"

"No," said Harry Kane. "I'd like to, but no."

Millard Parlette was near exhaustion. He'd moved into Jesus Pietro Castro's office on Sunday night, even before the outer wall was replaced, and he'd lived there ever since. His meals were sent in, and he used Castro's cot when he slept, which was rarely. Sometimes it seemed to him that he was at the end of his life, that he'd waited just long enough to meet this—the crisis he'd foreseen a hundred years ago.

The *Planck* had done terrible damage to the Hospital, but the work of rebuilding was well in progress. Parlette had hired a construction firm himself, paying them out of his personal fortune. Eventually he would push a bill through the Council to reimburse him. Now workmen were painting the outer wall of his office, which on Sunday night had been yawning space.

His immediate problem was that half of Implementation wanted to quit.

The events of the previous week had had a disastrous effect on Implementation morale. Having the Head accused of treason and deposed by force was only part of it. Elaine Mattson and Matthew Keller had done their part, infiltrating the Hospital with bombs and stealth. The vivarium prisoners had been freed to make slaughter in the Hospital corridors. The destruction of the *Planck* had affected not just Hospital personnel but all of Alpha Plateau, for the *Planck* was half of history.

Now Implementation was faced with a dreadful confusion. All raids on the colony plateaus had been canceled. Known rebels moved freely through the Hospital, and no one could touch them. Their attitude toward the police was rude and contemptuous. Rumor had it that Millard Parlette was drafting new laws to further restrict police power. It didn't help that the rumors were true.

Parlette did what he could. He spoke to every man who wanted to resign. Some he persuaded to stay. As the ranks dwindled, he found new ways to use the men he had left.

At the same time he was dealing with the Plateau's four power blocs.

The Council of the Crew had followed Parlette in the past. With luck and skill and work he would make them follow him again.

The crew as a whole would normally follow the Council. But a colonist revolt, in these days of a weakened, disheartened Implementation, might send them into a full panic; and then the Council would mean nothing.

The Sons of Earth would follow Harry Kane. But Kane was beyond Parlette's control, and he didn't trust Millard Parlette at all.

The nonrebellious majority of colonists would remain nonrebellious if Kane left them alone. But the Sons of Earth, with their privileged knowledge of the ramrobot gifts, could stir them to killing wrath at any time. Would Harry Kane wait for the New Law?

Four power blocs, and Implementation too. Being Head meant an endless maze of details, minor complaints, delivery of reprimands, paperwork, petty internal politics—he could get lost in such a maze and never know it until a screaming colonist army came to storm the Hospital.

It was a wonder he ever got around to Matt Keller.

Matt lived on his back, with his right side encased in concrete and his right leg dangling in space. He was given pills that reduced the pains to permanent, aggravating aches.

The woman in the organ-bank smock examined him from time to time. Matt suspected she saw him as potential organ-bank material, of dubious value. On Wednesday he overheard someone calling her Dr. Bennet. He had never thought of asking her name, as she had never thought of giving it.

In the early morning hours, when the sleeping pills were wearing off, or during afternoon naps, he was plagued by nightmares. Again his elbow smashed a nose across a man's face, and again there was the awful shock of terror and triumph. Again he asked the way to the vivarium, turned, and raised his arm to see the skin beaded with bright blood. Again he stood in the organ banks, unable to run, and he woke drenched in perspiration. Or, with a stolen sonic he dropped uniformed men until the remembered sonic backlash turned his arm to wood. He woke, and his right arm had gone to sleep under him.

He thought of his family with nostalgia. He saw Jeannie and her husband every few months; they lived not twenty miles from Gamma's major mining area. But he hadn't seen his mother and father in years. How good it would be to see them again!

Even the memory of mining worms filled him with nostalgia. They were unpredictable, yes, but compared to Hood or Polly or Laney . . . at least he could understand mining worms.

His curiosity had been as dead as his right leg. On Wednesday evening it returned with a rush.

Why was the Hospital treating him? If he had been captured, why hadn't he been taken apart already? How had Laney and Kane been allowed to visit him?

He was frantic with impatience. Dr. Bennet didn't appear until noon Thursday. Somewhat to his surprise, she was not at all reluctant to talk.

"I don't understand it myself," she told Matt. "I do

know that all the live rebels have been turned loose, and we aren't getting any more organ-bank material. Old Parlette's the Head now, and a lot of his relatives are working here too. Pure crew, working in the Hospital."

"It must be strange to you."

"It's weird. Old Parlette is the only one who knows what's really going on—if he does. Does he?"

Does he? Matt groped at the question. "What makes you think I know?"

"He's given orders that you're to be treated with an excess of tender loving care. He must have some reason, Keller."

"I suppose he must."

When it was obvious that that was all he had to say, she said, "If you've got any more questions, you can ask your friends. They'll be here Saturday. There's another weird thing—all the colonists wandering through the Hospital, and we've got orders not to touch them. I hear some of them are proven rebels."

"I'm one myself."

"I thought you might be."

"After my leg heals, will I be turned loose?"

"I suppose so, from the way you're being treated. It's up to Parlette." Her treatment of him had become curiously ambivalent. By turns he was her inferior, confidant, and patient. "Why don't you ask your friends on Saturday?"

That night they hooked up a sleepmaker at the head of his bed. "Why didn't they do that before?" he asked one of the workmen. "It must be safer than pills."

"You're looking at it wrong," the man told him. "Most of the patients here are crew. You don't think a crew would use a vivarium sleepmaker, do you?"

"Too proud, huh?"

"I told you. They're *crew*."

There was a listening bug in the headset.

To Parlette, Matt was part of the paperwork. His was

one of the dossiers lying on Jesus Pietro's desk. Its cover was scorched, like the others; but the Head's office, on the second floor, had escaped most of the damage from the *Planck*'s wildfire drive.

Parlette went through all those dossiers and many more. By now he knew that the worst threat to his "New Law" was defection by the Sons of Earth. Only they, with their presumed control over the colonists, could make it work; and only they were beyond his control.

Matthew Keller's dossier was unusual in its skimpiness. There wasn't even a record of his joining the rebel organization. Yet he must belong. Castro's notes implied that Keller had freed the vivarium prisoners. He had been badly hurt invading the Hospital a second time. He must be partly responsible for the *Planck* disaster. He seemed to be connected with the mystery of the bleeding-heart symbol. A very active rebel, Matthew Keller.

Then there was Harry Kane's disproportionate interest in him.

Parlette's first evanescent impulse was to have him die of his injuries. He'd caused too much destruction already. Probably the *Planck*'s library could never be replaced. But getting Harry Kane's trust was far more important.

On Thursday Dr. Bennet sent him word that Keller would be receiving visitors. Installing a listening bug was an obvious precaution. Millard Parlette made a note of the coming interview—at Saturday noon—then forgot it until then.

When Hood had finished talking, Matt smiled and said, "I told you they were little hearts and livers."

It didn't go over. The four of them looked solemnly back at him, like a jury circling his hospital bed.

When they'd first come in, he'd wondered if they were all slated for the organ banks. They'd been so deadly serious, and they moved with coordination, as if they'd rehearsed this.

Hood had talked for almost half an hour, with occasional interruptions from Harry Kane and no comments at all from Laney and Mrs. Hancock. It still seemed rehearsed. *You do all the talking, Jay*, someone must have said. *Break it to him gently. Then ...* But what they'd told him was all good.

"You've still got that bad-news look," he said. "Why so solemn? All is roses. We're all going to live forever. No more Implementation raids. No more being hauled off to the organ banks without a trial. We can even build wooden houses if we're crazy enough to want them. The millenium has come at last."

Harry Kane spoke. "And what's to keep Parlette from breaking all his rash promises?"

Matt still couldn't see why it should involve him. "You think he might?"

"Look at it logically, Keller. Parlette has Castro's job now. He's the Head. He runs Implementation."

"That's what you wanted, isn't it?"

"Yes," said Kane. "I want him to have all the power he can grab, because he's the only man who can put the New Law across—if he chooses. But let's just back off a little and look at how much power he does have.

"He runs Implementation." Kane ticked it off on a finger. "He's trained his own clan to use hunting guns. That gives him most of the weapons on Mount Lookitthat. He can twist the Council around his little finger. Parlette is well on his way to being the world's first emperor!"

"But you could stop him. You said yourself that you can raise the colony against him any time you like."

Kane waved it off. "We can't do that. Sure, it's a good threat, especially after what we've already done to Implementation. But we don't want a bloodbath any more than Parlette does, or says he does. No, we need something else to hold over him."

Four solemn faces waited for his reply. What the Mist Demons was this all about? Matt said, "All right, you thought up the problem; now think up an answer."

"We need an invisible assassin."

Matt raised himself on one shoulder and peered at Harry Kane around the white pillar of his traction-bound leg. No, Kane wasn't joking. The effort was exhausting, and he dropped back.

Laney put a hand on his arm. "It's the only answer, Matt. And it's perfect. No matter how powerful Millard Parlette becomes politically, he'll never have a defense against *you*."

"It's you or civil war," Kane put in.

Matt found his voice. "I don't doubt you're serious," he said wonderingly. "What I doubt is your sanity. Do I look like an assassin? I've never killed anyone. I never intend to."

"You did pretty well last weekend."

"What—I used a stun gun! I hit some people with my fist! Why does that make me a pro killer?"

"You realize," said Hood, "that we never intend to use you as such. You're a threat, Matt, nothing more. You'll be one leg in the balance of power between the Sons of Earth and Millard Parlette."

"I'm a miner." Matt gestured with his left arm, the one that didn't pull cracked ribs. "A *miner*. I use trained worms to dig for metal. My boss sells the metal, and buys worms and worm food, and with luck he makes enough to pay my salary. Wait a minute. Have you told Parlette about this idea?"

"No, of course not. He'll never know about it unless you agree, and then we'll wait until you're out of the Hospital."

"Mist Demons, I should *hope* so. If Parlette gets the idea I'm dangerous to him—and me on my back like this—I want to be on Delta before you tell Parlette. Hell, I want to be on *Earth* before—"

"Then you agree?"

"No, Kane! No, I do not agree to anything! Don't you realize I've got a family? What if Parlette takes hostages?"

"Two parents and a sister," Hood amplified. "Parents on Iota."

"Don't worry," Laney said soothingly. "We'll protect them, Matt. They'll be safe."

Kane nodded. "If anyone so much as harms a hair on your head, or threatens any member of your family. I'll declare total war. I'll have to tell Parlette that; and to make him believe it, I'll have to mean it. And I do."

Matt thought very seriously about shouting for Dr. Bennet. It wouldn't work. Even if she threw them out, they'd only come back later.

And Matt Keller was a man on his back. He could move three inches to the side if he was willing to endure the pain. Four inches, no. A captive audience.

"You've really thought it out, haven't you? Why did you wait so long to tell me?"

Jay Hood answered. "I wanted to be here. This is my day off."

"You're back teaching school, Jay?"

"It seems appropriate to teach history while we're making it." In the dry voice there was a barely concealed jubilation. Hood was in his element. Strange that he'd never suspected the size of Hood's ego.

"You got me into this," said Matt.

"Sorry. My apologies. Believe me, Matt, I only picked you as a probable recruit." When Matt didn't answer, Hood continued, "But we do need you. Let me show you how much. You were dying, Matt—"

"Stop, Jay."

"He has a right to know, Laney. Matt, those ribs you broke tore up your lung and your diaphragm. Harry had to talk Parlette into—"

"Jay, *shut up*."

"All right, Laney." He sounded hurt.

"Matt, we weren't going to tell you. Really we weren't."

Dead man's flesh was a part of him, forever. Living under his rib cage: a strange, partial resurrection.

Matt said, "All right, Laney. How do you stand on this?"

Laney looked down, then up to meet his eyes. "It's your choice, Matt. But if we don't have you, we don't have anyone." She seemed to stop, then hurried on. "Listen, Matt, you're making a big thing out of this. We're not asking you to rush right out and murder someone. We'd be perfectly happy to see you go back to your mining worms. For all we care, you can stay there the rest of your life, with a small extra income"—"Thanks"—"For being on standby alert. Maybe Parlette's honest. Maybe he really does want to make the Plateau a paradise. Maybe all is roses. But just in case"—She leaned forward in the uncomfortable hospital chair, gripping his wrist with one hand, looking deep into his eyes. Her nails cut the skin—"just in case Parlette is ambitious, then we'll need you to stop him. Nobody else will be able to do it.

"We must let him have his power now. Somebody has to take power, or there'll be civil war. But if he needs to be stopped, and you don't stop him, you'll be a coward."

Matt tried to pull his arm away. Torn muscles reacted; it was as if he'd been kicked in the side with a lead boot. "You're fanatics! All four of you!" And he was trapped, trapped . . .

Laney let go. Slowly she sat back, her eyes soft and dreamy, with pinpoint pupils.

Matt relaxed. The others were looking at nothing. Jay Hood was humming under his breath. Mrs. Hancock scowled at some unpleasant thought.

"The luck of Matt Keller" had given him a breathing space.

"The luck of Matt Keller." A joke, a shaggy-dog story. If he hadn't used the power to "rescue" Polly, she might be alive now. If he hadn't come running to Jay Hood for explanations, he'd be back tending his mining worms. No wonder this form of "luck" had never appeared before. Perhaps it never would again.

It was a detrimental mutation. It had kept him virgin

until he was twenty-one. It had killed Polly and caused Laney to see him as a tool instead of a man. It had sent him into the *Planck;* he'd never have tried that without his psychological invisibility. Into the *Planck* to die; out, by blind luck, with a dead man's lung.

A man should have the sense to hide his differences.

Too late. They would forget him, again and again, as often as he desired. But always they would come back. Matt Keller, tool, captive assassin.

Not likely!

"You," he said. "Mrs. Hancock."

The others stirred, turned to face him, returned to the world in which Matt Keller was a factor to be considered.

"Mrs. Hancock. Do you have anything to say to me?"

"I don't think so," said the middle-aged rebel who should have been a shrewish housewife.

"You didn't say a word while the others were browbeating me. Why did you come?"

She shrugged. "Just to see what would happen. Keller, did you ever lose someone you loved?"

"Sure."

"To the organ banks?"

"My Uncle Matt."

"I did my damndest to stop you from getting a transplant, Keller. Dr. Bennet says you'd have lived without it, but of course you'd have been a cripple."

"I'd have been just as glad," said Matt, though he wasn't sure it was true.

"I wanted to smash the organ banks the first chance we got. Nobody else seems to feel that way. Maybe nobody else had a husband cut up for the organ banks."

"Make your point."

She shrugged again. "I don't know if you're as important as Harry says. It seems to me nobody could be that important. You got us out of the Hospital, right. Parlette would never have found us otherwise, right. We're grateful, right. But did we have to cut a man up to show how grateful we are? You didn't do *him* any good.

"Well, he's dead, and we can't break up the organ banks yet. But we're trying to change the laws so less people go into them, and then only the ones that deserve it most. If you were any kind of man, you'd be wild to help us. I say it's all you can do for that dead man."

"For sweet charity."

Mrs. Hancock's mouth closed like a trap.

"I'm going to join you," said Matt. "But not for sweet charity. And now I'll give you my reasons."

"Go on," said Harry Kane. He was the only one who didn't show surprise.

"I can't go back to my mining worms. That's absolute. But I'm no hired killer, and that's for sure too. I've never committed murder. I haven't wanted to, not often. If I ever kill a man, I'll want to know just why I'm doing it.

"There's only one way I can be sure I will.

"From now on, the five of us are going to be the leaders of the Sons of Earth." That he saw, jolted even Harry Kane. "I'll want a hand in all decisions. I'll want all the information available to any of you. What do you say, Harry?"

"Keep talking."

Matt's mouth was dry. Harry Kane didn't like this, and Harry Kane was a bad enemy. "The Sons of Earth can't commit murder without my consent, and I won't give it unless I decide murder is necessary. To make that decision, I'd have to know everything, always. One more thing. If I ever decide one of you is trying to cheat me, I'll kill him, because cheating me of information will be murder."

"What makes you think you can handle that much power, Keller?" Harry's voice was dispassionate, merely interested.

"I have to try," Matt pointed out. "It's *my* power."

"Fair enough." Harry stood up. "One of us will be here tomorrow, with copies of Parlette's New Law, in full. If we decide to make changes later, we'll let you know."

"Let me know before you make the changes."

Kane hesitated, then nodded. They went.

Millard Parlette sighed and turned off the receiver.

Invisible assassin? An odd phrase to come from a practical man like Harry Kane. What could he have meant?

Kane would tell him eventually, of course.

Even then it wouldn't matter. Kane could be trusted now, and that did matter. Now Kane had a hold on Millard Parlette. Be it real or imaginary, he would use that hold before he started a civil war.

And Millard Parlette could concentrate on the man waiting outside. Implementation had selected one of their number to present a set of grievances. The man must be getting angrier and angrier as he waited for the Head's attention.

Parlette used the intercom. "Send him in, Miss Lauessen."

"Good."

"Wait. What's his name again?"

"Halley Fox. Corporal."

"Thank you. Would you please send to Gamma and Delta and Iota plateaus for records on Matthew Keller."

"Done, mine ancestor."

Mist Demons! How had Castro put up with the woman? Parlette smiled. Why not? Let him take care of Implementation and the Council, and Harry Kane would take care of the rest. An invisible assassin had just lifted half the load from his back.

"It'll be one strange balance of power," said Harry Kane. "Parlette's got every weapon on the planet, except for what we've built in our basements. He's got all the electrical and medical facilities, and most of the wealth. And what have we got? Matt Keller."

"And lucky to get him," said Laney.

A red-haired girl in an iridescent dress passed them, walking quickly down the corridor. A crew girl, probably visiting a relative. They stopped talking until she had passed. Harry Kane grinned after her, grinned at her startled expression and at the way she'd quickened her step to leave them behind. They'd all have to get used to this someday: to the sight of colonists in the hallowed corridors of the Hospital.

Jay Hood said, "Well, we've got him. Or has he got us?" He slapped the wall, making gunshot echoes. "Can you imagine what the historians will say? They may never figure it out."

Matt lay on his back and contemplated the ceiling.

He'd made the right decision. He was sure of it. If he had a power, then *someone* had to have a use for it.

He himself had none.

A detrimental mutation is one that prevents the organism from surviving long enough to breed. Matt's only hope of becoming a father lay in suppressing the "luck" entirely, at least in his private life. An invisible man goes nowhere in a civilized society.

Someone entered. Matt's eyes jerked hard over, caught by the iridescent blue of her dress.

"I beg your pardon," she said, and turned to leave. She was tall and slender, and young, with dark red hair curved into impossible contours. Her dress was of a type never seen on Delta Plateau, loose and clinging, and it *glowed*. A face lovely in its strangeness, with flared nostrils and pronounced cheekbones, marked her as pure crew.

"Just a minute," Matt called.

She turned in surprise, not at what he'd said, but at his colonist accent. Then her back straightened and her chin lifted and her mouth became a hard, angry line. Matt flushed.

And before her eyes could coldly leave him, he thought, *Look at me.*

Her eyes didn't turn. Her chin came down and her face went soft and dreamy.

Keep your eyes on mine, he thought at her. *I fascinate you, right? Right. Keep looking.*

She took a slow step toward him.

Matt dropped the control. She took another step forward, and then she looked horrified. She turned and ran from the room, followed by Matt's pealing laughter.

Detrimental mutation?

Maybe not.

The Outsider ship was a Christmas decoration, a ball of tinsel ribbons looping over and under and around one another, never touching. It was the diameter of New York City, with about the same population, in beings like black cat-o'-nine-tails with thickened handles.

Miles ahead at the end of its tethering cables, the fusion drive spread dim light over the ship. The basking ramps cast vacuum-sharp shadows across each other, and in the borderlines between light and shade lay the crew. They lay with their heads in sunlight and their branched tails in shadow, soaking up energy through thermoelectric currents. Fusion radiation sleeted through their bodies, unnoticed. It was a peaceful, lazy time.

Between stars there was little to do.

Until actinic blue flame flashed across their course, throwing high-energy particles and electromagnetic fields about with carefree abandon.

In moments the object was out of sight, even to an Outsider's sensitive eye. But not to the ship's instruments. In an hour the Outsiders had it nailed: position, velocity, mass, design, thrust. It was metal, mechanical, pushed by fusion, and fueled by interstellar hydrogen. Not a primitive device, but . . .

Built by potential customers.

In every arm of the galaxy were Outsiders, using everything from photon sails to reactionless, inertialess drives to push their ships; but always they traveled through Einsteinian space. Hyperdrive was vulgar. The Outsiders never used hyperdrive.

Other species were different. They preferred not to dawdle in space, enjoying the trip, sightseeing, taking their time. Usually they preferred the speedy convenience of the hyperdrive Blind Spot. Hundreds of times over, alien races had bought the secret of the hyperdrive from passing Outsiders.

The trade ship swung easily toward Procyon and the human colony on We Made It, following Interstellar Ramscoop Robot #144. No chance of catching up, not at the customary .01 gee. No hurry. Plenty of time . . .

In two sparks of fusion light, an industrial revolution moved on We Made It.

DEL REY *Catch a Rising Star!*